KEITH GRAY

OSTRICH BOYS

Definitions

In association with
THE BODLEY HEAD

OSTRICH BOYS
A DEFINITIONS BOOK 978 0 099 45657 5

First published in Great Britain by Definitions,
an imprint of Random House Children's Books
A Random House Group Company

This edition published 2008

5 7 9 10 8 6 4

Copyright © Keith Gray, 2008

The right of Keith Gray to be identified as the author of this work has been
asserted in accordance with the Copyright, Designs and Patents Act 1988.

The Random House Group Limited supports the Forest Stewardship
Council (FSC), the leading international forest certification organization.
All our titles that are printed on Greenpeace-approved FSC-certified paper
carry the FSC logo. Our paper procurement policy can be found at
www.rbooks.co.uk/environment.

Set in Garamond Book

Definitions are published by Random House Children's Books,
61–63 Uxbridge Road, London W5 5SA

www.kidsatrandomhouse.co.uk
www.rbooks.co.uk

Addresses for companies within The Random House Group Limited
can be found at: www.randomhouse.co.uk/offices.htm

THE RANDOM HOUSE GROUP Limited Reg. No. 954009

A CIP catalogue record for this book is available from the British Library.

Printed and bound in Great Britain by CPI Bookmarque, Croydon, CR0 4TD

For Carolyn.
For fourteen years of friendship and support.

Part One
Ash

One

Our best friend was ash in a jar. Ross was dead. Kenny, Sim and I were learning to live with it.

And this was all Sim's idea. It was just that Kenny and I weren't convinced exactly how great an idea it was.

We'd had to wait for it to get dark, which at this time of year wasn't until after half-ten. We'd given it until eleven. Now we were crouched whispering in the shadow of some scraggy fir trees in the front garden of the history teacher's house. We had branches jabbing at us, needles in our hair and down the backs of our collars. But no matter how much we shuffled and hunkered, the shadow wasn't quite big enough. We were still wearing our dark funeral clothes, and that helped. The problem was Kenny, who kept squirming, shoving bits of me and Sim out into the glare of the streetlights. All it would take was one eagle eye to look our way and we'd be seen for sure.

A car sped by and we ducked our heads. It wasn't just the warm June night making me sweat.

'This is for Ross, remember,' Sim whispered. 'We can't flake out now – we all agreed. You agreed too, Kenny. Don't say you didn't.'

Kenny made a noise – not quite yes, not quite no. 'Can't we just put a note through his door or something? I'm telling you: if we get caught—'

Sim looked disgusted. 'Christ-on-a-bike, Kenny! You want to write a poem in a card too? A card with love hearts and rabbits wearing hats on the front?' He shook his head, popped the lid off the can of spray-paint he was clutching. 'No. It's got to be *big*.'

Kenny opened his mouth to argue but I nudged his arm, hushing him.

Mr Fowler's house was a corner terrace with a small square of scrappy garden on Brereton Ave – a busy enough road within walking distance of the pubs and clubs along the sea front. It was Friday night in Cleethorpes and for most people the only place to be were those pubs and clubs. We could hear giggling and chatter from a group of girls clacking along the pavement in their heels. We huddled down even further under the fir trees, ignoring another showering of needles. One of the girls wanted to get a taxi, her feet were killing her – but her friends said it wasn't worth it, they were nearly there now. We waited for them to decide. I stared hard at the ground, hoping they wouldn't look at us if we didn't look at them.

At last they walked on and I whispered, 'Either we do it or we don't, okay? We can't stay here all night arguing about it.' I didn't care how edgy I sounded. More edgy than nervous. Of course I was worried about being seen, but more than that I still wasn't convinced this was the right thing to do. For Ross, I mean. I didn't give a damn about Mr Fowler.

Two, three cars swept by.

'I don't want to do it,' Kenny said. 'We shouldn't do it.'

'I'm gonna do it,' Sim said.

'Well, yeah,' Kenny agreed. 'It's your idea, so you should do it.'

Sim looked to me. 'Blake?'

'You're gonna do it whatever I say.'

He grinned. 'I know.'

Kenny felt brave enough to poke his head out from under the low branches, looking towards the house's dark front windows. 'D'you think he's in?'

Sim shrugged. 'Maybe, maybe not.'

'There're no lights on,' I said. And then, just like that, one went on behind the front-room curtains. I ducked my head and swore.

'He's in! He's in!' Kenny hissed. He scrabbled as far back under the fir trees as he could get, pushing me and Sim out into the open again. I had to elbow my way back into hiding.

We kept our eyes on the glow of light behind those curtains. What was Mr Fowler doing in there? Watching TV? Reading a book? Eating takeaway pizza? How come he still could but our best friend was dead?

He'd been hit by a car, knocked off his bike. At the funeral the vicar had called it an 'accident'. But somehow the word wasn't enough. It wasn't big enough, powerful enough – didn't *mean* enough. He hadn't spilled a cup of tea, he hadn't tripped over his own feet. He'd had his life smashed out of him. It felt like there should be a whole new word invented just to describe it.

Sim didn't seem in the least bit worried that the teacher being home might make his plan riskier. Although I didn't think I'd ever seen Sim get nervous about anything much. He was more comfortable being angry. He had these dark brown eyes that hardened like snooker balls whenever he got mad. And he'd always had short hair but only yesterday he'd had it shorn to within a millimetre of its life, leaving his freshly exposed scalp much too pale compared to the rest of him. In his funeral get-up he looked like a fifteen-year-old version of the bouncers who guarded the doors to the rowdy clubs along the sea front.

'We should've brought disguises,' Kenny whispered.

Sim rolled his eyes.

Kenny ignored him. 'I'm telling you: even balaclavas or something. You two are all right, you could be anybody. But I'm so obviously me.'

I wasn't sure what he was trying to say, unless he was talking about the fact that he was the shortest, blondest kid in our year. He had a furry mop of hair and an almost perfectly round baby-face, making him look more like twelve than fifteen. His biggest hates in life were sitting still and keeping quiet. He was like one of those little dogs that scurried around your legs, nipping at your ankles, yapping all the time.

I said, 'Whatever happens, everybody'll know it's us three anyway.'

Sim nodded. 'Yeah, exactly. I don't even see why we're hiding.' He stood up in full view of the house and the street, brushed pine needles off his shoulders and out of his Velcro hair.

Kenny panicked. 'God, Sim. Get *down*, you idiot!'

Sim pulled the collar of his jacket high up around his face. 'Just run when I tell you to.'

Kenny was quick to get on-your-marks, like a sprinter. 'Maybe you'd better get a head-start,' he said to me.

Which confused me at first. Then, when it clicked, I punched him.

I've always been touchy about my size, my weight. I'd fight anybody who called me fat. And I've had the thesaurus thrown at me: portly, rotund, stout . . . I prefer to think of myself as *heavy*. And Kenny wasn't meaning to be spiteful; he wasn't the nasty type. Just sometimes his honesty deserved a punch.

Sim turned his back and lowered his face as a taxi drove by. He waited for it to get far enough away down the road. 'Don't go without me,' he warned.

Then he was running across the patch of lawn to

the front door. He drew the can of spray-paint like a gunslinger. He fired and the spitting hiss of it sounded so loud. Kenny and I watched him, watched the window, watched the road, watched the window. And begged inside our heads that Mr Fowler wouldn't suddenly appear.

We had a few nice enough, decent enough teachers at our school. There were a couple who even looked like they enjoyed being teachers and were willing to have a laugh now and again during lessons. Mr Fowler wasn't one of them. He was still quite youngish for a teacher, yet he already had a shiny saucer of baldness at the back of his head and a beer-gut that arrived in a classroom several seconds before the rest of him. We knew this was his house because Sim biked by it every day on his way to school. And once upon a time Sim used to say 'Hello' or 'Good morning' – he was in Mr Fowler's history class after all. But he'd stopped as soon as he'd realized his teacher was always going to pretend he hadn't heard and was never going to reply. Mr Fowler preferred to believe his pupils didn't exist outside of school time. He was the reason Kenny and I had dropped history the first chance we got. Ross and Sim hadn't been quite so quick off the mark. And over the past couple of weeks the man had made the last of Ross's life a genuine nightmare.

So this was payback – Sim-style. This was revenge. Pure and simple.

It felt like it took him an age to do it, but it could only have been thirty seconds at most. Then he was back across the garden and shoving through the fir trees out onto Brereton Ave. Kenny and I leaped up after him. But before I turned to run, I looked at what he'd sprayed in hasty, spiky, harsh black letters that bled down the history teacher's door:

Haunted by Ross Fell

Two

It was eleven thirty by the time we got to Sean Munro's. He lived on Brooklands Ave – a short but posh road just off the sea front. Posh because there were gates either end that could be closed to stop people using it as a short cut, or maybe just to keep undesirables out. There was no traffic and everything should have been quiet, but even as we climbed over the locked gate we could hear voices, laughter, music from the top end of the street. Not too loud, but probably far too loud for this time of night in this kind of neighbourhood. There was a bunch of kids hanging around outside the house with the brightest lights – so bright they lit up most of the narrow road.

'Three guesses,' Sim said.

'Munro, Munro, Munro,' Kenny and I answered together.

'Kind of makes it all a bit more difficult,' Sim said.

'Maybe we should go do Nina's house first, then come back.'

'I've got to be in by twelve,' Kenny said. 'You know what my mum's like. I'm telling you: she'll go mad if I'm late.'

Sim wasn't happy. But I jumped in to back Kenny up. 'I've got to get home soon as well. We're not gonna have time for Nina's.' Which wasn't strictly true. The thing was, if I didn't feel right doing this to Mr Fowler or Sean Munro, no way did I want to do it to Nina.

'Let's get a bit closer,' Sim sighed. 'Maybe they're gonna be going home soon.'

The gardens along either side of the road were small but they all had trees and bushes and it was easy to creep along. The road forked before it hit the sea front and Munro's house was the first house on the left-hand side. The house on the opposite side had a hedge big enough for all three of us to hide behind as long as we stayed on all fours. Kenny moaned about his new suit getting filthy, and after crawling under fir trees and sneaking through bushes, I knew I was going to have to hide mine from my mum too.

Looking towards Munro's we realized the bright

lights illuminating most of that side of the road were the high beams of a sleek, gorgeous sports car sitting in the driveway. The engine wasn't running but the music was also coming from the car. The driver's-side window was down and the stereo was pumping it out.

We recognized all four of the lads. Munro, obviously, and like us still wearing his funeral clothes – but it felt disrespectful from him somehow, like he'd forgotten he had them on. He was the biggest kid in our year. As tall as Sim, as wide as me, with no neck but extra face to make up for it. He kept walking around the sports car, pawing at it, polishing it with his sleeve. I guessed it was his dad's new toy and Munro Junior couldn't keep his hands off it, was dreaming of being seventeen and burning up the streets in it.

An age our best friend would never reach. An experience he'd never have.

We couldn't see the car's badge from this distance. 'What kind is it?' Kenny wanted to know.

'The seventy-grand kind by the look of it,' Sim said.

I didn't have a clue about exotic cars – but I did know a bit about music. 'Why is it that all these blokes who insist on having their car stereos turned up loud enough to annoy people always have such crap taste in music?'

'Is he stroking it?' Kenny asked.

Sim just growled his contempt. His dislike of Munro far outweighed that for Mr Fowler.

The other lads were Munro's most recent goons. I couldn't even be bothered remembering their names. It wasn't as though they were his friends – more like hangers-on. He had a different set each year. I guessed these three had already done all their 'oohing' and 'aahing' over the car, had done enough fawning for one night, and were now bored. One was swinging on the front gate, another was lying along the low garden wall with his arms dangling down on either side, while the third was sitting on the grass verge plucking at his laces. They reminded me of chimps in a zoo.

I nudged Sim. 'What d'you call a bunch of monkeys?'

He grinned when he realized what I was getting at. Knowing this stuff was his speciality. 'Either a troop or a tribe,' he said. Which didn't sound insulting enough. 'But it's a *flange* of baboons.'

I nodded, grinned back. That was more like it.

As we watched, the front door of the house on the

far side of Munro's opened and an elderly man with wispy grey hair, wearing a tartan dressing gown and slippers, stepped out onto his drive. 'Can you turn that music down, Sean? Do you know how late it is?'

Munro's monkey mates all perked up – at last there was going to be something worth taking notice of. But Sean ignored the old man.

'Sean? Sean! I'm asking you to turn your music down.'

With practised disrespect Munro deigned to look across at the man.

'Sean. Are you listening?'

Munro leaned in through the car's open window, but only to turn the music *up* a notch. His goons thought it was hilarious.

The old man didn't come any closer so had to shout louder. 'Sean! Sean! Where's your father?'

Munro continued to paw and polish the car but did it in a weird jerking fashion. It took me a couple of seconds to realize it was him trying to move to the music, his version of dancing. His monkey mates gibbered and chortled, thought it was pure cabaret.

'Sean!' the old man shouted. 'For God's sake, boy!'

And then Munro's dad appeared, barging out onto

his own doorstep. 'What's all the noise about? Doesn't
anybody give a damn what time it is?' He was bare-
foot, wearing stripy pyjama bottoms and a white vest.
He had a gold bracelet as thick as cable on one hairy
wrist and more chunks of gold on several fingers. You
could see who little Seany had inherited his good
looks from – necks must have been rare in the Munro
genealogy.

'Can you please ask your son to turn that down?'
the old man from next door shouted.

'Go to bed, Gerald,' Munro Senior bawled back.

'It's nearly midnight and—'

'Yeah, yeah, I know. It's nearly time for you to turn
into a bat, you old vampire. Just go back to your
coffin, will you?'

Sean glanced at his goons to make sure they were
watching and seeing how cool his dad was. They
grinned back at him in wide-eyed, head-bobbing
pleasure – this had so been worth hanging around for.

The old man stood there for a few seconds longer.
The music banged on. 'I'm calling the police,' he
threatened. 'It's nearly midnight.' But the Munros
stood shoulder to shoulder, unmoving. 'You've
dragged this street right down since you arrived,' was

his last riposte before scurrying back into his house. 'Right down.' And he closed the door firmly behind him.

Munro was laughing. 'I think he's just jealous of our new car,' he said to his dad. 'Old git.'

Munro Senior smacked his son around the head with a ringing blow. Kenny, Sim and I winced at the sound of it. 'What the hell d'you think you're doing running my battery down?'

Sean staggered back, hand to his ear, scrunching his face up in pain. 'I was just showing it to my mates.'

His dad's hand flew at him again. And he almost ducked it. Almost.

'Do I want a new car with a dead battery? Eh? Do I?' He didn't wait for an answer. He was quick to turn off the stereo and the lights, letting calm night return to the street. 'Get inside,' he told Sean.

'But my mates . . .'

Munro Senior glared at the three of them hovering at the bottom of his drive. 'They can piss off too.' He shoved his son hard in the back and marched him indoors.

For a few long seconds Munro's monkey mates didn't know what to do. They usually only did things

Munro told them to, and this seemed like a new and confusing situation. But at last it dawned on them that Sean wouldn't be coming out again tonight and they sloped off down the road, dragging their knuckles behind them.

Kenny, Sim and I had watched it all unfold with a kind of amazed horror. And if it had been anybody else, maybe we would have given a damn.

Sim pulled the spray-can out of his pocket.

Three

'You shouldn't have done it on the car,' I said.

We'd leaped the gate at the sea-front end of Brooklands Ave and legged it across Kingsway, dodging taxis. We didn't slow as we jumped down the steps in between the ornamental flowerbeds on the opposite side. Down to the path that ran the length of the beach from the lifeboat station to the leisure centre. Only when we reckoned we'd put enough distance between us and the Munros did we stop and lean back against the sea wall to catch our breath. The tide was out and the beach was dark. I was glad I wasn't the only one red-faced and sweaty.

'Sim. I said you should've just done it across his door, like Mr Fowler's.'

'Yeah, yeah. I heard you the first time.' Sim took his suit jacket off and tied it around his waist by the sleeves. 'Look, Munro's a shitweasel. His dad's obviously an even bigger shitweasel. Are you telling me you really give a toss?'

He waited for me to answer. I didn't.

He checked his watch. 'Come on, we've still got time to do Nina's if we're quick.' He started to walk away with Kenny in tow.

I didn't follow. 'We haven't got time to do Nina's.'

'It'll take two minutes, if that.'

'I don't think we should do Nina's. I'm not coming.'

Sim carried on walking but Kenny hovered between us, hopping from foot to foot, unsure what to do. 'Sim, Blake says he's not coming.'

I saw the set of Sim's shoulders and knew that he wanted to keep going – he'd do it by himself if he had to. But our friendship was too strong. His shoulders slumped and he turned back to face us. 'What?' He didn't come to us but waited for Kenny and me to walk to him.

I shook my head. 'Not Nina.'

'Why not?'

'Honestly? Because I don't think Ross would want us to.'

He pulled a face.

'Look, if we were gonna be spraying stuff anywhere it should probably be school, right? You know he hated it.' I saw his eyes narrow as he considered the idea. 'But I don't think Ross would want us to do it *anywhere*,' I added.

Sim looked like he was ready for an argument. 'How come you reckon you know him better than us all of a sudden? You didn't even meet him until you moved here. Kenny and I knew him in primary.'

'That's not what I'm saying.' I didn't want to get into some ridiculous argument about who was our best friend's best friend.

Kenny obviously did. 'I knew him longest. He always told me stuff he never told anybody else.'

'It's not a competition, Kenny.'

'I'm just telling you he did. Remember, he told me first about the time when he was trying to run away.'

'He wasn't trying to run away,' I said. 'He just wanted to get to that place in Scotland.'

'He told me he was trying to find himself.'

'Only because he was going to a place that's actually called *Ross*. He thought it'd be cool to *be* Ross *in* Ross. But he wasn't running away.'

Kenny was adamant. 'But that's what he told me –

kept going on about it, about wanting to "find him-self".'

'And did he?'

Kenny shrugged. 'He said he got as far as Leeds.'

Sim was gripping the can of spray-paint. 'Look, we agreed. For Ross.'

'It just doesn't feel right,' I said.

'What's that supposed to mean?'

I was struggling to explain it in my own head, never mind out loud. 'It means, it doesn't feel right.'

He wasn't impressed. 'You were there too, Blake.' He was talking about the funeral.

'And I'm telling you,' Kenny said. 'Ross would've hated it.'

But Kenny didn't have to tell me anything. I'd sat in between my mum and dad in that cramped and claustrophobic crematorium, feeling my stomach twist itself into hot knots, getting tighter and tighter as my best friend's farce of a funeral dragged on. People who hardly knew him reckoning they could tell us about him, a stupid vicar, patronizing hymns . . . Ross would have loathed every single second of it.

'You were there,' Sim repeated. 'And half the other

people shouldn't have been. The kids from school who turned up? They probably never once even spoke to him, just wanted to get out of this afternoon's lessons. Bunch of hypocrites. And his mum or dad or sister just never said anything, did they? But for me the real killer was seeing Fowler, Munro and Nina. The three people who'd made Ross's life the biggest misery ever! What the hell did they think they were doing there?'

'Ross hated them as much as they hated him,' Kenny said.

I shook my head. 'You can't include Nina. You can't say she's as bad as Munro and Mr Fowler.'

'You weren't there when she dumped him,' Kenny told me. 'I was, and I saw the look on his face. I'm telling you: really bad, really cut up.'

I couldn't answer that; didn't know how to.

Sim said, 'Out of all the hypocrites that went this afternoon, those three are the lowest of the low.' He counted them off on his fingers. 'Nina told him she loved him, and then went and dumped him. Fowler hassled him and picked on him in class, getting him even worse grief from his mum at home. And then Munro goes and beats the crap out of him. No way on earth should any of them have been there.'

He waited, watching me.

I shrugged.

'It was a disgrace, you said so too. It was shit.'

I nodded. I agreed with him – up to a point. But for me it was the *whole* of the funeral that was the problem. I wished I'd had the courage to stand up there and then, right in the middle of the crematorium, and say something. What we were doing now was Sim's idea of revenge, not mine. I wasn't even sure that I wanted revenge. I wanted something *bigger*. Something more *Ross*. But I couldn't figure out what.

'You can't flake out, Blake,' Kenny said.

'I'm not flaking out. I'm not scared of spraying up somebody's house. And if we get caught, get done – fine, I'll take my share. I always have done, haven't I? It's just, you know . . .' But again I struggled for what I wanted to say.

And that wasn't like me. I know Ross was the one who wanted to be a writer, but I was top in English and couldn't ever remember getting stuck for something to say before. I knew some pretty big words. But this was infuriating, exasperating. I waved my hands about as if trying to gather up my thoughts and knead them into a proper sentence. Then felt stupid with the other two staring at me.

With a shrug I turned away from them towards the beach and the sea. Out there I could see the bulky silhouettes of tankers waiting for the tide to turn so they could head out onto the North Sea proper. Our sea's not the real sea, just the choppy grey River Humber. But the beach is sandy and there's a pier and candyfloss and rock and a funfair – so it's close enough. Beyond the tankers, across on the other side, was the steady, slow blink of the lighthouse at Spurn Point. I watched it, let it hypnotize me for a few seconds.

Kenny and Sim were expecting me to say something. I waited for one more blink of the lighthouse and still the best I could do was: 'It just doesn't feel *right*.'

Kenny pulled a face like I was a moron. And maybe I was. Who knew?

'I don't want those three ever to forget what they did to Ross, okay?' Sim said. His eyes had taken on their snooker-ball stare. 'I want all their neighbours and anybody who walks past their house to know all about it too. And every time they clean it off, we're just gonna go back and spray it on again. And again. Every night if we have to.'

Kenny wasn't too sure he liked that. 'I can't do it on school nights. You know my mum won't let me out if it's school the next day.'

Sim gritted his teeth. 'Christ-on-a-bike, Kenny . . .' He turned and stalked away towards the leisure centre.

Kenny looked at me.

'You've pissed him off,' I said.

He looked worried. 'You started it.'

And we had to run to catch up.

'You know what I thought was weird about the funeral?' Kenny asked. 'The vicar. Didn't you think he was weird? He could've been talking about me, couldn't he? Or anybody really.'

'I bet he'd never even met Ross,' I said.

'Yeah, exactly. That's what I mean. He was going on and on about this kid who walked and talked and went to school, but it could've been anybody. He made Ross sound like this paint-by-numbers person who hadn't been painted in yet.'

'Vicars probably use the same speech for

26

everybody,' Sim said. 'Doesn't matter who you are.'

'They should have asked *us* to say something,' Kenny said. 'We knew him best.'

And that was the real point, wasn't it? As Ross's best friends we felt we should have been included. But we'd been lost in the crowd.

'Maybe we should have been the only ones there,' Kenny said.

Sim laughed through gritted teeth.

We kept to the walkway alongside the beach, round the back of the leisure-centre car park, wanting to stay away from the main road in case someone had discovered our graffiti and a Munro was on the hunt. Then when we crossed the miniature-railway lines and turned away from the beach I realized that, despite what I'd said earlier, Sim was still leading us to Chichester Road and Nina's house.

Kenny said: 'They definitely should've stopped teachers from going. All except his mum, I mean.'

'She's not a teacher,' I told him. 'She's a lecturer, at the college.'

'Same difference. But I suppose it was all right Miss Dean being there. Ross always said he thought she was okay.'

'She's a librarian,' Sim said. 'They're not teachers; they don't give you half as much hassle. If there's a fire in the school and I've got to choose who I'm gonna save – a teacher or a librarian – the teacher's gonna burn every time.'

Kenny and I agreed. Harsh but true.

'He didn't fancy Miss Dean, though,' Kenny said. 'She just let him borrow loads of books all the time.'

'That's kind of what librarians do, Kenny.'

'Funny, Blake, funny. You know what I mean. She let him have extra books – more than other people. He was *always* reading.'

'He wanted to be a writer,' I said. 'I guess you have to read a lot of books to be a writer.'

Sim was angry again. 'And that was something else about the funeral, wasn't it? When they got that girl from Year Eleven to read out his story.'

'Janine somebody,' I said. 'They chose her because she's always in the school plays. I heard she's supposed to be going to drama school next year.'

Sim didn't care who she was or what she did. 'Smug cow – I can't stand her anyway. They should've asked one of us to read it. And it wasn't even his best story, was it? I've read all his stories; I would've chosen a better one.'

'Didn't his dad choose it?'

'Yeah, well, proves what *he* knows. And it was the way everyone was clapping that really pissed me off.'

Kenny didn't understand what he meant.

'People were always having a go at him about wanting to be a writer, weren't they? People like Munro. Always giving him grief. But after that smug cow read his story they all sat there clapping and saying how good it was.'

'She probably thought they were clapping her,' Kenny said. 'I was clapping the story. And they were all pretenders. Hypocrites, I mean.'

'Everyone there was a hypocrite,' Sim said.

'Except us.'

'Obviously.'

We walked by the abandoned paddling pool – these days the only thing to paddle in was litter – and headed down to the boating lake. The water was still, black and shiny. It might have been painted on. Ducks grumbled at us for coming so close, unimpressed with being disturbed.

I believe I've been let down a lot by adults: by

parents who don't listen, teachers who don't care and strangers who *presume*. But this afternoon had felt like a genuine betrayal. How could they have let it happen? It was shit to think that Ross would have been disappointed in his own funeral.

And nobody had even bothered to ask us our opinion. We were his best friends, we knew him better than anybody. When his parents were giving him hassle, when he got into trouble at school, when Sean Munro and the other morons were battering him, he came to us. Because we were his friends. We knew everything about him. But after they'd burned him up, they didn't even ask us how we felt.

'Maybe you're right, Kenny,' I said. 'Maybe it should've just been us there today.'

We crossed over the lake on the wooden double-humped bridge in single file, our feet loud on the planks. Kenny spat over the side and watched the small ripple he made on the water's surface. We used to hang around here a lot when we were younger, during the summer holidays, what with Ross and Kenny living not so far away. I wondered what we'd be doing this summer without Ross. For the first time ever, I wasn't looking forward to it. We skirted the kiddies' sandpit and scrambled up the small grass slope back onto the main road. The Wellow Hotel at the top of Chichester Road was opposite.

'Maybe that's what we should do,' I said. 'Have the kind of funeral that Ross would really want.'

And that was when it all fell into place: the light bulb lit up.

'In *Ross*,' I said. I grabbed Sim's arm. 'We could give him a real funeral. A proper one.' I got hold of Kenny too. 'But we do it in Ross, in Scotland.'

They looked at me like I was cracking up.

'Don't you get it? We'll take Ross to Ross, just like he always wanted. There'll be no vicars, no teachers, no parents – just us, his best friends. Doing something for him he always wanted to do. A proper memorial.'

Even in the dim light I could see Sim liked the idea. He nodded, beginning to understand what I was getting at. 'We could, couldn't we?'

Kenny seemed less convinced. 'But he's dead. He was cremated.' He spoke like I was a child. 'How're we supposed to take him to Scotland when he's in an urn?'

Sim let a slow grin slide across his face. 'We steal him. Right?'

I grinned too. 'Exactly.'

Kenny groaned.

Four

Ross's urn was sitting on the table in front of me. And as soon as his sister turned her back I was supposed to steal it. And him.

At the moment she wouldn't even let go of it. She kept touching the smooth sides, rubbing it like Aladdin rubbed his lamp – as if she was hoping Ross might leap out, same as the genie always did.

It was old-fashioned-looking, squat but curvy, marble-white with swirls of grey. I couldn't stop staring at it. And weird thoughts kept popping into my head. Like, did he fill it to the brim? He was a skinny fifteen-year-old; if he'd been a twenty-eight-stone fat knacker, would he spill over? Would it matter if I shook him up? Could you tell the difference between arm ash and leg ash? Freaky thoughts – but I couldn't stop myself thinking them.

Yet, in a way, they were the easier thoughts too. The truth of Ross being gone for ever, of my best friend being nothing more than ash in a jar, still felt impossible and bizarre.

'I don't like thinking this is really my little brother,' Caroline said, as if reading my mind. 'I want to pretend it's more like something he's left behind to remember him by.'

I nodded and mumbled something close to an agreement, and felt thankful she was willing to talk over my awkwardness. I'd been scared she might think it was kind of sick, kind of creepy for me to turn up and ask if I could see the urn. But now I reckoned she couldn't stop wanting to look at it either. It was horribly magnetic that way.

She brushed her hair out of her eyes, pulling it back into a hasty ponytail. She had a wide forehead, a thin, straight nose and a point to her chin. She was a slice-of-birthday-cake prettiness. But it was crumbling away beneath the tears.

It was a glorious June Saturday morning and the sun streamed into the kitchen through the window over her shoulder, making her untidy hair glow in a hazy mess. It was hot out there, and it was close and stuffy in here. My T-shirt was sticking to me. I'd been in this kitchen a hundred times at least, enough that I never noticed what stood on the shelves any more. But it didn't feel like the same kitchen today. All the doors and windows were shut tight. The whole house felt claustrophobic. The sadness that filled it was like a suffocating pillow pushed down over my face.

'Yesterday made it true,' she said. 'I think up until the funeral yesterday I could pretend it wasn't real. Or was just some kind of stupid mistake.'

It was the way I'd felt too. The funeral had made the past week solid, undeniable fact. Which was yet another reason for hating the crappy funeral.

She dug in her pocket for a tissue, then turned away from me as she blew her nose and wiped at her tears. Seeing her cry made me wonder if I should admit to her what we were planning. I liked her. If there were going to be sides, maybe she should be given the chance to choose ours.

Not that I got to say anything because Sim's face appeared at the window behind her. He was wearing sunglasses, peering inside. He waved to get my attention and tried to mouth something at me but I couldn't read his lips. Then Kenny poked his head up next to him and the two of them started waving, signalling, desperate to tell me something. Caroline was digging for a second tissue. I glared at Kenny and Sim, hoping they'd get the message to 'get lost' before she saw them.

'I honestly thought I would have run out of tears by now,' she said. Half smiling, but not meaning it. 'Do you think you'll ever get used to it?'

I was too busy trying to figure out what Kenny and Sim were telling me.

Caroline looked up. 'Blake?'

I nodded, ducking my head so she'd follow my eyes back to Ross on the table instead of to the window over her shoulder. 'Yeah. Sorry, I'm, you know . . . What did you say?'

'It doesn't feel right without him,' she said, reaching out to touch the urn again. 'The house feels empty; I don't know if I'll ever get used to him not being here. It must feel weird for you too, because you were his best friend. School must be strange without him. Do you think you'll ever get used to him not being there?'

I stared at the urn. 'No.' I shook my head hard enough to stop any slippery tears of my own from escaping. 'No.'

'Because you were always together, weren't you? You and Sim, and that other boy.'

'Kenny,' I told her. 'Kenny England.'

She nodded and I looked back over her shoulder at the two of them waving and miming at me. Kenny was wearing a bright orange T-shirt that was far too big for him. He was drowning in it, the baggy sleeves coming down to his elbows. He kept shaking his arm at me, flapping the sleeve like a wing.

Caroline nodded. 'Ross was lucky to have friends like you.'

I met her eyes, wanting to know if she really meant that. She'd always called him 'Little Brother', never Ross. She was seventeen and I'd expected us to be just stupid kids to her; she only put up with us because she had to, because we were her brother's friends. And, of course, Kenny, Sim and I fancied her – much to Ross's amusement (and sometimes annoyance). She was on the county netball team and we went to watch her play every chance we got. We didn't give a damn who won. She just looked fantastic in her PE kit.

I remembered Ross once saying, 'I bet I wouldn't have any friends at all if my sister was a dog.' And with hindsight, maybe one of us should have told him it wasn't true.

She didn't look much like my stunning netball

fantasy today. She was wearing a shapeless jumper and stretched, scruffy jogger's pants. Her eyes were red-rimmed and puffy. Her sadness made her ugly. And I knew she'd had a big bust-up with Ross last week, and she might just be feeling guilty about that. But she didn't seem to be feeling sorry for herself. The way she talked was the way I felt. It made me feel kind of protective towards her – I wanted to cure her of her grief like Kenny, Sim and I were going to cure ourselves of ours.

She gripped the urn in both hands. 'You know, I can remember so many things about him now. Little things, I mean. Things that happened on holidays or just funny things he said that I swear I'd never have remembered in a million years if he hadn't . . . if he was still . . . It's like, if he was still here, I wouldn't need to remember them. Maybe wouldn't have even wanted to.' She gave that half-smile, which was nothing like a smile really. She was fighting the tears again. 'Weird, isn't it?'

I nodded and decided I really was going to tell her about our plan. I even opened my mouth to spill everything, but we heard keys rattling in the front door, and then the door open.

'My dad's home,' she said, getting up. 'He'll want to see how Mum is. But you can stay – he'll be really pleased you're here.'

I'd hoped I could avoid having to see Ross's mum or dad. 'I thought your dad was at work.'

'No, he's been at the police station. They called really early this morning.' It was lucky she was already halfway out the door because then she couldn't see the look of sudden horror on my face.

All I could think was either Munro Senior or Mr Fowler had called the police about the graffiti. And of course the first people the police would contact about it would be Mr and Mrs Fell. It was their son's name sprayed over other people's property after all. I waited in the kitchen, expecting Mr Fell to come charging through to accuse me. I racked my brain for a convincing alibi. But I heard footsteps going upstairs and guessed he wanted to see Mrs Fell first. But did that mean he didn't know what we'd done last night? Or was he just asking her opinion on what to do with us? She'd always been the strict one.

Kenny and Sim were still at the kitchen window. I had to lean over the sink to reach it and open it a crack.

'What're you fannying about at?' Sim hissed. 'We've just seen his dad's car. He'll be home any minute.'

'He's *already* home,' I hissed back.

'So hurry up then.' He pointed at Ross on the table. 'Come on, pass him through.'

'And he's been to the police station.'

Sim recoiled. 'What?' He pushed his sunglasses up on top of his head, where they were held fast by his Velcro hair. 'What for?'

'Don't know. But I bet I can guess.'

Kenny was at Sim's shoulder. 'That's it, then. We shouldn't do it. Let's just go. Leave Ross. I'm telling you: we'll just get in even more trouble.'

I shushed him. I could hear footfalls in the room above. 'No,' I whispered. 'We've got to do this. But maybe we can get Caroline to help.'

Sim wasn't happy. 'Really bad idea, Blake.'

'She's really cut up,' I said. 'I can tell just by the way she's talking how bad she feels. I mean, genuinely. And I reckon she'd probably want to come with us.'

'Yeah? Well, I'm not doing it if she is,' Kenny said, almost climbing in through the window to make his point. 'So she can't. Tell her she can't. *I'll* tell her if you want.'

Sim shoved him out the way, warning him with a glare to keep his voice down. 'What about what she did to him last week? Remember? In front of everybody at school? She wasn't all that cut-up taking the piss out of him then, was she?'

I shrugged. 'Yeah, but . . .'

'If she wasn't his sister she'd be just as bad as Fowler and Munro.'

Kenny got his nose in again. 'After what she did, I bet she's half the reason Nina dumped him.'

I knew that wasn't true, but I also knew I couldn't explain why not either.

'She won't understand,' Sim said. 'She was there at the funeral same as everyone else, and she didn't do anything, did she? No one's gonna do anything because no one else knew him like we did. So no one else is gonna understand.'

I nodded. Maybe he was right.

He slipped his sunglasses back down into place. 'Look, if we don't go now, we get done for the graffiti. And then we're never gonna be able to do this. I've already told my mum I'm staying at Kenny's tonight, and he's said he's staying at mine – we're already doing it. Just get Ross and let's go.'

'Yeah, Blake,' Kenny said. 'Come on, it's nearly ten.' He pushed his watch in my face. 'The train goes at half-past.'

I checked over my shoulder again. 'Okay, but how am I supposed to sneak him out now his dad's here?'

'Just pass him through.'

'I've got to get out too, don't forget. I can't still be here when they come back and see Ross isn't.'

'Climb through with him.' Sim stepped back to give me room.

'Can you fit?' Kenny asked. Which wasn't particularly fair.

'Of course I can *fit*,' I hissed. 'But I'll make a hell of a lot of noise doing it.' I pointed out the crockery and glasses in and around the sink that I was bound to smash trying to climb over. 'I'm gonna have to leg it out the front door while they're upstairs. Wait for me on the corner, okay?' I turned back to the table to grab Ross.

But Kenny stopped me. 'Do we need all of him? Can't you just scoop some out? No one's going to notice if there's just a scoopful missing.'

Sim and I weren't impressed.

'Are you sick?' Sim asked. 'And what're we meant to carry a "scoopful" in anyway?'

Kenny shrugged. 'There must be some Tupperware somewhere. He had a lunch box, didn't he?'

'D'you really think he'd want bits of him here, bits of him there?' I remembered my earlier thoughts, wondered if we'd be able to tell whether we'd taken some arm or leg or whatever. 'No way am I gonna get into this much trouble just so we can end up with his big toe!'

Kenny was ready to argue again, but I heard footsteps coming back down the stairs and waved at him to shut the hell up. I swore, realizing it was too late to pass the urn through without getting trapped in here. 'Now what am I meant to do?' I said.

They both shrugged.

I swore again. 'Just meet me on the corner in five minutes, okay? And get ready to run.'

They nodded. Then ducked their heads quicker than if someone was aiming a gun at them. Caroline had walked back into the kitchen, with Mr Fell behind her.

Yesterday at the funeral was the first time I'd seen him since Ross's accident, and there had been a weird little bit of me worried he might resent me for still being alive when his son was dead. I'd just avoided him. And now I was scared he'd hate me for spraying Ross's name on people's doors and cars. But he smiled at me, came over and shook my hand, pumped it hard. 'Blake, good to see you. Wonderful of you to come round.'

I didn't know how to reply. So I said something stupid. 'I, er, just opened the window a bit. I wanted to let some air in.' Anything to distract him from the guilty flush on my face.

'It is a bit stuffy, isn't it?' he said. 'Push it all the way up if you want. We seem to keep barricading ourselves in at the moment.'

I opened the window as high as it would go, and leaned over far enough to see Kenny and Sim scrambling away through the flowerbed on their hands and knees, dragging our rucksacks through the dry earth behind them. When I turned back Caroline was sitting at the table, holding Ross in both hands again. Mr Fell was pouring himself a glass of orange juice. He offered me some but I shook my head. If he was going to get mad at me about our graffiti he was going an odd way about it. I guessed he didn't know what we'd done – not yet anyway. I couldn't work out why he'd been to see the police.

He was a tidily shabby man, always wearing what appeared to be the same baggy cords and old-fashioned cardigan with patches on the elbows – although Ross had told us he had a wardrobe full of them. He had a thick but neat, greying beard and half-moon glasses on a chain around his neck. Like Ross, he wanted to be a writer, and I supposed dressing like one was halfway towards actually being one. He was the opposite of Ross's mum, who never seemed to be able to switch off her bossy-lecturer mode, even when at home. She spoke to everybody like they 'could try harder'. And this past year Ross had somehow got it into his head that he was adopted. No way did he think he had any of the same genes as either of his parents. He'd made a long, long list of all his differences. The shared ambition with his dad being the *only* similarity.

'Penny says to say hello,' Mr Fell told me, nodding his head at the bedroom above, where Mrs Fell had confined herself since Ross's death. Caroline had already told me that the funeral yesterday was the only time her mum had left the house this past week.

'She's sorry she can't get up to see you. Doctor's got her on so many pills she's beginning to rattle. She's still . . . still struggling, unfortunately.'

He was talking to me in a particularly adult manner, as if confiding in me. I nodded in what I hoped looked like an understanding way and wondered how on earth I was going to prise my best friend out of his daughter's grasp.

'I'm glad you came round, Blake. I've been meaning to get in touch because there's something I'd like to ask you.' He'd been staring at his orange juice but now he looked straight at me. There was a worry in his eyes that I didn't understand. 'I'm not quite sure how to put this . . . but, how did Ross seem to you? In the days running up to his accident, I mean.'

I was confused. I looked from him to Caroline. She kept her eyes on Ross.

'Okay. I think.'

Mr Fell nodded, scratched his nose. 'Anything bothering him? That you know of? Anything in particular that he might have told you?'

I thought about Mr Fowler, Munro, Nina. Caroline was quite defiant in her not looking at me and I also thought about the way she'd taunted her brother, embarrassing him in front of most of the school last week.

I said, 'Just school and stuff, I suppose.'

Mr Fell kept nodding and even gave me a brief smile. 'The usual things you lot have to put up with?'

'Well, yeah. I suppose so.' I wasn't lying, I just wasn't going into detail.

'He didn't seem . . . anxious?'

I couldn't see where this was leading. 'I don't think so.'

Mr Fell was silent. He drank his orange juice in one long gulp and sighed.

'Can I ask why?'

He looked up at me again, surprised. 'Yes, of course. Of course you can.' But it took him a while before he answered. He stared hard at Ross's urn – like it was a crossword, sudoko and Rubik's cube all rolled into one.

'The police, well, they needed to talk to me about something – something that hadn't really crossed my mind.' His eyes flicked between his daughter and me. 'Anybody's mind, for that matter. But it has very much upset us – Caroline, Penny and myself.' It still took him an effort to spit it out. 'It's the driver of the car that hit Ross who's brought the matter up. He seems to think Ross may have purposely caused the accident. That he intended to ride into the car. On purpose.'

I still didn't get it. I waited for him to explain.

He lifted his glass to drink again, but there was only the tiniest of drops left. It took an age for it to dribble along the inside of the glass to his open mouth. All I could do was sit there and watch. At last he put the glass down on the counter.

'He was your friend, Blake. I'm sure he talked about lots of things with you that he'd never dream of telling his mum and me. I'd very much appreciate your honesty. Do you think Ross could have taken his own life?'

I felt like I'd been punched. The air was knocked out of me.

'No!' I said it immediately, didn't even have to think about it.

Then, when I was able to think for a second or two: 'No. No way. That's . . .' I shook my head as hard as I could. 'No.'

Mr Fell's eyes searched mine.

'No,' I repeated.

He seemed to snap out of himself. He stood upright. 'Good. Exactly. That's exactly the way I feel too.' He gave me a clenched smile. 'Thank you for that. I think I can understand why the driver would rather believe . . . But Penny, it's upset her terribly, I'm afraid.'

'Ross wouldn't have,' I said. Not just to Mr Fell and Caroline, but to myself as well.

'Good. Thank you, Blake. Thank you.' His smile widened behind his beard as he fortified himself. He nodded at me. 'And wonderful to see you again. Tell Kenny and Sim they're both welcome here any time too. Tell them to be sure to come and see us. We want to keep up with what you're up to, don't we?'

I gave the urn a guilty glance.

'This house would feel even stranger without the three of you getting under our feet.' He was talking far too much and was in a hurry to move on, wanting the subject changed. 'In fact, tell Kenny I need his help, can you? A favour. He's the one who's good with the old computers, isn't he? Mine's gone a bit loopy, you see, and whisked my novel away somewhere. I'm sure it's still lurking in the damn thing, hidden in a file God knows where. But Kenny'll be the one to sort me out, won't he? Yes, he's the chap. A good few years I've been working on that novel and I'm not going to give up on it now, by God.' His laugh was too loud.

I nodded vaguely. I was fighting to get my head around what he'd asked me about Ross and didn't give a toss about his precious novel or broken computer. He'd lit a fuse in my head; I could feel its hot fizz and sputter.

'So, well, let yourself out when you're ready.' He came over and shook my hand again. 'Good to see you, Blake. Good to see you're well.' And he held on a little too long for comfort. I saw his eyes were wet, shiny, and I had to look away, scared and embarrassed he might cry in front of me.

When at last he let go, he said, 'Caroline, love, would you bring a fresh jug of water for your mother? I'll see if I can get her up for a bit.' Then he ducked out of the kitchen and headed back upstairs.

It seemed to be a real effort for Caroline to let go of the urn. She took a clear plastic jug from one of the cupboards and moved over to the sink.

'Did you hear this thing about Ross too?' I asked.

'It's a lie.' She ran the tap, filled the jug with cold water. 'My mum's really suffered since Ross's accident, and this has made her even worse. Of course the driver doesn't want it to be his fault. I've tried telling them, but my dad wanted to ask you too.'

I could feel myself getting angry. Maybe if he knew his son as well as I did he would never have had to. I looked at Ross on the table.

Caroline stepped towards the door through to the hall. 'I'll be back in a minute.'

Blinking and focusing on what I was meant to be doing here, I realized this was my last chance to steal Ross. And I even reached out for the urn in my eagerness, like I was reaching for the biggest slice of pizza. Caroline saw me and hesitated at the door. I whipped my hand back but it was too late, she was already suspicious, and the guilty blush on my face didn't help matters.

'Blake?' She took a step towards me, as though she was going to take the urn herself.

So I picked it up before she got the chance.

She was confused. 'What are you doing?'

'Look, I'm sorry,' I said. 'We're doing it for Ross, I promise.'

She stood in the doorway, frowning. Her

bewilderment cranked up my guilt another notch or two. She was blocking my way.

I repeated how sorry I was, tried squeezing past her into the hall. She wasn't going to let me get by. But as I pushed against her I knocked the jug in her hand, splashing icy water over both of us. It was a shock in the stuffy house; we leaped away from each other. I turned for the front door.

'Blake? What're you . . . ?' Her voice rose in alarm.

Mr and Mrs Fell were on the landing at the top of the stairs. She was wearing a long dressing gown and leaning on Mr Fell's arm as if she was ten times older than what she really was. I'd always thought of her as strict and spiky – had always been kind of glad she wasn't my mum. She didn't look like a short-tempered lecturer this morning, however. She looked more like a ghost than the woman I remembered as Ross's mother.

I ran for the front door at the end of the hall, clutching that urn so tightly I worried I might shatter it.

Both Mr Fell and Caroline were shouting at me.

I wanted to stay and explain, I really did. I knew what we were going to do was bound to hurt them, but we were doing it for Ross. I might have told them everything if I'd had the chance. And yet I guess I believed Sim: nobody else would understand why we wanted to do this, so no way would they agree to letting us do it. I slammed out the front door and ran onto the street without looking back.

Kenny and Sim were waiting at the corner. 'Come on! Come on!' Kenny urged and beckoned me to hurry. Sim grabbed our rucksacks. Then we were all running. All four of us. Me, Kenny, Sim . . . and Ross.

Five

'It's not really kidnapping, is it?' Kenny said. 'He'd have to be alive, wouldn't he? For it to be proper kidnapping, I mean.'

'I suppose so,' I said. 'But I doubt that means we're in any less trouble. You know how it's going to go: Ross's dad'll ring up my house, and my mum'll ring Sim's, who'll ring yours. Sim's mum'll find out he's not really staying at your house, yours'll find out you're not staying at his—'

'And then everybody goes ape-shit,' Sim said, making it all sound so very inevitable anyway.

Kenny was looking much more worried. 'I thought you were going to sneak him out. That was what you said. You said you'd—'

'Caroline wouldn't let go of him. Maybe if I'd had some chloroform or a couple of tranquillizer darts I could have prised him out of her unconscious fingers. Apart from that, what else was I meant to do?'

'Pass him to us, like we said.'

'Yeah, great, then I'd have been the one trapped in there trying to explain how come the urn had upped and disappeared into thin air all of a sudden.'

Kenny was quiet, but he wasn't happy.

Ross's house was on Hardy's Road, but we'd run all the way, and going by the clock tower on the train station's roof had made it with five minutes to spare. The day was getting hotter and I wasn't the only one panting for breath. But I didn't want us to start squabbling and bickering now; we had to get on the train and get moving.

'Look, be glad the police didn't want to talk to Ross's dad about the graffiti, okay?'

'Yeah, what did the police want anyway?' Sim asked.

'Just some mad bullshit – I'll tell you about it when we're on the train. Can we just get our tickets and get going before anyone thinks of following us?'

Kenny grumbled, but went through to the ticket office.

Last night Sim had been easy to persuade. Straight away he'd grasped just how brilliant and meaningful and cool it would be to take Ross to Ross. And how brilliant Ross would have reckoned it was too. 'Just like one of his stories,' Sim had said. Ross wrote adventure stories and even though he changed the names, we knew the characters were based on us. I'd managed to persuade Sim not to spray Nina's house and we'd made our plans for today.

Kenny's reasons to be worried were good ones. The biggest being that what we were doing now was far worse than spraying a bit of graffiti. Which meant we could land up in even bigger trouble. Sim had first used the story argument to try and sway him. Hadn't he ever wanted to live out one of Ross's stories for real? And then I'd resorted to emotional blackmail. If he'd hated the funeral as much as he reckoned he had, and thought all those people were as big hypocrites as he said he did, then wasn't giving Ross a real, proper, fitting memorial exactly the right thing to do? Kenny's problem was one minute he said yes, one minute no. It was why me and Sim had to make up his mind for him most of the time.

But standing on the station waiting for the train, we were all tense, jumpy. Even Sim, no matter how cool he thought he looked with his shaved head and trendy sunglasses. He was checking over his shoulder, watching the clock as often as me and Kenny were. The train was late and we were anxious we might have been followed. Getting stopped before we even got started wouldn't be the smartest idea.

The trouble with Cleethorpes station is that the platforms are so open, there's nowhere to hide. You can see the beach, and what we call the sea. I've never understood why people would want to come here on holiday – there must be half a million more exciting places. But at this time of year, and on sunny Saturday mornings, there are plenty of trippers wandering around. I kept thinking people were looking at us. It was difficult to go unnoticed standing next to Kenny in his horrible orange T-shirt – it was the orangest T-shirt I'd ever seen. No wonder Sim was wearing sunglasses.

There were about a dozen others waiting on the platform with us; I didn't recognize any of them, so hoped they didn't recognize us. We felt guilty knowing Ross was tucked deep inside my rucksack and conspicuous with our tickets to Scotland. Cleethorpes is also a dead-end: the trains only come this far. They don't even turn round, just go back out towards Grimsby the same way they came in. And the train coming in was late, so we knew it would be even later going out again. We shuffled our feet, fidgeted, squirmed, stared along the track – willing it to hurry up.

When my mobile rang Kenny and Sim leaped away from me quicker than if they'd heard the sudden ticking of a bomb. I didn't want to even touch it at first – guessing who was on the other end. I had thought it was funny to pick the noisiest, nastiest ringtone I could. But I wasn't laughing now. And some of the other waiting passengers turned to glance at us. Waiting was boring; they were quite happy to be nosy. I killed the call without even taking the phone out of my pocket, just fumbling for the button. Then, reluctantly, oh so reluctantly, I took it out to read the caller display.

Sim stayed at a safe distance when he asked, 'Your mum?'

I nodded.

He swore. Then went pale when his mobile burst out ringing too. He hurried to shut it up. Looking a little pale he said, 'My dad. They must have got him out of bed – he was on night shift last night.'

'Please God don't let them call my mum,' Kenny prayed. 'Please, God. Please, God . . .'

He shook his fist at the sunny blue sky when his mobile finally went off.

We switched our phones to silent. Maybe they'd be easier to ignore. But the way they buzzed and vibrated was like trying to hold angry pins and needles in the palm of your hand.

So now we knew: Ross's parents had been quick to contact ours. In my mind's eye I got a flash of the look on my mum's face as she gripped the receiver of our phone in the living room at home. I stopped the call but she kept ringing back. There was no way I was going to answer, yet I didn't quite dare switch the phone off either. Ignoring my mum's call was dangerous enough; switching it off altogether was close to mutiny.

I decided to let her shout at the voicemail instead of me and was grateful when at last it kicked in. My phone went still. I grinned at Kenny and Sim in relief. But only for a second or two. Mum wasn't going to be ignored quite so easily.

Kenny was dancing on the spot, juggling his mobile like it was on fire.

'Don't answer it,' Sim told him. 'Don't you dare!'

'But . . . my mum . . . she'll go mad if I don't.'

'That's exactly *why* you don't.' Sim waved his own phone high, and with an exaggerated devil-may-care grin held down the power button, blanking the screen and killing its furious buzz. He shrugged and pushed the phone deep into his jeans pocket. 'My dad's gonna kick my arse. But I reckon it'll be worth an arse-kicking.'

Kenny didn't seem so sure. 'You know my mum. You know what she's like. I'm telling you: she'll *kill* me.'

'She's just going to tell you to come home, right? D'you want to go home? You're not flaking out on us already, are you?'

Right then I think Kenny was tempted to say 'yes', but he knew Sim and I would never give up so easily. So he shook his head. 'No, course not. Just . . .' He danced a bit more, pointing at his phone.

Sim snatched it from him. 'It's got an "off" button too, you know.'

'Maybe, yeah. But my mum hasn't.'

Sim ignored him, turning the phone off. Then he looked at me.

I nodded, forced the image of my mum's angry face out of my mind and pressed down hard on the power button. I felt a little shaky with my defiance but didn't let it show. I held the phone up to Sim to prove the screen was blank.

'Right,' he said. 'Now this is the deal. We don't turn them on again until we get home, okay? We don't need them. It's not like anything's going to happen to the three of us together, is it? We'll take whatever crap they throw at us when we get home. But by then it'll be too late to stop us, because it's already going to be done, isn't it?' He seemed pleased with his logic.

Kenny and I didn't get a chance to argue because that was when the train decided to arrive. We hurried on board. And I felt that bubbling, nervy defiance I had inside become a definite rush. I realized I'd never been this rebellious before. My parents would stop me in an instant if they could, and they'd certainly punish me now that they couldn't. But here I was, doing it anyway. Doing it with my friends.

Who'd have guessed it could feel so good?

Six

I let out the big breath I didn't even realize I'd been holding when the train at last dragged itself away from the station. No one could stop us now – no turning back.

It was a short, noisy train. We managed to find a free table in the second carriage out of two and huddled around it like the conspirators we were; Sim blocking the fourth seat with his rucksack to discourage anyone else from joining us. An old lady with spider-web hair sat at the table across the aisle and was watching us, but when I met her stare she took out a glossy magazine to read.

Kenny pressed his face to the window, trying to keep an eye on the station as it disappeared behind us. 'We've not been followed,' he said. He sounded like he was expecting his mum and a whole host of SWAT police to come charging onto the platform as we escaped just in the nick of time. I reckoned he'd been watching too many movies. 'No one we know spotted us.'

'Which is a miracle for you in that T-shirt,' Sim said.

Kenny turned round in his seat. 'What d'you mean by that?'

'It's not exactly camouflage, is it?'

'It's designer.'

'It hurts your eyes if you look at it for too long,' I said.

Sim asked, 'Did someone give it to you?'

'No, I bought it.'

Sim acted amazed. 'With your own money?'

But Kenny refused to bite. He stroked a hand across his chest, smoothing rumples. 'It's my favourite. And you're so jealous I can smell it.'

Neither Sim nor I had a clue what that meant. We burst out laughing.

Kenny grinned at us, pleased that he'd been funny. He pushed his messy blond fringe out of his eyes and said, 'Come on, Blake. Get the map out. I want to know where we're meant to be going exactly.'

But Sim shook his head. 'No. Get Ross out first.'

We cleared up the newspaper and half-eaten

sandwich crud left by the passenger before us; Kenny even scrubbed away a dried coffee splot from the tabletop. We didn't want our mate sitting in litter. Then, checking to make sure we weren't being watched by the old lady across from us, I carefully took Ross out from where he'd been wrapped up in my jumper at the bottom of my rucksack and placed him on the table. I had to keep hold of him because of the rattling and swaying of the train. And just like it had been with Caroline, we couldn't take our eyes off him.

'This is the closest I've ever been to someone who's dead,' Kenny said.

'I can't get over how small it is,' Sim said. 'Ross was as tall as me, and now he fits in *there*.'

'How do we know it's all of him?' Kenny asked. 'How could you tell if they've missed some?'

'Can you believe somebody even has that job?' Sim was incredulous. 'How did work go today, darling? Well, it was a bit slow; I only collected four burned-up dead people.'

'D'you reckon they'd fit you in there?' Kenny asked me.

I looked at him to make sure he wasn't taking the

piss. 'Maybe,' I said. 'If they tamped me down a bit, you know?' With my fist hitting my palm I made the action of squeezing a dead chubby kid into a confined space – or something similar. And Kenny laughed.

Sim reached for the urn's lid.

Kenny blocked him. 'What're you doing?' he said, shocked.

Sim's hand hovered. 'I want to have a look inside.'

'No, you can't. That's wrong, that is. *Disrespectful.*'

'Says the one who was going to put him in a lunch box!'

Kenny looked to me. 'We can't . . . can we?'

I knew what he meant. But when I'd been with Caroline, hadn't I also wanted to look? 'Aren't you just a little bit curious? If you've never been this close to a dead person, you've definitely never *seen* one before.'

Kenny thought about it. 'I don't know,' he said. 'What if you spill him?'

'I'll keep hold while Sim takes the lid off, okay?'

He still wasn't keen. 'Okay. But we've all got to cover our noses too. Because I'm telling you: we're really shittered if anybody sneezes.'

Sim pushed his sunglasses up on top of his head, stretched his neck to look around, double-checking that none of the other passengers were paying us any attention, then took hold of the urn's lid. Kenny watched me to be sure I kept a tight grip on the base. Sim struggled at first, before realizing the lid was meant to be screwed off. He waited for the clattering train to get over a bumpy section of track. Kenny and I leaned as close as we could. And finally he lifted the lid away.

We peered inside.

It was ash.

Of course it was. But we'd been expecting . . . I don't think we knew what we'd been expecting. And none of us knew what to say. We didn't know whether to feel disappointed, humbled, or just that little bit stupid. We were all quiet.

Then I remembered what Caroline had told me about the weird memories that kept popping into her head. 'It's what *can't* be fitted in there that counts,' I said.

Kenny nodded hard, sitting up in his eagerness. 'Yeah. Yeah, that's right, isn't it? And that's why we're doing all this stuff. Because of all the other stuff.'

Sim put the lid back on. 'We're doing it because of everything they *didn't* say at the funeral yesterday – everything that everybody else forgot.'

'Or didn't even know in the first place,' I added.

I noticed the old woman with cobweb hair was watching us over the top of her magazine. I turned my back on her, wrapped Ross up in my jumper and pushed him down to the bottom of my rucksack again.

At the top of his voice, Sim said, 'Some people are just really dead nosy, aren't they?'

When I turned round again the old woman looked like she'd been sucking lemons, but her eyes were back fixed on her magazine. Now that we were moving I wanted to talk to Kenny and Sim about what Ross's dad had asked me. I could still feel the fuse he'd lit fizzing away inside my head.

'That thing about the police . . .' I whispered, leaning across the table. 'About why they wanted to see Ross's dad? You're not gonna believe what's been said. The driver reckons Ross did it on purpose.'

Kenny was confused. 'Did what on purpose?'

'The accident.'

But he still didn't get it. 'How? How d'you get

knocked off your bike on purpose? That's why it's called an accident, isn't it?'

Sim was getting angry. 'The driver said it?'

'Yeah. And Ross's dad was asking me if Ross was all right, if he had any *problems*.' I was surprised how hurtful I found it. It felt like an attack on us, his friends.

'Yeah, Ross had problems,' Sim said. 'A dad who's a moron for one thing. Why's he want to believe Ross killed himself?'

'I don't think he believed it,' I said. 'But it definitely felt like he was checking up.'

'He shouldn't have had to. It's obvious the driver's just trying to get himself out of trouble. What a shitbone!'

'D'you think he should have been there yesterday?' Kenny asked. 'The driver, I mean. My mum told me he sent a wreath. But how do you say sorry for, you know . . . for what he did?'

'I'm glad he wasn't there,' Sim said. 'So it was an accident and everything, okay, but he's still the one that knocked Ross off his bike and killed him. No way should he have been allowed anywhere near. And especially if he was gonna spread bullshit too. I've thought about it, right. And I bet Ross was coming round that corner fast and just reckoned he could beat him. How many times have you dodged in front of cars on your bike?'

'Millions,' Kenny said.

'Every day on the way to school,' I said.

Sim nodded. 'Exactly. Everybody does it. Ross was just unlucky.'

We sat there in silence contemplating our own luck compared to that of our friend. But it's always un-comfortable thinking that luck can be the fine line between life and death. We jogged along with the train, not looking at each other. We thought about Ross's mangled bike. TV had filled us full of images of solitary wheels spinning, crowds gathering, broken bodies bleeding – we didn't need too much imagin-ation to put Ross's face in amongst it all.

I'd never admitted to the others that I'd cried when I'd found out about his death, but no way did I think for one second that I was the only one who had. Still, I doubted we'd ever talk about it. We claimed we were the closest friends in the whole world, yet there were certain things we couldn't share – there was always a front to keep up. We'd stand shoulder to shoulder, no hesitation, fighting against the rest of the world. But the crying would always be done in private.

We stopped at Grimsby Town station. I hoped old Mrs Cobweb Head opposite would get off but she didn't move. A handful of people got on – nobody we recognized. As the train pulled away again the conductor appeared.

We acted innocent; probably looked guilty as hell. I realized he couldn't know what we were doing, it was impossible for him to know. I told myself to stop being paranoid. But it didn't stop the prickling nerves.

He towered over us in his uniform, feet planted firmly but the rest of him swaying with the movement of the train. He was sweating in the summer heat and had his sleeves rolled up, displaying half a blue tattoo on his forearm. He checked Sim's ticket first; punched it. 'Quite a journey you've got there,' he said. 'You all going?'

We nodded but didn't speak.

He took Kenny's ticket. 'That's your return,' he said, and Kenny had to ferret around in his rucksack for his outgoing stub while Sim and I rolled our eyes at each other. 'You know all your connections?'

We nodded again.

But: 'Change at Doncaster,' he told us anyway. And checking his watch he added, 'You might need to run when we get there if you want to make the next train.' He wasn't apologizing for this train being late, I noticed. Taking my ticket he asked, 'Holiday, is it?'

I said the first thing that came into my head. 'We're visiting a friend.'

He handed me my ticket again. 'Heck of a long way to go.' He turned his back on us, leaned his arse against our table as he checked the old lady's ticket too. And from over his shoulder we heard him mutter, 'Must be a bloody good friend, that's all I can say.'

Seven

Sim glared at the back of the conductor's head as the man walked through to the next carriage. 'What's it got to do with him? We've paid for our tickets. What's he care where we go?'

'*I* paid for the tickets,' Kenny said.

Sim rolled his eyes. 'I said I'd pay you back, didn't I?'

Kenny didn't answer.

'I said I'd pay you back, okay? I always pay you back, don't I?'

Kenny shrugged.

Sim forced a casual laugh. 'Come on then, when? When haven't I paid you back?'

Kenny seemed reluctant; he looked at me. I held up my hands – staying out of it. I made a point of never getting involved in any of Kenny and Sim's little *tiffs*. 'Lovers' tiffs', Ross called them. We used to bet on the outcome. Sim usually won, but I reckoned he was on shaky ground today.

'When?' he said. 'Name a time. Any time.'

'That time we went swimming,' Kenny said.

'Swimming?'

'Yeah, with Sally Shaw and her brother.'

'That was two years ago!'

'Okay: I bought you a pizza last week. I've bought you loads of pizzas. You've never paid me back for them.'

'That's rubbish. You were buying them for yourself, and just let me share.'

'I don't buy large pizzas just for me, do I?'

Sim looked as though he knew he was cornered. But then he grinned, clicking his tongue the way he did whenever he was feeling pleased with himself. 'Yet.'

Kenny was confused. 'What?'

'Yet. I haven't paid you back *yet*. I promised I'd pay you back, but you never set a time limit, did you? And you can't call me a liar unless I *never* pay you back. You can't call me a liar unless I die tomorrow and you still haven't got your money back.'

Kenny wasn't happy. 'But—'

'It's true. Tell him, Blake.'

I had to admit I admired the way Sim had wriggled his way out of that one.

Kenny pointed a finger at him. 'Yeah, well, I'm telling you, okay? I'm going to kick your arse.'

Sim leaned back in his seat, put his sunglasses on and spread his hands. 'See what I'm doing? I'm waiting.'

'I just haven't done it *yet*,' Kenny said. 'But I will. Just not *yet*.'

Sim only grinned wider. He and I passed several enjoyable minutes winding Kenny up.

Thing was, Kenny had also paid for my ticket – no way would we be able to do any of this if he hadn't agreed to put up the cash for all three of us. We knew we were going to have to stay overnight somewhere, and we'd need to eat too, and Sim and I were relying on Kenny to help us out.

To be fair, he was loaded. He was an only child. Mr and Mrs England had divorced when he was eight or nine and his rich businessman dad had moved to Canada, meaning Kenny hardly got to see him any more. He once told me he'd seen his dad a total of five times since the divorce. And Kenny wasn't as daft as he looked: he reckoned the only reason his dad forced money on him was out of guilt. And what was he meant to do? Refuse it?

Not so long ago I asked him if he missed his dad.

'Sometimes,' he'd told me. 'But whenever I do get to see him, he's never as nice as I thought he was when I was little.'

Sim's mum and dad are still together, but in Sim's eyes might as well not be. His dad's a security guard, night shifts mostly, while his mum's on the checkouts at Tesco – one on the way out the door as the other's coming home. Since his older brother moved out they even have their own bedrooms so they won't disturb each other. Sim finds it easy enough to dodge in between them. If he plans his days well he can go for maybe as long as a week without seeing either one of them, only communicating by notes stuck to the fridge. His brother's a bouncer at some club over in Hull, but he doesn't seem interested in having anything to do with anyone south of the Humber any more and Sim never talks about him. Sim just suits himself a lot.

I'm part of a mixed-up web of a step-family. When my mum and dad split they'd made an agreement to stay close for my sake. Which means occasional but pretend happy Christmases, or forced smiley picnics with Dad and Kim and her two kids, and Mum, Pete and me with my new baby brother Harry. I get on with Kim better than Mum sometimes – which upsets Mum, obviously. And I have to get on with Pete because I live with him, but it can get kind of strained. I'm sure there's been plenty of times he's wanted to clout me for being a clever little git, yet he manages to hold himself back somehow.

It always seems like strategy and tactics with my parents anyway. Pretending to still get on, pretending to like each other's new family. Then Mum and Dad playing me off against each other.

They'd both come to Ross's funeral: Dad had brought Kim, but Mum was alone. And believe it or not, this had caused an argument. Because I'd said I'd like Kim to be there, but I'd not told Mum she could bring Pete. It was only because Kim had met Ross a couple of times and had *offered* to come. I didn't mean it as a slight against Pete that I hadn't hand-written an invitation asking him to come and have fun at the funeral. I'd always thought avoiding funerals was most people's main aim in life. But when I'd told Mum this she'd warned me that I tried to be far too clever for my own good sometimes, and one day I'd find myself knocked down a peg or two.

'Like Ross?' I'd asked (but not out loud).

Maybe I wouldn't dare tell my parents but Kenny, Sim and Ross had always felt like my real family anyway. I'd chosen them as friends because I liked them, and they liked me. Nobody had allowed me to choose my family. They'd just been dumped on me.

We felt the train slow as it pulled into a station and craned our necks to see where we were. Sim spotted the sign first. 'Scunthorpe already. Get your map out, Blake.'

I dragged my rucksack from underneath my seat and rummaged for the map of Britain I'd sneaked out of Pete's car this morning. I waited until any passengers getting on or off had squeezed by down the aisle and then spread it out in front of me. It appeared to be only the size of an exercise book but unfolded noisily, endlessly, becoming as big as a duvet.

'You'll have to move your bag, Kenny,' I said. He'd left it on the table after digging through it for his ticket. He had to stand on his seat to push it onto the rack above his head, which drew an evil look from the web-headed old woman across from us. We ignored her and struggled to huddle over the massive map.

'You should have just got one of Scotland,' Sim said.

'It was all Pete had. And I had to sneak this out without him knowing.' I leaned across it trying to find the place again, wishing I'd marked it with a big cross. 'There,' I said, just as the train pulled away from the station, stabbing my finger at the south-west coast of Scotland. 'That's where we're going.'

Sim and Kenny both peered. I had to remove my finger because it completely covered the dot that was the place called Ross.

'That's it?' Sim asked. 'That's *Ross*?'

I nodded. 'Yep. That's it.'

'What's there?' Kenny wanted to know.

'About three houses, going by the size of it,' I said.

'Looks like there might be a beach,' Sim added, sounding far too hopeful to me.

'Are you sure that's Scotland?' Kenny said. 'I thought Scotland started up there somewhere. Look, there's Edinburgh there.'

'The border's just above Carlisle on the west coast,' I told him. 'And this bit that sticks out towards Ireland? This is all Dumfries and Galloway – definitely Scotland.'

'It's not as far as I thought then,' Sim said. 'I was thinking we'd be going all up around here somewhere.' He was pointing north of Loch Ness.

'It's something like two hundred and sixty miles from Cleethorpes. But that's why I said we can be home tomorrow. Day there, day back. If we hadn't messed up stealing Ross—'

'If *you* hadn't messed up stealing Ross,' Kenny said.

'– then nobody would have even noticed we'd gone.'

'So if we've just left Scunny now . . . ?' Sim was tracing our route on the map. 'We've got to change at Doncaster; then where?'

'Doncaster to Newcastle, Newcastle to Carlisle, Carlisle to Dumfries. But then we have to get a bus. I looked it up on the Internet, and we can get a bus fairly close, but we might have to walk some of it.'

'Because it's in the middle of nowhere,' Kenny said.

'Pretty much,' I agreed. 'But that's where Ross always said he wanted to go.'

Kenny pulled the map closer to him. 'When he first told me about it, I just thought he was making it up.'

'It looks real enough on here.' I noticed his eyes were down at the bottom of the map, around Plymouth somewhere.

'It's up here, Kenny.' I pointed again. 'Scotland.'

'Yeah, I know. I was just looking to see if there's a place called Kenny. I might want to go there too one day.'

Sim and I exchanged a look. 'What's your surname?' Sim asked.

Kenny was running his finger along the Cornish coast. 'England. You know it is.'

We stayed quiet – let it sink in. It took almost a full minute.

Then he started laughing. 'England! Right . . . I don't need to go there, do I? I *live* there.' He thought it was the funniest thing ever. In fact, he laughed most of the way to Doncaster.

He made me and Sim laugh too, and suddenly we were having a good time. We were searching the map for stupid place names, like Farleigh Wallop, Nempnett Thrubwell and Nob – shouting them out to each other, fighting over the map to find one even more ridiculous than the last. We were enjoying being loud, acting up – we even saw it as a compliment when the miserable old woman across the aisle scowled and tutted at us. And it felt good, great, brilliant to be acting stupid with mates (like most lads, it was what we'd always been good at after all). It was a release. The past week since Ross's death had been dark and claustrophobic, full of crying parents and sleepless nights. But now, because we were doing the right thing, doing the thing we knew Ross would have wanted, it felt like we could allow ourselves to loosen up again. It was just such a pity he wasn't here to join in.

I pointed out the old woman's hair, said that it looked like a mass of spiders' webs. 'What do you call a bunch of spiders?' I asked Sim.

'A clutter,' he said.

'She doesn't go to the hairdresser's,' I whispered. 'At night, while she's sleeping, a clutter of spiders scurries across her bald scalp re-doing her hair for the morning.'

And we laughed like a pack of hyenas.

We swayed and rattled the last few miles before Doncaster. I'd forgotten all about our train being late and the conductor's warning that we'd be pushed to make our connection. It didn't even cross my mind until his voice came over the intercom to announce that we were now arriving in Doncaster station, apologizing for the delay.

I dived into my rucksack, looking for the scrap of paper with our connections and times scribbled on it. We were supposed to arrive at 11:36, the train for Newcastle leaving at 11:49. But my watch said it was gone quarter to already. And when I looked out the window I could see a long, sleek 125 already waiting at another platform.

'Quick! Get your stuff!'

Kenny and Sim looked confused.

'We've got about two minutes. We're going to miss the next train!'

There was panic as Sim grabbed his rucksack and Kenny struggled to fold the map back up. This train was trundling in alongside the platform, its brakes whining. Kenny couldn't get the huge map to do as he wanted, swearing at it as it crumpled, and he had to start all over again. I tried to help him but the two of us made an even bigger mess of it in our rush. I ripped it along one crease, tearing Norfolk in two. The other passengers were up and heading for the doors.

Sim was on his feet. 'Stop fannying around. Who cares if it's folded properly?' He tried to squeeze past the old woman with as polite a shove as he could.

I yanked on Kenny's arm. 'It doesn't matter. Don't

worry about it.' I threw my rucksack over my shoulder and followed Sim. If we missed our connection then I had no idea how long it would take us to get to Ross. Kenny bundled up the map as best he could. The two of us followed Sim – angering the other passengers as we pushed by.

As soon as the train door slid open the three of us were out onto the platform and running for the subway at the end. We had to get down and through the subway to the northbound platform on the other side of the tracks. Sim led the charge, skipping and dodging between the people coming up the steps as we were leaping down. 'Sorry. Excuse me. Sorry.' I was hot on his heels. Kenny wasn't far behind with the huge map flapping and fluttering around his head like a ripped sail. And even though we were running, even though it must have been obvious to any idiot that we were in a rush, people still didn't help us by simply stepping out the way to let us through. Sim weaved in between them. Our banging footsteps echoed off the subway's walls. I wasn't as light on my feet and ended up smacking shoulders with quite a few. Kenny couldn't see a thing with that map flying around his head and knocked one bloke flat on his backside.

We raced towards the end of the tunnel, then, leaping for the light two steps at a time, burst up onto the northbound platform. There was already a station guy with a whistle in his mouth all set to move the train off.

'Wait! *Wait!*' the three of us shouted at once, scared we couldn't be heard over the engine noise.

He spotted us and waved for us to hurry – was good enough to give us those couple of extra moments to jump aboard. But the split second we did, the doors bleeped rapidly and slid into place with a clunk. Kenny almost got the edge of the map trapped, and that would have been the Isle of Man and most of Wales lost for ever. We heard the whistle blow, and with a lurch the train got itself moving.

We stood in the connecting area between the carriages, the rumble of the train much louder here, Doncaster station sliding out of view from the window. We were grinning at each other, slapping each other on the back – excited by our nick-of-time timing. I was out of breath. I may be big, but I can run when I need to – it just takes the wind out of me. I had to bend over and put my hands on my knees to ease a stitch. We were all sweating.

Then Sim said: 'Are you sure this is the right train?'

The three of us instantly panicked again. All swearing and fussing at once. We could be going to Farleigh Wallop, Nempnett Thrubwell . . . anywhere. We could be going back to Cleethorpes for all we knew. I'd just *assumed* this was the right train.

But Kenny spotted the notice on the door listing the different stations along the train's route. THE ROUTE OF THE FLYING SCOTSMAN. It was going all the way to Edinburgh, but would be stopping off at Newcastle too.

The relief felt good, our grins and bravado returned. Another catastrophe avoided. This was seat-of-the-pants stuff, but we were doing okay. Sim said we should try to find somewhere to sit. Kenny and I at last managed to fold the map back up and I told him to put it in his bag.

'My bag,' Kenny said, white-faced. '*My bag!*' He looked like he'd been smacked on the back of the head with a plank of wood. 'I've left it on the other train. It's got all my stuff in it. It's got all my money in it!'

Eight

The train hurtled north, taking us with it. We stayed in the connecting area between the carriages where the noise of that hurtle was loudest. Other passengers staggered past towards the toilet or the buffet, keeping a hand to the wall as the train rocked. We stood close together, heads bent and whispering, but doing our best to look inconspicuous.

'We can't go back,' Sim said. 'It's impossible.'

Kenny hopped from foot to foot and whined.

I met Sim's eye; he was thinking the same as me. As if this trip wasn't going to be difficult enough ... Without Kenny's cash it could go a bit nightmarish all too easily.

'We've got to go back,' Kenny said. 'I'm telling you: we—'

'How?' Sim was pissed off. 'Are you gonna ask the driver to turn the train round or am I?'

'But my bag ...'

'The train we were on was going all the way to Manchester,' I said. 'It's not even going to be back at Doncaster any more.'

'It's got everything in it.' Kenny was almost pleading. 'I mean, not just my money. I had my iPod and my mobile . . . I'd got a waterproof in case it rained.'

'At least you were wearing your favourite T-shirt,' I said. 'You've still got that.'

Sim shot me a look to tell me I wasn't helping. Kenny said, 'I'd thought of everything. I'd got my toothbrush. I'd got Travel Scrabble.'

Now Sim looked stunned. 'Christ-on-a-bike, Kenny! What the hell did you want . . . ?' He shook his head. 'You amaze me, you know? How can you think of stuff like that, but not even remember to keep hold of your bag?'

'Tell me you've at least got your ticket on you,' I said.

'Of course I've got my ticket.' Kenny pulled it out of his back pocket and waved it at me.

I took it from him to get a better look. 'That's the return part,' I said.

He snatched it back, not sure if I was still trying to

be funny. But I was telling the truth. He closed his eyes, hung his head.

I felt bad for him then. He was a real *trier*. If Kenny ever died it would probably say 'I tried' on his gravestone. He was the cleverest person I knew when it came to computers and stuff like that; he'd just never had any common-sense software uploaded, that was all.

'We might be able to get you another ticket,' I said. 'We only need enough for a single there, right? How much money have we got on us?'

We dug as deeply into our pockets as we could. I had two £10 notes crushed up at the very bottom of mine.

'Just over a fiver,' Sim said, counting out shrapnel. 'Five pounds thirty-eight.'

Kenny didn't have anything any more. 'I had easily a hundred quid in my bag – at least.'

'Twenty-five pounds thirty-eight,' Sim said. 'Nowhere near enough for another ticket.'

'True, but at least it's something.' I was desperate to sound positive. 'It'll do us for food – a couple of Maccy Ds each.'

'What about for a hotel tonight?' Kenny was morose.

'Do you really think there's going to be a hotel at Ross? You saw the map – that spot the size of gnat crap?'

'But—'

'And who needs a hotel anyway? It's summer out there, isn't it? Haven't you heard of sleeping out under the stars?' I was laying it on thick. 'This is an *adventure,* right?'

Kenny perked up enough to insult me. 'We could always use your pants as a tent.'

'Yeah, and burn your radioactive T-shirt to keep us warm.'

Sim said: 'What about his ticket?'

They both looked at me, both eager for me to make everything all right again. This was my idea after all. 'Maybe we can get away with it,' I said. 'We only need to get as far as Newcastle on this train, right? We might have enough for a ticket from Newcastle to Dumfries. The closer we get, the cheaper a ticket's going to be.'

'But we've got to get to Newcastle first,' Kenny said.

'Just keep your head down, pretend to be asleep or something,' Sim told him. 'Hide in the bogs if you have to.'

Kenny wasn't happy. 'What'll happen if I get caught?'

'I'm sure they'll stop the train before they throw you off,' I said.

We went looking for seats.

The train charged through the countryside, fields and trees speeding by the windows. It was busy but not packed. We weren't worried about being recognized now, had no fear of bumping into anyone we knew. There were families with young kids, students sitting by themselves and backpackers in twos or threes. Most of them wore their 'travel face' – kind of blank, a bit bored, mostly tuned-out. We made our way through two then three separate carriages hoping to find a free table where the three of us could sit like before. But without any luck. It was when we reached the carriage where the conductor was checking tickets that we panicked, spun around and stumbled over each other in our hurry to get back the way we'd come. And we ended up exactly where we'd started.

Kenny was so worried he bounced. 'So, you know . . . So, what do we do? I might as well get off at the next stop, right?'

'Don't chicken out on us now,' I said.

'But I'm the one who's going to get kicked off. Not you.'

I looked at Sim. 'What do you call a load of chickens?'

'Brood,' he said. 'Or peep. Some people call it a peep.'

'Don't "peep" out on us, Kenny,' I said. 'It's all part of the adventure, right?' I was worried he might give up and go home, and I believed this trip was meant to be all three of us. I felt sure Ross would have wanted all three of us together.

Kenny was a long way from happy. He didn't like me picking on him, and liked being labelled a whole bunch of chickens even less.

Sim was wearing his sunglasses again, keeping his cool. 'You'll just have to hide in the bogs.'

'But what if I get caught? They might get the police – it's against the law, right? I'm telling you: someone's bound to tell my mum.'

'So don't get caught.'

'Great. Thanks. That's easy enough for you to say, isn't it?'

'So what am I supposed to say? You weren't worried about the law last night when we sprayed up Fowler's house and Munro's car.'

'Yes I was. I was the one who said we—'

'And you're the one who's lost his ticket, so stop whining.'

Kenny scowled and turned as though he was going to stomp away. But maybe he remembered there wasn't really anywhere to stomp away to. Instead, he sagged.

'Why's it always happen to me? It's true, isn't it? It's always me stuff like this happens to. Why am I always getting the crappy end of the stick?'

Sim didn't like Kenny's sudden self-pity. 'Get over it.'

'Yeah, thanks. Thanks for that. You're a great friend, you are.' He saw Sim was about to bite back so got in there first. 'Don't say it. I don't care what you say. Because I'm the unlucky one, aren't I?'

'I can't help thinking that out of all the people I know, Ross is probably the unluckiest.'

But Kenny wouldn't stop. 'You're not the one who's just lost a hundred quid.'

'I wouldn't be lucky enough to have hundred quid in the first place,' Sim scoffed.

'It wasn't just the money! What about my other stuff – my iPod?'

'And Travel Scrabble,' I reminded him.

'All of it!' He was getting red-faced and worked up. 'It's always *me*. I'm telling you: over and over again, it's always me who all the crappy stuff happens to.'

Part of me knew he was right. Teachers could think he was rude, girls sometimes called him weird: he wasn't either. The truth was that the real world seemed to move at a quicker pace than Kenny's head sometimes, and he was always too busy trying to catch up to see what was actually going on around him. So part of me did feel sorry for him – yet I couldn't help thinking he brought a lot of it on himself.

You've got to learn to deal with your own problems, haven't you? Moaning about it won't help. How messed up would you be if you didn't get a grip and get over it?

But he was anxious and miserable. 'I want to go to Scotland as much as you, you know. It's not just about the stuff I've lost. I want to do this funeral thing too – do it for Ross, same as you. But I'm the one messing everything up. It's true, isn't it? I am, aren't I? It's my fault.' He kicked the train wall. 'God, I hate myself sometimes. Maybe I'm the one should be dead instead of Ross.'

'Don't be so pathetic,' Sim growled.

'How d'you know I'm being pathetic? You can't say that.'

'Kenny, you sound like a dick.'

'Piss off, Sim! Shut up, okay. You can't say that. You can't! How d'you know I don't mean it?'

But there was no sympathy from Sim. 'So just grow up then.'

Kenny bristled. 'I'm older than you.'

'By five months – big wow. But you're acting like your nappy's on too tight.'

The train bumped and we stumbled against one another, Kenny and Sim almost banging heads. And Kenny gave Sim a vicious shove, gritting his teeth as he did so.

Against my better judgement, I threw my weight in between them. 'Come on, leave it.' I knocked Sim's fist to one side before he could aim it at Kenny. 'It's happened, it's done – okay, Kenny? So you've been unlucky, now we've got to figure out what we're going to do about it. Right, Sim?'

But that ended up being the worst thing I could

have done, because then I couldn't stop myself from getting sucked into the argument too. We were all shouting at each other, bickering like idiots. And nobody saw the conductor coming until it was too late.

'Tickets, please.'

Part Two
Friends

Nine

Standing on the platform at York station with our rucksacks at our feet (well, mine and Sim's anyway) we watched the train aim north without us. I could imagine myself looking down on the three of us like in one of those weird out-of-body experiences people talk about. We'd appear to be in a silent space all our own, even though we were in the middle of the busy platform, with hurrying people streaming around either side. From above I'd see the invective flying out of Sim's mouth in daggers and blades, luckily not aimed at anyone in particular, just catching the sun as they spun away. Kenny's moroseness would be a sodden grey quilt around his shoulders, heavy enough to bend his knees and his back. While my own crestfallen figure was punctured, deflated, my skin creasing and sagging as all my hot air escaped. But the image only lasted a nanosecond or so because when I blinked I could hear the station's bustle and see out through my eyes again.

We stood there. Watched the train dissolving with a glint into the sunny distance.

The conductor had had a weird little moustache and a twitchy eye, but he'd been less intimidating than the one on the Cleethorpes train. He'd listened to us as we'd fallen over each other trying to explain our predicament. And even agreed that it was indeed an unfortunate predicament to be in. But had still said Kenny couldn't travel on his train without a ticket.

We'd waved the return part at him, Sim and I had shown our tickets with matching times and dates printed on them, we'd argued hard. Maybe Sim had argued that bit too hard. The upshot was, Kenny had to get off at the next stop and go see someone at the station's travel centre who might be able to issue him with another outward ticket – it wasn't something the conductor could do himself. We'd tried to explain about our connections, said we were pushed for time. We'd begged. For a second or two I'd thought he might crack, might let us stay on all the way to Newcastle. And then Sim had called him a 'miserable jobsworth git'. And now here we were.

York. A long way from Newcastle. A longer way

from Ross. Staring at the place where our train used to be.

Sim's tirade finally ran dry. He took a deep breath, blew it out. 'Right. Okay.' He shook the anger out of him like a dog shakes water off its coat. He gathered himself, put his sunglasses back on. 'When's the next bastard train?'

York's a large, good-looking station compared to Cleethorpes. Several long, long, wide platforms with a huge, arching roof high above them. An ornate foot-bridge spans the tracks. Some of the shops and cafés are either really old or just made to look that way. It's a hectic station too. Always a train coming in as another's going out. Loads of people milling around. Sim strode straight through the crowds; Kenny and I followed, weaving in between them. The massive electronic departures board is on stilts in the middle of the main concourse. The three of us stared up at it.

'There's another one in just over half an hour,' Sim said, pointing. 'Twelve forty-six to Aberdeen. Stops at Newcastle.'

I nodded. 'Let's hope it gets us there in time.'

Kenny hovered, looking anxious. 'What about my ticket?'

'Well, you'd better be quick,' I told him.

'What d'you mean?'

I was looking around. 'It's over there,' I said, pointing.

'What is?'

'The travel centre. You've got thirty-six minutes.'

'Thirty-five,' Sim corrected me.

Kenny was worried, confused. 'But I don't know . . . What if . . . ?'

'*Run!*'

He leaped away from me, his face stuck somewhere between shock and miserableness. 'But . . .'

'Run, shithorn! *RUN!*' Sim shouted.

And Kenny ran, edging and dodging through the crowd towards the travel centre.

Sim and I watched him go. Then Sim said: 'We should've left him. Me and you – we should've stayed on the train.'

'You reckon?'

'Yeah.'

'But you never would have, would you?'

He sighed. 'I'd never drown a puppy either.'

We picked up our rucksacks and followed the way Kenny had gone.

This was meant to have been a straightforward kind of journey after all. Kind of there-and-back-again before anyone noticed we'd gone. But the problems seemed to be piling up on top of one another, higher and higher, building a big wall of hassle to block our way. I was surprised and then disgusted at myself when I wondered whether it was all going to be worth the effort. I crushed the thought. I remembered I had my dead best friend in the bag over my shoulder.

And for a split second I thought I saw him. Just in front of me, through the crowd. Out the corner of my eye. The back of his head.

It stopped me in my tracks. But when I looked again it was a much older bloke – just the same colour hair, same height, kind of.

Not that this was the first time I'd thought I'd seen him. It threw me to begin with, sent a genuine streak of icy lightning up my spine. Now I reckoned it was something I was just going to have to get used to.

'You okay?' Sim asked.

I nodded. 'Yeah. Fine. No worries.' But my smile felt awkward.

Inside the travel centre was a long, winding queue

with Kenny at the very end of it. I counted and he had twenty-eight people in front of him. Sim rolled his eyes, muttered something about hating waiting and wandered back out the way we'd come. I went to stand with Kenny.

'Is Sim really mad?' Kenny asked, craning his neck to try and follow him.

'Mad insane? Or mad angry?'

But Kenny wouldn't laugh. He didn't look at me when he asked, 'Are you going to go without me? If the train comes before I get another ticket?'

'It's tempting,' I admitted. 'The problem is, things would've been so much simpler if we'd stayed on that train. I had all the times worked out. But if we want to catch up a bit and get to Ross before tonight, it's gonna be a whole lot easier if we can make that connection at Newcastle.'

'But how much does it matter if we don't get there tonight?'

'We can easily get there tomorrow,' I said. 'That's not the problem. But the train times just don't fit for us to get there *and* all the way back to Cleethorpes tomorrow as well. It's too far. Which means we won't get home till Monday. And staying out another night is something we definitely can't afford. Never mind the fact that the longer it is before we go back to Cleethorpes, the deeper the trouble we're in is gonna get.'

Kenny stared at his feet. 'We're shittered, aren't we? I'm sorry, you know? Honest, Blake. I didn't mean . . .'

I knew he felt embarrassed because of his freak-out on the train. It wasn't the right time to make him feel worse. 'Yeah,' I said. 'I know.' The time to really make him squirm would be when he had another ticket and we were on that connection from Newcastle, back on schedule. That's when I was planning on completely ripping the piss out of him.

But I checked my watch, twice. The queue inched forward; we shuffled a couple of steps with it. And I couldn't help doubting we were going to get any further north than we already were.

At the front of the room was one long counter with at least ten windows where the station staff sat at computers, checking timetables and issuing tickets. The frustrating thing was, only four of the windows had anyone sitting there. I craned my neck to scan the queue, counting everyone in front of us again. There were only twenty-six now. Weighing them up I reckoned some people were in pairs, and there was definitely a threesome – three backpackers with bright, shell-like packs. So maybe it wasn't the full twenty-six in front of us. In reality perhaps there were only twenty, twenty-one. That sounded better. Not brilliant, but better. I checked my watch again. Just under half an hour to go.

Sim appeared behind us. 'What's happening?'

'Not a lot.' The queue moved on another single shuffled step as if to prove it. Twenty-five people in front of us now. 'Where did you go?'

'There's an information kiosk-thing out there. I asked the bloke if he could do anything.'

'And?'

Sim pulled a face. 'Kenny needs to see one of them.' He pointed at the staff behind the windows. 'I got him to check when this next train gets into Newcastle, though. Three minutes before the one to Carlisle leaves.'

'That's tight,' I said.

He nodded, turning away from me. I realized he was also counting the people in the queue. 'And there's no way we're going to make it just standing here,' he said.

An idea popped into my head, but it took me a few seconds to say it out loud. 'Maybe we could call Caroline.'

Sim wasn't amused.

'I'm just saying: we could give her a ring and ask her to drive us.'

'That's the most stupid—'

I tried to defend myself. 'I told you what she was like this morning. I really think she'd help us if she knew.'

'Yeah, but would Ross want her there? Think about that.'

Kenny said, 'I reckon all that stuff because of her with his notebook and poems was why Nina finished with him. I'm telling you: that was definitely the start of it.'

I remembered this morning, the way Caroline had hid her face from me when Mr Fell was asking if Ross had any big problems. I was being truthful when I said no, but I knew he and Caroline weren't talking.

He'd had this little notebook he always carried around with him, where he wrote down his story ideas and stuff like that. He'd also been writing love poems to Nina. And last week Caroline had stolen his notebook and read the poems out to everyone at lunch time. There'd been a load of us on the grass behind the dining hall and she'd really gone to town with the amateur dramatics. I think it was meant to be a joke at first, but the way people started ripping into Ross and taking the piss had been vicious. I hate to say it, but I'd been glad I wasn't him right then. Or Nina. Talk about having to crawl under a rock somewhere . . .

But when I'd spoken to Ross afterwards he seemed all right about it. He said his sister was just jealous – which was true. She was older, cleverer, much more popular, but he always got loads of attention because of his stories. He'd just won that big story competition too. Most of the teachers thought he was greater than great because of that; the head made everybody give him a round of applause in assembly. So I could believe Caroline was jealous – she never received that kind of attention when she got yet another A-star in some exam. But I also saw Ross tear up his notebook and throw it away when he thought nobody was watching.

Kenny and Sim were waiting for me to say something. 'It was just an idea.'

Sim snorted his derision. 'Yeah. A stupid one.' He scanned the queue again; but with a click of his tongue seemed to have an idea of his own.

He took off his sunglasses and tapped the shoulder of the elderly woman in front of us. She was wearing a heavy brown coat despite the June sun outside and seemed squashed with old age. She smiled at us and all her wrinkles bunched up at the corners of her eyes.

'Hi, excuse me. Sorry to bother you, but we're in a really big hurry.' Sim was using the same voice he used for teachers when he hadn't done his homework. 'We've only got a couple of minutes before our train and if we don't get it we're gonna be really stuck.'

The woman looked from Sim to me and Kenny. We both smiled our best, politest smiles. Luckily Kenny's T-shirt didn't scare her and she was kind enough to let the three of us push in front. We thanked her several times too many.

Sim tried it on the next people in line, a young guy and his girlfriend. But the guy didn't even look at Sim when he said, 'You're not the only ones in a hurry, mate.' He couldn't have been that much older than us, was even a bit shorter than Sim, and for a second I thought Sim was going to square up to him. I saw

Sim's eyes harden and thought, Oh God, here we go. I got ready to stand at his shoulder – whatever happened. I was never much good in a fight; it was just that my bulk sometimes put people off.

But Sim took a step back, saying, 'Thanks for nothing, *mate*.' He stood to one side, weighing up the whole queue. And I was thinking, Is he going to fight them all?

'Excuse me!' he shouted. 'Excuse me! Hello!' When they were all looking his way he said, 'I know you're all in a rush and fed up of queuing and everything, but my friends and I really are in a big hurry. If we don't get the next train to Newcastle we're gonna be in trouble – big time. If you'd just let us get served next it'd be fantastic. We'd really appreciate it; you'd be doing us a massive favour.' He stood there with his face half needy, half demanding.

There was a bit of shuffling and bustle in the queue, shrugs and murmurs. There were still twenty-odd people in front of us, and to be fair maybe at least half of them seemed willing to let us push in. But not everybody was happy, or generous of spirit.

'I've been here half an hour already,' an old man in

a flat cap whined. 'I've not asked anyone if I could push in.'

'We're *all* in a hurry. We've *all* got somewhere to be,' someone else said.

'The sign says you've got to wait in line.'

'Everybody will want to go in front of me if I let you.'

In the end one of the station staff called out from behind his window: 'If everybody could just be patient we'll get to you as soon as we can.'

Sim looked disgusted with the whole lot of them. He came back to stand with me and Kenny again. 'How long we got?' he growled at me.

'Twenty minutes.'

'Great.' He ground his teeth, glared at as many people in the queue as he could, then stalked back out into the station. 'Bunch of shitflickers,' he said, far too loud for our comfort zone.

Kenny and I were on the receiving end of evil stares and mutters from the rest of the queue. We kept our heads down, shuffled a couple of steps forward every time we got the chance. Didn't even speak to each other, just kept checking our watches as the time ticked by. But it was pointless – there were still fifteen or so people in front of us.

'We're going to miss it,' Kenny said.

'Yep,' I agreed. I was annoyed with Sim for wandering off; wondered where he'd got to. And I was tempted to leave Kenny with the excuse of going to look for him.

'So . . . should I still get a new ticket?'

'Depends how you feel,' I said. 'If we try to sneak you onto the next train, we might get as far as Newcastle without being caught – if we're lucky. But then we've got the train to Carlisle *and* the train to Dumfries. Do you feel lucky three times over?'

'I want to go to Ross,' he said. 'Whatever it takes. I don't care what my mum says.'

'Even if we don't get home until Monday?'

He hesitated, then: 'Yeah. I mean, like Sim said: it's worth an arse-kicking.'

He'd smashed the ball into my court. After the graffiti and urn-theft it would be ridiculous to worry about skipping school. I admit I was worried about staying out a second night without any money. But I reckoned if Kenny was prepared to deal with it, then I should be too. And Sim? It would probably cheer him up to know we were skipping school.

I pushed the worry about where on earth we were

going to spend our two cashless nights right to the back of my mind. Same as when getting on the train back in Cleethorpes, there was an excitable bubbling of rebellion in my belly. 'Okay. Then we should get that new ticket. Make sure there's no other problems along the way.'

We waited as the last few minutes before that next train ticked by.

And that was when Sim burst back into the travel centre. 'Come on. We're going.'

I thought he'd given up waiting. In fact the announcement for our train sounded out over the tannoy – it was approaching platform five.

'Don't worry about it,' I told him. 'We'll get the next one. We need Kenny's ticket.'

'Forget the train,' Sim said. 'I've got us a lift.'

We had to run to catch him up. Onto the busy station concourse and then dodging the crowds out through the barriers towards the car park.

'To Ross?' I said. 'Sim? Sim!' I grabbed at his arm. 'All the way to Ross?' It was too good to be true. 'Or just as far as Dumfries?' Because even that would be brilliant.

He shook his head. 'Blackpool.'

'Blackpool?'

Kenny was confused. 'I didn't know we went to Blackpool.'

'We don't,' I told him. 'Sim, what—?'

'It's closer than here,' he said. 'Think about it. We'll be on the right side of the country, yeah? And can probably just get one train all the way to Dumfries – straight up the west coast.'

I wasn't sure. Maybe he was right. Kenny had pulled the map out of my rucksack's side pocket and was struggling with it as we walked, trying to find Blackpool.

Sim led us into the car park and towards two older lads standing smoking beside a big black taxi cab. 'Okay, we're ready,' he greeted them. And pointing out me and Kenny: 'These are my mates.'

The tall lad with the scruffy ponytail nodded at us. 'Right. Better get moving then.' He looked about nineteen, twenty; far too young to be a taxi driver. He flicked his cigarette away towards the tracks – towards the train that was just pulling into the station. It was the train we should have been on.

I stood there, incredulous. 'We're getting a taxi?'

Sim swung the door open like he was my chauffeur.

'Twenty-five pounds thirty-eight,' I reminded him.

'It's not a proper taxi,' he said.

'Looks a hell of a lot like one to me.'

He seemed far too pleased with himself. 'Stop fretting and get in, will you?'

Kenny yanked on my arm. 'Blackpool's here,' he said, crumpling up the map to point it out to me.

I nodded. 'Yeah. I know.'

'But it's nowhere near Ross.'

'Yeah,' I sighed. 'I know.'

Ten

There were a couple of size-ten muddy footprints on the back seat of the taxi, crushed fag ends, scrunched-up crisp packets and several empty beer cans on the floor. The lanky, ponytailed lad shrugged a quick apology as he swept the cans and crisp packets into a plastic bag. 'Bit of a party last night,' he said. He looked around for a litter bin, but it was obviously too far away for him, so he shoved the bag full of rubbish underneath the neighbouring parked car instead. He winked at me.

'Sim,' I said, close to his ear. 'Are you sure this—?'

But he was all grins and hustle. 'Get in, get in.' He clicked his tongue; so pleased with himself.

The second lad held the door for us.

Still kind of unsure, I slid onto the back seat. Kenny climbed in next to me. He whispered, 'Do we know them?'

'I don't reckon so, no,' I said.

116

'So why . . . ?'

'Exactly,' I agreed. I was hoping Sim knew more than he was letting on.

The one with the ponytail was driving. He was really tall, really thin, pale like he never saw the sun, with really *really* blue eyes. The stockier dark-haired lad climbed in the back with Kenny, Sim and me. He was a brick: oblong and hard. He had a pointy little goatee that could have been a paintbrush glued to his chin. He and Sim sat on the fold-down seats with their backs to the driver, heads resting against the Perspex partition, facing me and Kenny. Even with our rucksacks there was plenty of room. And, with more of a chug than a roar, we were headed for Blackpool.

We were well on our way west, halfway to Harrogate, before Sim told us what was going on. And by then it was too late to turn round. But by then I don't think any of us wanted to.

Joe was the driver; he did most of the talking, in between puffs on a cigarette, either throwing glances over his shoulder or looking at us in his rear-view mirror. He was cocky and loud, but in a funny way. He said they'd given a couple of their mates a lift to the station – ones who'd been in no fit state to find their own way after their party last night. He had a strong Liverpudlian accent, and because I'd never met anybody from Liverpool before, I thought he sounded like someone off the telly. Gus was the guy in the back with us. I didn't know where he came from, he never said. He just smoked. So it was Joe who told us they were Sports Science students who'd just finished their first year at York Uni, and said they were going to meet a friend in Blackpool who could offer them summer work at one of the amusement parks.

'How lucky was it I ran into you?' Sim shouted.

'Thought it was me who ran into you,' Joe replied.

The ride was noisy. The taxi wasn't the quietest vehicle ever invented and we had to keep the windows down because of the heat. But Sim was glowing anyway. Not only with his own good fortune, but also with the newfound knowledge that you could go to university to study kicking a football about – it sounded like the perfect waste of time and energy to him. At last he had an ambition.

Joe shouted over his shoulder: 'When you're running around in a taxi you soon get used to picking up the waifs and strays.' He grinned at us in his mirror. 'That's what you keep saying, right, Gus?'

Gus nodded; sucked on his cigarette.

'We were desperate,' Sim said.

'You looked it,' Joe agreed.

'And I'm dead sorry, for . . . for acting up and that.'

'No worries. No harm done, was there, Gus?'

Gus shrugged; blew smoke.

Apparently, after Sim had gone storming out of the travel centre, he'd had the idea of checking bus times, just to see if there was anything helpful going our way. But as he'd followed the signs to the bus stands, head up, trying to work out where they were meant to be pointing, he'd walked straight into the car park and been knocked flat on his backside by Joe reversing. And Sim, being Sim, hadn't taken it well. There'd been shouting and swearing and a kick aimed at the side door. Gus had been quick to want to calm Sim down. But luckily Joe had been quicker to hold Gus back.

Joe said, 'After knocking Sim here on his arse and hearing about your ticket problems, we just reckoned the least we could do was offer you a lift.'

We were on the A59, a busy single carriageway. There were mostly hedgerows and fields either side of us, occasional roundabouts to break the monotony. Kenny had the map open across his knees. He was watching for names on signposts then following our progress. We passed one that read NUNMONKTON 3.

'Where are we?' I asked him.

'Only here. How long d'you think it'll take us to get to Blackpool?'

I didn't have a clue. I looked to Sim, but he was ignoring us.

'So whose is the taxi?' he asked Gus.

'Bit of a story, really,' Joe said. Our side of the road was blocked by roadworks and he slowed to join the queue of cars waiting at the temporary traffic lights. He pulled on the handbrake and twisted in his seat. 'Suppose the cab's mine now – more or less. My uncle moved to Australia. He was a cabbie but got fed up with it. Got sick and tired of all the morons on a weekend who can't handle their beer, puking up and fighting all the time. He had girls swinging their Gucci handbags at him, screaming and swearing, trying to dodge paying for trips to the KFC. And then there was this time he had his nose broken by some bloke after trying to kick him out for dropping his kebab all over the back seat.' He shook his head. 'Crazy world. Pissed-up kebab-heads: they were driving him nuts, he said. So he decided he was off. Said it was okay to borrow his cab for a day or two, to move all my stuff to uni, but then decided to let me keep it anyway. Said he wasn't coming back – no way.'

'What's he doing in Australia?' I asked.

'You'll laugh,' Joe said.

'What d'you mean?'

'He's driving a taxi.'

We all laughed.

The light went green and Joe followed the rest of the traffic past the roadworks, shifting through the gears. 'He says it's different, though. Loves it out there. He's somewhere out in the middle of nowhere and reckons he has more trouble with kangaroos than kebab-heads.'

'It must be great,' Kenny said. 'Having your own taxi to drive around in.'

'We have a laugh, don't we, Gus?'

Gus chuckled; smoke curled from his nostrils.

We chugged along; there was plenty of time to watch the scenery slide by. The taxi was no hotrod and the glorious sunshine had brought out plenty of countryside day-trippers to clog up the way ahead. I couldn't ignore that niggling, anxious part of me that was still worried about missing trains and being behind schedule. But maybe Sim was right and we could get a train up the west coast. Then again, maybe not. He was joking around with Joe; he didn't seem worried. Even Kenny had relaxed. He still had the map open but had stopped noting every single signpost and place name. I guessed that, either consciously or not, we were all coming to the realization that this trip was going to take its own sweet time.

Joe plugged his iPod into the cab's radio. Led Zeppelin – Gus's favourite, apparently. He moved his lips to the lyrics, played a bit of air guitar.

Kenny wasn't impressed. He rolled his eyes at me and Sim.

Ross had liked Led Zeppelin – he'd been into all that old-school rock stuff. David Bowie, Pink Floyd. He used to argue with Kenny about it because Kenny was the kind of person who thought anything that had been around longer than a few months, anything not bang-up-to-date 'now', was a waste of space. Kenny was keen to think of himself as a trend-setter. Ross reckoned anything any good had already been discovered, done or invented years ago. Which made Kenny call him a 'depressive'. Which made Ross call Kenny a 'victim'.

'So what's at Blackpool for you three then?' Joe asked.

Kenny, Sim and I exchanged looks. Nobody spoke.

Joe kept flicking glances at us in his mirror. Waiting for one of us to reply. Or say anything. I pulled my rucksack closer into my feet, wrapped my legs around it as if to protect what was inside.

At last Sim said: 'You know. Just . . .'

'O-kay . . . Dodgy question,' Joe said. He kept one hand on the steering wheel while he lit himself a cigarette. 'Change the subject, right? So what do you do when you're not going to Blackpool? What do you get up to back home?'

'We're still at school,' Kenny said.

'Right. But what's your story? What're you into? School can't be everything.'

We weren't sure what he meant. Then Kenny said: 'Do you mean other stuff like computers? It's computers for me, I suppose. I'm good at all that stuff.'

'Stuff like programming?' Joe asked.

Kenny blushed, clashing with his T-shirt. 'I invent my own games . . . sometimes.'

Sim gave Kenny a playful punch in the arm. 'He's

really good. He's not as stupid as he looks.'

I remembered Mr Fell wanting Kenny to help him out. 'Ross's dad wants you to go round and fix his computer. He says he's lost his novel.'

Sim groaned, shook his head. 'Not the greatest novel ever written!'

Joe laughed too, but only because of the way Sim said it. 'What's this?'

'This bloke we know,' Sim explained, skipping mentioning who the bloke was. 'He wants to be a famous writer and he's been writing the same book for, like, seven years or something. It must be a million pages long by now. And it's all he ever talks about.'

Ross used to call it the most famous book never written. The thought made me laugh, but Kenny looked furtive, uncomfortable.

'So you'll help him, right?' I asked. 'You can't let him lose his masterpiece.'

'I kind of already know about it. Ross phoned me. It was him who lost it.'

'What? When?'

Kenny leaned forward, wanting to exclude Joe and Gus. Not that Joe could hear up front unless we shouted and Gus couldn't have looked less interested if he'd tried. 'Last week,' Kenny said. 'He was panicking a bit, but I was really busy. I couldn't go round.'

'How could he completely wipe it?' I asked.

'Well, he probably didn't. He'd probably just accidentally buried it somewhere – you never really completely wipe stuff. I told him to try a couple of things, but he didn't understand what I was on about.'

'I bet he was shitting it,' Sim said. 'His dad would not have been happy. All that work lost.'

Kenny looked glum.

'So why didn't you go round and help?'

'I was busy.'

'Christ-on-a-bike, Kenny. You could've helped him at least.'

'I would've gone later. But that was the day when . . . you know?'

Sim and I were amazed. 'Last Saturday?'

Kenny nodded.

The weird thing was, I was jealous. The last thing I'd seen or heard of Ross was at school last Friday. Kenny had been the last one to speak to him, but I wished it had been me. Maybe if he'd been with me he wouldn't have got knocked off his bike . . .

'And you didn't even help him,' I said. 'Great mate you are.'

Kenny squirmed, but couldn't defend himself because Joe was watching us in his mirror.

'Everything okay?'

Kenny, Sim and I shrugged, nodded, shrugged again.

Joe was curious, but must have decided not to ask. Gus, on the hand, still looked bored.

'So what about you? Blake, yeah? What's your story?' Joe tried to continue the previous conversation.

But the problem was, I was stuck. What was I into? Not computers or writing. Most of the time it was just school in my life. Shit. Was that a bad thing?

Sim tried to rescue me. 'He's the clever one. He's always top of the class and getting the teachers to kiss his backside.'

'Not much wrong with being clever,' Joe said.

Kenny nodded. 'Maybe, yeah. But he's a smart-arse with it. I'm telling you: he never lets you forget how clever he is.'

'You just wish you were cerebral too,' I told him.

Kenny pulled a face. 'See what I mean? Big words give him a boner.'

'So that must mean you're the dark horse, right?' Joe said to Sim. 'What're you? Shakespearean actor, or ice-skater – something like that?'

'In your dreams.'

'He's always playing footie,' Kenny said. 'But he's crap at it.'

Sim punched his arm, hard this time, making Kenny yelp. 'I reckon I'm gonna do what you and Gus are doing,' he said. 'Sport at university.'

'Trust me, you don't need to be any good at football to do Sports Science. That's right, right, Gus?'

Gus nodded.

'I'll tell you what Sim does,' I said to Joe. 'Name an animal – any animal,' I told him.

Joe drew on his cigarette. 'Giraffe.'

'A tower,' Sim said.

Joe frowned. 'A what?'

'Say another,' I told him. 'Come on, make it difficult.'

Both Joe and Gus were intrigued now. 'Hippopotamus.'

Sim didn't even hesitate. 'A bloat.'

The two students were confused. Kenny and I were laughing. 'He knows them all,' I said. 'What do you call a load of giraffes? A tower. What do you call a big bunch of hippos? A bloat.'

'Right, yeah. Someone told me about this before,' Joe said. 'There's a special name, right?

'Collective nouns,' I said.

'That's it, yeah. Hedgehogs?'

'A prickle,' Sim told him.

Joe beamed at us in the rear-view mirror. 'Yeah? A prickle of hedgehogs. That's fantastic. Where'd you learn this stuff?'

'It's just something I remember from primary school. The teacher made us write a poem about them or something. But I thought they were funny, you know? I've got a massive list of them somewhere.'

'There was this kid at my school who could tell you every capital city of every country,' Joe said. 'No matter how weird the country. The two of you should get together – you'd be great in pub quizzes.'

Sim grinned, a little embarrassed.

'Snails,' Joe said.

'A walk.'

'Hamsters.'

'A horde.'

And that kept us amused right up until we needed to stop for diesel somewhere near Skipton.

Eleven

We stopped at a small garage, still on the A59, some-where between Skipton and Clitheroe, going by the map. There were two other cars filling up alongside us. One was a boxy people carrier with the parents up front and a bunch of kids squabbling in the back. At the pump on our other side was a flashy couple in a flashy convertible. Kenny, Sim and I didn't so much as glance at the people carrier. I reckon we were all thinking the same thing: that we'd rather end up like Ross than driving one of those things. We were much more interested in the convertible, and the blonde woman in its passenger seat. She may even have been good-looking, but it was difficult to see her through all that fake tan.

Sim said to Kenny, 'That's the kind of car you reckon you're getting, isn't it?'

'Changed my mind,' Kenny said. 'I've decided I don't want the sort of car Munro's dad drives, do I?

I'm having one of these instead. I'm telling you: the very next second after I pass my test, I'm having a taxi.'

'Yeah? Why?'

'It's obvious, isn't it? Look at him: he can only get one girl in his convertible. You can fit loads in one of these.'

Sim shook his head. 'Like you'd ever have loads.'

We climbed out to stretch our legs. I took my rucksack with me – it just didn't feel right leaving it lying around, out of sight. My T-shirt was sticky and uncomfortable, like the weather. This was turning out to be the hottest day I could remember. It had felt cooler in the cab with the wind rushing in through the open window.

Gus unhooked the diesel hose, pushed the nozzle into the cab's tank and pulled the giant trigger. The pump rumbled into life and the display's numbers began flickering ever upward. The smell of the fuel in this heat wasn't pleasant and I stepped away towards the grass verge, watched the traffic shooting by on the road.

Kenny and Sim followed me. 'What time is it?' Sim asked.

'Half-two,' I said. 'Just after.'

'What time d'you reckon we'll make it to Blackpool?' he called over to Gus.

Gus looked to Joe, who had his wallet open, counting his cash.

'Four-ish?' Joe said without looking up.

Sim turned back to me. 'What d'you reckon? We should still be able to get a train then, yeah?'

'How should I know?' I said. 'This is your plan now. I thought you knew what you were doing.'

'It's got to be easier just getting one up the west coast. We don't have to be fannying around in Newcastle or anything.'

'Kenny still needs another ticket,' I reminded him.

He put his sunglasses on; nonchalant. 'Bet you we've still got time.'

'I'm going to get something to eat,' Kenny said, turning towards the garage shop.

'What with?' I asked.

Kenny was halted in his tracks. 'Lend us a quid, will you, Blake? I'm starved. I'll get some crisps or something so we can share.'

Joe came round the side of the taxi. 'Talking of money . . . hate to mention it, but can you help out with the diesel a bit?' He had a twenty in his hand. 'A tenner should do it.'

I looked at Kenny and Sim: we all knew exactly how little we had. 'Each?' I asked Joe.

'Between you's fine.'

'We can't,' Kenny started, 'because—'

I cut him off. 'Yeah, no problem. That's fine. A tenner's fine.' I didn't want to argue in front of Joe and Gus. It would have been embarrassing, demeaning. I didn't want them to think we were scrounging off them. I dug for one of the notes I had in my pocket. 'Here.'

Joe didn't take it. He was watching Kenny pull faces.

'Honestly,' I said, holding out my note. 'It's fine.' I nudged his hand with it. 'It's really good you could give us a lift and—'

'How much have you got?' he asked me.

I pretended to count in my head. 'About twenty-five. Something like that.'

He asked Sim, 'And what have you got?'

'Er, yeah, about the same. About twenty-five.'

Then to Kenny: 'And you've not got anything?'

Kenny shook his head.

'Fifty quid between the three of you? Jesus. Hope you're not planning on . . .' But he saw the look on my face. 'No? Twenty-five *between you*? How far're you hoping to get on that?'

'I lost my bag,' Kenny said. 'I had about a hundred, but . . .' He trailed off.

Joe thought for a second then called over to Gus. 'That should do it, yeah?'

Gus cut the pump off at £19.

I felt small, mean. 'Honest, Joe. We don't want to rob you. Why don't you give us your address and we can send it to you?' Kenny and Sim both nodded.

Joe walked away to pay without answering, whispering something to Gus as he passed. The first thought that raced through my mind was that they might leave us here.

It was Sim's too. 'They're gonna leave us,' he said. 'I don't even know where we are. I mean, I've never even heard of Clitheroe before.' And of course he blamed Kenny. 'I can't believe you were stupid enough to lose your bag. This wouldn't have happened if—'

Kenny bit back. 'Me and Blake were going to get another ticket. It's you who said go to Blackpool. And Blackpool's not even anywhere near—'

'Christ-on-a-bike, Kenny! Can't you—?'

I left them to it, went after Joe.

The garage shop had air-conditioning. The cold was a shock at first, then a relief. There was some horrible soft rock playing over the speakers – the kind of stuff dads who watch car programmes on telly think is cool. Joe was down one of the short aisles, picking a bag of party-sized Mars Bars off the shelf. I still had my tenner out in front of me.

'Joe,' I said. 'Joe, listen, we—'

'Are you on the run or something?'

'What? No.'

'You've not all run off from some home somewhere and there's going to be social workers and police chasing you?'

'God, no. It's not like that. We ... you know? We're just wanting to go to Blackpool. We love all that deckchair and donkey stuff.'

He laughed and pointed at his T-shirt, plucked at the material. 'Sorry, should've said. This is my bullshit-proof vest.'

He waited for me to say something. I didn't know what I should say.

He seemed to weigh me up as he tugged the elastic

band out of the back of his hair; tucking the bag of Mars Bars under his arm, he used both hands to scrape loose strands of hair off his face and re-do his ponytail. He pinned me with those sharp blue eyes of his.

I tried to stare at my feet but still felt obliged to say something. 'It's just not what you think.'

'But with all that whispering about your other mate going on a few miles back – you're in trouble, right?'

I almost laughed. But couldn't. 'Yeah. But not the way you think we are.'

'You going to get me and Gus into trouble?'

'No, no way. I swear.'

He pursed his lips, blew out a short breath. 'Okay, we'll take you as far as Blackpool. But you're going to tell us what's going on, right? Because we don't know you, do we? We don't know why you're all so wound up and jumping at your own shadows. And we've not got a clue why you can't let go of your bag there, even for one second.'

I flinched, and knew I looked guilty – caught red-handed.

I wasn't sure I wanted anyone knowing what we were doing. I liked Joe, thought I could trust him – but who knew? And I didn't know how Kenny and Sim would feel about explaining everything either. What we were doing felt personal, between the three of us. I didn't think I wanted to share it.

Joe shrugged. 'You've got some story going on. Sorry, but it's obvious. And let's just say you've got me intrigued. Gus too, probably. So we want to know – the truth, right? And my guess is you three are going to tell the best story me and Gus have heard all year.'

That was what changed my mind. I liked the way he kept using that word: 'story'.

Ross writing all those adventures with us as the characters. Ross once saying, *You've got to keep making stories you can tell about yourself. What's the point in life if you're not making stories?*

'Okay,' I said to Joe. 'But I'm warning you: this story doesn't feel like we're even halfway through.'

'Yeah, well. Plenty of time yet.'

I followed him to the counter but he still wouldn't take my money. I saw he didn't have the bag of mini Mars Bars any more and was tempted to run back to get them, to keep Kenny happy. But Joe was too quick paying and I didn't want to push my luck and hold him up.

When we walked back to the taxi Kenny and Sim were quiet, twitchy.

'Get in,' Joe said. 'Gotta get moving.'

They both looked at me, then were quick to scramble in when I nodded. The relief flooded their faces.

We were back on the road when Kenny asked, 'Don't suppose you got any crisps, did you?'

Before I could answer, Joe pulled the bag of Mars Bars out from under his T-shirt and tossed it to him. I hadn't even noticed him shove it up there in the first place. He was full of minor miracles.

'Come on, then,' he said to me in that thick accent of his. 'Jackanory – tell us your story.'

Twelve

Me telling the story of why we were doing what we were doing (including plenty of interjections from both Kenny and Sim) had taken over half an hour. Led Zeppelin were starting up on their second go around. Our route had bypassed Blackburn and Preston, we'd turned off the A59 and hit the M55 at a decent speed – Gus's driving keeping us in the middle lane like we were on rails. It was going to be a straight cruise all the way to Blackpool from here. And I realized I was in a part of the country I'd only ever heard about or seen on TV, never been to. We were getting further and further away from what we knew.

They'd taken some persuading that our story was the truth and I'd taken Ross out of my rucksack as proof. Gus had recoiled at the sight of it. He kept shooting backward glances at the urn like it was full of actual flesh and blood rather than just ash. Maybe he was worried I might spill it. But Joe was more philosophical.

'Yeah, Mickey Gee,' he said. 'He was just like that.'

I guessed he meant like a really close, best friend. Not like one who was carried around in a marble jar. Even so, I was confused.

Sim too. 'You had a mate that died?'

'No. There was this lad I grew up with called Mick, Mickey Gee, and we went everywhere together. My mum always said we were joined at the hip. It was like, if people saw me they knew Mick couldn't be far behind. And vice versa. We used to have a right laugh.' He laughed to himself as if to prove it.

'What happened to him?'

'Don't know really.'

'Don't you still see him?'

'Not for ages. He didn't stay on at school like me, just left first chance he got. He still lives our way though, so my mum says. She still sees his mum in the supermarket, or the bingo, wherever.'

I could tell by the looks on Kenny and Sim's faces that they were as shocked by this as I was. 'He couldn't have been a good friend,' Kenny muttered.

'What was that?'

Kenny was embarrassed. 'Just, maybe, that he

wasn't that good a friend. You know, if he doesn't keep in touch any more?'

'No, he was great. We grew up from little together; virtually lived in each other's houses – me at his, him at mine. We became blood brothers too. We were eleven or twelve or something and did all the cutting each other's hand and stuff. Still got a scar some-where.' He searched his palm for the evidence.

'So why don't you see him any more?' I asked.

'Suppose it's just one of them things. Kind of drifted. Just the way it goes.' He knocked on the Perspex partition behind Gus's head and grinned. 'Got new mates now. Right, Gus?'

Gus nodded; smoke leaked from between his lips.

Kenny, Sim and I looked at each other. We weren't impressed. It would never happen to us.

'What did you say your mate was called?' Joe asked.

'Ross,' Sim said. 'Ross Fell.'

'And did he?'

'He was run over.'

'Nasty,' Joe said.

'Some people reckon he did it on purpose,' Kenny said. Then shrank away from the dirty looks

Sim and I threw at him. 'But it's not true,' he mumbled.

'Why? What happened?' Joe asked.

'It's all bollocks,' Sim told him.

I said, 'It's just the bloke who was driving the car saying stuff. I mean, of course he doesn't want to take the blame. Who would? But if everybody knew Ross like we did, they'd know him doing something like that on purpose is a totally stupid thing to think.'

'No smoke without fire,' Joe said, looking at the tip of his cigarette.

'But it's rubbish,' Kenny, Sim and I said at once. 'No way. He'd never.'

'I'll tell you the kind of person Ross was,' Sim said. 'He got me out of loads of trouble last week. He let me copy his history homework, yeah? We got found out because our answers were too much alike, which was obviously my fault. But our teacher, Mr Fowler, he just picked on Ross. And Ross could've easily said I was the one who asked him, but he didn't. Even when he got a letter sent home and his mum had a go at him too, he never once dropped me in it. That's how good a friend he was. Does that sound like somebody who'd go and kill themselves to you?'

'He'd just won a story competition too,' Kenny said. 'He was going to get one of his stories published in a book. He had his picture in the paper and everything. He'd always wanted to be a writer.'

Sim jabbed a finger at Joe. 'And where's his note then? Suicide people always leave notes, don't they? Saying why they did it? So where's Ross's?'

Joe held up his hands in submission. 'You knew him better than me.'

'What really pisses me off,' Sim went on, 'is that there's gonna be some people who'll believe it. They'll even *want* to believe it.'

'People like Munro,' Kenny said. Both Sim and I nodded.

Joe wanted to know who Munro was.

'This kid who seemed to get his kicks picking on Ross,' I said. 'That thing Sim just told you about – with Ross getting done by the history teacher? Well, Munro went and made it even worse. He sprayed this graffiti on the back of the bike shed and Mr Fowler blamed Ross for it, thinking he was doing it out of spite because of all the homework trouble.'

'We knew it was Munro,' Sim said. 'Just couldn't prove it. We were in the dining hall when Fowler cornered Ross and accused him, but Ross didn't even know what he was talking about at that point. And Fowler was virtually screaming at him – his face like this, like it was gonna explode. And everyone watching. Then Ross went and said he wished he *had* written it.'

Kenny thought that was fantastic. 'Did he? Honest? I didn't know that.'

Sim nodded. 'He said it under his breath as Fowler was walking away, but he heard him. Sent him to the head, who had a massive go at him too, and made him take another letter home to his mum and dad.'

'His mum went even madder than before,' I said to Joe. 'I was there. He kept telling her he hadn't written anything on any shed, but she was just going mad at him for having two letters sent home – didn't care whether he'd done it or not. She said he had to apologize to Mr Fowler, and Ross said no way was he was going to apologize for something he hadn't done.'

'What did it say?' Joe asked. 'On the bike shed?'

' "Fat Twat Fowler".'

Joe laughed out loud. Gus found it funny enough to cough out smoke. 'Yep,' Joe said. 'That's gonna get you in trouble all right. And is he?'

'What?'

'Fowler. Is he fat and a twat?'

'Hundred per cent,' Sim growled.

'But he was being bullied then?' Joe said.

'What d'you mean?'

'Your mate, Ross. He was being bullied by this Munro kid. That's a reason some kids have for suicide, isn't it?'

I shook my head. 'Yeah, but not Ross. He never backed down from anything. Always said he wanted to fight his own battles.'

I remembered Munro and his goons had got Ross the day after. They'd cornered him in Haverstoe Park and beat the crap out of him – it was a threat to make sure Ross didn't grass anyone up about any graffiti. Ross had come round to my house to try and clean up a bit before he went home, not wanting his mum and dad to see him like that. He got blood from his nose on our towels and I'd had to chuck them out before my mum saw them and asked awkward questions too.

I'd said to Ross, 'You ought to get Sim to have a go at Munro back.'

But Ross wouldn't do it. He'd said, 'The day I can't stand up for myself any more is the day I might as well roll over and die.'

145

It didn't sound anything like a kid who was going to kill himself by the end of the week to me.

'We got both Fowler and Munro back, though, didn't we?' Kenny said. He told the story of our own graffiti exploits.

I couldn't tell if Joe was shocked, amused or simply amazed. He said, 'Listen, it's cool what you're doing, okay? Kind of a bit mental, but very cool. You've got balls – got to give you that. Hey, Gus! You ever met kidnappers before?'

'You can't kidnap him if he's dead,' Kenny said.

Joe shrugged. 'Urn-nappers then. Ash-nappers.'

Kenny was worried. 'Can they arrest you for that too?'

Sim rolled his eyes.

The conversation shifted then – Kenny, Sim and I kept on telling Ross-stories. About the time we'd sneaked into the girls' changing room at the local leisure centre; about the time we'd built a tree house only to have it hospitalize Ross when not only the house but half the tree fell on him; about the way Ross had somehow talked a really good-looking girl from Humberston into going on a date with Kenny.

I re-wrapped Ross in my jumper and pushed him

deep down inside my rucksack. There was a stab of realization – again – that we were talking about someone who was dead. These realizations came in different shapes and forms, sneaking up on me. And some hurt more than others.

This one was maybe the most painful so far. This one reminded me that our stories of Ross were about someone who'd no longer be around to make stories for us to tell. Never again.

Thirteen

We made it to the outskirts of Blackpool just after four, so Joe's prediction was pretty much spot on. We got lost coming off the M55 and ended up going the long way round to get into the town itself. And the trouble was, none of us had any idea how to find the train station. We kept our eyes peeled for signs but without any luck.

'There're two stations, I think,' Joe said. 'Do you know which one you're after?'

Kenny, Sim and I did synchronized shrugs.

'Tell you what then. We'll go see my mate who's getting me and Gus jobs. He should know; he's been here long enough. And he'll still be at work so you'll get to see the sights as well.'

Gus aimed for the sea front, ignoring two lots of people who tried to wave us down as if we were a real taxi. It was still a perfect, hot and glorious day, so we reckoned they shouldn't be lazy and should be enjoying the weather. There were plenty of others who were. Lots of shorts and sunburn.

Kenny was the first to spot the famous tower. We drove along the wide main street – Central Promenade onto South Promenade – with the beach on one side and a never-ending façade of pubs, chip shops and amusement arcades on the other. We could hear the hullabaloo of greedy slot machines through the taxi's open windows. We dodged a couple of trams, which was fun. The long piers striding out into the Irish Sea looked impressive in an old-fashioned kind of way. Seagulls perched on top of lampposts draped in coloured lights or squabbled amongst the litter. The donkeys on the beach looked bored. And massive hoardings for Burger King or McDonald's tried to intimidate the candyfloss kiosks.

Up ahead a scary scaffolding of roller coasters filled the skyline. It was the world-famous Pleasure Beach and where I assumed this mate of Joe's worked. But Joe pointed across the road from the amusement park to the real beach. At first I couldn't work out what I was looking at – it was some kind of tall crane planted in the sand, a crowd gathered around. But then some-one hurled themselves off the top . . . And bounced before they hit the beach – snapped back into the air by the thick elastic cord tied to their ankles.

'Bacon runs the bungee jump,' Joe said. 'His old man owns a bingo hall and a couple of arcades. But he gave Bacon the bungee business as an eighteenth birthday present.'

'Can't be bad if you've got a rich dad,' Sim said, looking at Kenny.

But Kenny just scoffed. 'Like my dad would get me a bungee. Where am I meant to put it? My back garden?'

'It's big enough,' Sim muttered.

We parked down a side street and walked back across South Promenade towards the beach and Bacon's bungee. Joe knew he might get a parking ticket, but seeing as the cab still officially belonged to his uncle – who lived a long, long way away – he couldn't be less bothered. I was thinking the sun on my back felt like an Australian sun anyway. I knew I had sweat stains under my arms and would have liked to change my T-shirt, but didn't want to get my pale barrel-belly out in front of everyone to do it.

'Is he really called Bacon?' Kenny asked Joe.

'It's what everybody calls him. Bacon was always

his dad's favourite thing, apparently. So he started calling his son Bacon too, and it just kind of stuck.'

I carried my rucksack and Ross. We climbed over some railings to drop down onto the beach, kicking up sand where we landed, and headed for the gathered crowd of onlookers and the loud music. Closer to, the crane was more like an open cage-lift that took the jumpers way up to a narrow gantry or platform. It looked high enough to be able to grab a seagull. The sun was in our eyes as we approached, so when the silhouette of a jumper leaped from the top he reminded me of Icarus falling to earth. The onlookers on the ground whooped.

'Who?' Kenny asked.

'Icarus,' I repeated.

'Is he that clever Polish kid from Mr Mitchell's class?'

I shook my head. 'Forget it.'

'Cool job to have,' Sim said to Joe.

Joe nodded. 'Be a laugh. Right, Gus? Might meet some nice girls. And if the summer stays like this, we'll get back to York with tans like we spent it in the Canary Islands.'

To one side of the bungee lift was a small wooden

hut that had been painted garish colours and clashed with the golden sand. BUNGEE! BLACKPOOL!! BUNGEE! was splashed across the side. CONQUER YOUR FEAR! LEAP INTO THE UNKNOWN!! I DARE YOU!!! There were two crate-sized speakers in front of its door pumping out bass-heavy music. Joe stepped inside, looking for Bacon. Kenny, Sim and I stayed with Gus, watching the attendant lower the jumper the last couple of metres to the ground now that he'd lost his bounce. He had his ankles untied. And even though he looked a little shaky on his legs he received another whoop from the crowd when he got to his feet, safe and sound, grinning with lopsided relief.

'Will you get a free go then?' I asked Gus. 'Seeing as you're working here. D'you fancy giving it a try?'

He dropped his cigarette and scuffed sand over it with his toe. He had to lean back to look all the way up to the top of the platform. He shaded his eyes. Then sucked his teeth, shrugged and went into the hut with Joe.

'I'd do it,' Kenny said. 'If I hadn't lost my money.'

Sim and I didn't bother to answer him because we didn't believe him.

'Yes I would,' Kenny said, knowing full well what

our silence meant. 'I'm telling you: if we had the cash to spare, I'd do it.'

'Lucky for you we don't have the cash then, isn't it?' Sim said. 'Makes it kind of difficult for us to call you a chicken-shit liar.'

'Would you do it?'

Sim shook his head. 'Not if my life depended on it. Not even if *your* life depended on it. Have you heard how much you can die from bungee jumping?'

'You can only die the same amount, can't you? Surely.'

'You know what I mean. I heard you can yank your legs from their sockets. The pressure can make your eyes burst. And they reckon you can even pull your spine right out of your arse.' He made a sound like a spine being pulled out of an arse – it wasn't pleasant. 'It's for nutters, and nutters alone.'

I watched the next nervy jumper being taken up in the lift. I let my eyes travel all the way up to the top again. It would have been nice to pretend I was that brave, but . . . 'Not something you're ever going to see me doing, that's for sure.'

'No need to go feeling bad about it, man,' a voice

said from behind us. 'I doubt I've got a bungee cord strong enough for you anyway.'

I spun round to see Joe and Gus with a real weird guy, about the same age as them, but taller. Bacon. He prodded me in the belly and laughed through his nose. He was skinny, wiry – streaky. With sunken cheeks and Shredded Wheat facial hair. He wore a red and black skull-and-crossbones bandanna tied tight around his head. His white sleeveless T-shirt had BUNGEE! BLACKPOOL!! BUNGEE! written in faded orange across the narrow chest. He waggled his eyebrows and grinned like a dirty uncle.

I counted to make sure – but I was right. Out of the six of us, he was the only one who thought he was funny.

He seemed to realize and started apologizing. 'Hey, look, sorry, man. Didn't mean, you know . . . ? Not the best thing to say. I know that now. I've learned, yeah?' He held out his hand for me to shake, to prove there were no bad feelings. And he grabbed my hand even though I didn't offer it, pumped it hard. 'Great. Awesome. Friends again.'

'I didn't realize we'd been friends in the first place,' I said.

154

Bacon took a step back from me. 'Wow. Bad vibes from the big guy. Heavy, man. And not just on the outside.' He was grinning, but his eyes were hard.

Joe stepped in between us. 'Leave it out, Bacon. He's a good kid.' Which was almost as insulting as what Bacon had said. Then to us: 'The closest station's just behind Pleasure Beach apparently. Me and Gus'll get you there if you want.' He turned to Gus. 'Then it's time for us to start looking for another job, right?'

Gus didn't look happy.

Bacon put a skinny arm around Joe's shoulders. 'Look, man, really sorry, yeah? I know what I said. But business, it's just no good right now. Look at him, that guy about to jump? You know, he's only the ninth person today. Not even double figures, man.' He looked at Kenny, Sim and me. 'Hey, but what about you dudes? Experience of a lifetime, yeah?'

I curled my lip at him. Sim shook his head. But Kenny asked, 'How much is it?'

'Forty. Total and absolute bargain, man. Hundred and sixty metres up, so that's only a quid for every four metres. Used to be fifty, used to be forty-five, but just forty for friends of Joe's. And you listen to me when I say no roller coaster can give you the kind of thrill this baby does.'

Kenny shrugged a poor man's apology – something he didn't often have to do – and looked awkward doing it.

Bacon threw up his hands in fake despair. 'See what it's like?' he said to Joe. 'I drop my prices so low it hurts, man. And they still don't bite. You can see it with your own eyes: I just can't take anyone else on right now, yeah?'

'Yeah, no worries. We understand, don't we, Gus?'

Gus didn't look very understanding about anything from where I was standing.

'Stick around, Joe, yeah?' Bacon said. 'If it picks up, man, you'll be the first to hear.'

'Not really got the money to stick around with, Bacon.'

'If the punters come,' Bacon said, 'you're top of my to-call list. That's a gold-standard Bacon guarantee.'

'You should advertise.'

Everybody turned to look at Kenny. Sim and I rolled our eyes at each other.

He cringed, tried to hide his head by burying it in

his shoulders. 'Just an idea,' he said. 'Just, you know, a thought.'

'Good thought,' Bacon said, throwing an arm around Kenny's shoulders now. 'Great idea, man. But d'you know how pricey that advertising malarkey is?' He rubbed his thumb and fingers together. 'Mucho moolah.'

I said, 'Come on, Kenny. Let's go.'

But Kenny stood his ground. 'You just need a big sign or poster people can see from up the road,' he said. 'We didn't even know it was a bungee until we got close. Just get a really good image that sticks in people's minds.'

I was as surprised as anyone that Bacon seemed to be taking him seriously. 'And you're the kind of dude that knows about this kind of stuff, yeah?'

Kenny shrugged. 'We did it in business studies at school.'

'Wow, business studies, man. I just knew I should've gone to that one.'

I was lost. Was he taking the piss? Was he serious?

'So Mr Business Studies, dude, give me an image. Something cool, something awesome. Something *Bungee! Blackpool!! Bungee!*'

Kenny looked at Sim and me, but we weren't going to help. 'Someone jumping?' he asked.

Bacon scratched at his stubbly chin. 'Well, now. I see what you mean. I see where you're coming from, but – and I don't want to crush your creative spirit, man – but that's—'

'Someone who you wouldn't expect to be jumping, I mean,' Kenny blurted. 'Someone funny, or weird. Like a businessman in a bowler hat waving his umbrella.'

I think it's fair to say that we were all a bit stunned. Who knew Kenny had it in him?

'I like it,' Bacon said. 'You're the dude!' he told Kenny. 'You're the *man*!'

Kenny beamed.

Then Bacon turned to me. 'But how about you?' He prodded my belly again. 'I can't get my hands on some business dude with a bowler hat, but you'd look good on a poster. And you get to jump for free.' He tried to prod me one more time.

But I slapped his hand away. 'Are you for real?'

'Now don't you go thinking it's all about you being fat, okay. No bad vibes from me. But who'd expect someone like you to jump? I can see it now. Yeah, man. Awesome poster.'

'Piss off.'

He opened his hands wide, palms up. 'Free jump and fame. Hey, what more can I give you?'

'A wide berth,' I said.

He laughed. 'So cool to see you digging the fat jokes, man.'

I picked up my rucksack and started walking away.

He wouldn't give up. 'You jump for me, let me take a picture, and I'll give you the forty quid. How's that for deal or no deal?'

'Which way's that train station?' I asked Joe.

Kenny and Sim followed me up the beach. I was fuming. I was burning up. Joe and Gus told Bacon they'd be in touch then followed along too.

'Honest, Blake, take no notice,' Joe said. 'He's a fart on the surface, but scratch underneath and he can sometimes smell a bit better.'

I didn't laugh.

'And he just told me he meant it. If you let him take a photo of you jumping, he's serious about paying you.'

'He's an arsehole,' I said.

Joe nodded. 'Yeah, okay, you got me. He's an arsehole. But there's a lot of them about.' He nudged Sim. 'Hey, what do you call a bunch of arseholes?'

Sim thought about it for a second or two. 'A stench,' he said.

And at least that cracked us up.

I didn't talk on the way to the train station; all my goodwill had pretty much drained away. I was embarrassed and annoyed that Bacon had managed to push my buttons so easily. When Joe parked up outside the station entrance I told Kenny and Sim to go in and check the train times, and to see about Kenny's ticket. I stayed in the back of the cab.

'Better check our tickets are okay too,' I called out the window after Sim. 'Last thing we want is some conductor thinking of kicking us off because he says it's a bit of a weird way of getting from Cleethorpes to Dumfries.'

Joe was still uncomfortable about what had happened with Bacon. 'Look at it this way,' he said. 'Who's going to tote *Bacon's* ashes around in remembrance? But you know one thing for sure: if it was you in that urn and not your mate Ross, he'd be doing the exact same thing for you. Kenny and Sim too.'

I nodded, thanked him. Partly because he meant it, but also because I reckoned it was true.

When Kenny and Sim came back they didn't look

happy. 'Good news, bad news,' Sim said. 'There is a train, so we can get to Dumfries tonight no problem. It goes at five to six, gets in at quarter to ten, and no problems for me and you with our tickets either.'

'So the bad news is . . . ?'

'They won't give me another ticket,' Kenny said. 'They say I've got to buy one.'

'Do we have enough? How much is it?'

'Thirty-nine pounds fifty,' Sim said.

I could have laughed at the spitefulness of the world. In fact, I did. But there was no relish in my voice when I said, 'Looks like I'm going to be taking Bacon up on his offer after all then, doesn't it?'

Fourteen

Long way down. Blackpool spread out on one side, the sea on the other. Stunning view of the whole Golden Mile. I was gripping the safety rail hard enough to put kinks in it.

'Yeah, that's right,' Bacon said. The tail of his red and black skull-and-crossbones bandanna fluttered in the breeze. 'That's what a hundred and sixty metres down looks like. You're as high as the tower, dude. But you'll fall it in less than five seconds. Hey, you never know. Maybe you'll even make it in three.'

I couldn't help taking a step away from the edge and he laughed at me.

The worst part had been getting weighed. No, that had just been humiliating. The worst part had been the consent form.

Bacon's cramped little hut smelled of sweat and weed. It had a small counter with a computer and printer. He'd printed out a crisp new consent form and had flourished it like it was the Magna Carta or something.

'Ready to sign your life away?' he'd asked, smirking.

I'd read the form with a frosty stomach despite the heat. Kenny had been peering over my shoulder. 'Oh my God, look at all that stuff that could happen to you. I'm telling you: that's scary shit, that is.' I'd given him a sharp elbow in the ribs to get him to back off. But only because he'd been right.

That's exactly what the form was: thirty types of suffering. Thirty injuries, afflictions, traumas. And I had to sign it to prove that no matter how neck-whipped, shoulder-wrenched, leg-yanked, knee-twisted, bowel-slackened, spine-snapped, back-cracked, heart-attacked I ended up, I wouldn't blame *Bungee! Blackpool!! Bungee!* and try to sue Bacon or his dad.

'There was some bloke in America who died, wasn't there?' Kenny said. 'I read about it somewhere. The cord snapped and he hit the ground. I mean, he wasn't killed straight off, but he was all messed up and couldn't talk and had to crap through this tube. It was really gross. But his mum—'

'Kenny! For Chrissake . . .' I gave him my rucksack and said to Joe and Gus: 'Take him outside and bury him in the sand or something, will you?'

Which at least just left Sim to witness my embarrassment on the scales.

'Sorry, man,' Bacon said without meaning it. 'Gotta weigh you. Need to get the bungee cord adjusted to your weight. And we've got to get it just right – it's a precision job, dude. If that crazy bungee's too long you're gonna smash face-first into the beach and be like that American dude Mr Business Studies was talking about.'

Kenny deserved one hell of a big punch, that's what I was thinking. If he hadn't lost his bag . . . If he hadn't gone on about posters . . .

Then, when I was on the scales Bacon had checked the reading, but sucked in a long breath and shook his head.

'Don't know if we've got a bungee strong enough.'

'If you're trying to wind me up—' I'd said.

'Hey, no. Come on, man, would I?' He used a big felt pen to write my weight on the back of my hand. 'Show this to Dunc at the top so he can adjust the bungee, but make sure he knows it's not a joke.'

I'd been quick getting off the scales. 'Let's just do it, okay?'

And I wasn't stupid, I knew what he was doing. Everything he'd told me, every word he'd uttered, it had all been aimed at frightening me. Because a scared face was going to make a better picture than a happy one. But I'd signed his form, and allowed him to wind me up some more, and then we'd taken the cage-lift to the top. We'd stood facing each other – there was no room to sit. And it had rattled and clanked all the way up. I watched the crowd on the ground getting smaller and smaller. I tried to focus on Kenny in the middle of it all – he was easy to spot because of his orange T-shirt. I eased my nerves by thinking of how much I'd enjoy punching him when I was back on terra firma again. And we went up a long, long way. It seemed to take for ever.

There were two small speakers at the top, but they managed to beat out music bass-heavy enough to keep your heart thumping. The lift had shuddered to a halt and we'd climbed out onto the narrow gantry. There was the hint of a breeze off the sea. My legs had felt weird. Not weak, but springy. If I stepped too heavily maybe I'd bounce like an astronaut on the moon and fly right over the edge. I didn't think I'd ever been so high. There were seagulls *below* me. The gantry didn't feel wide enough, stable enough, safe enough. Left, right, up, down – there was nothing around me except clear blue sky. It felt horribly easy to fall. That's why I was holding so tight to the single rail.

Bacon was watching me.

'We're up here now. Might as well enjoy the view,' I said, sounding braver than I felt.

We weren't the only ones up here. There was a jumper in front of me, just about ready to go. He'd already had the cord tied to his ankles and could only shuffle towards the gap in the rail at the end of the gantry. I had sudden pictures of pirate movies in my head – of walking the plank. He was being helped towards the edge by a surfer-tanned, blond-haired attendant wearing a BUNGEE! BLACKPOOL!! BUNGEE! T-shirt whom Bacon called Dunc. I noticed the jumper was older than me – looked harder, tougher, braver too. Sticking out from one side of the platform was a short pole with a camera attached, and once Dunc had the jumper teetering on the edge he took hold of the camera's cable and remote button, ready to take a souvenir snap of him in freefall.

'Why don't you use his picture?' I asked Bacon.

'Not the right image. Remember what your mate said, yeah? Got to be the right image. And that, dude, is you.'

Dunc was speaking to the first jumper. 'Look straight ahead, keep your eyes on the tower and the big wheel. I'll count down from three, then you go.'

Bacon was watching me to make sure I was watching them. But there was no way I would have been able to tear my eyes away even if I'd wanted to.

The jumper steadied himself. Fixed his eyes straight ahead.

Dunc shouted: 'Three – two – one. Go!'

And he went.

There was a flash from the camera, capturing the instant he flung his arms wide and dived into the empty air. Even above the music I heard the split second of silence from the crowd below. But I think I only imagined the *whoosh* as gravity stole him.

I followed his downward rush with bulging eyes, forgetting my own nerves as I leaned over the rail to see. He fell fast. Head down, hands reaching out for the ground. And as the crowd cheered the bungee cord stretched, stretched, stretched to its limit . . .

He was whipped up towards us again. Flung in a rag-doll pirouette, hurled high. He reached much higher than I was expecting. I could see he had his eyes closed, his teeth gritted. Then, at the pinnacle of his bounce, the height of the cord's recoil, he hung for a brief moment of weightlessness. But gravity was only teasing him like a cat might torture a mouse. And he fell again. But there was no way he could control what was happening, and no way he could stop or get off. It wasn't that kind of ride.

I realized I'd been holding my breath and half laughed, half swore in a burst of bubbling tension.

I watched until the jumper had at last lost enough bounce that he could be lowered the final few metres back onto solid beach. There was no way I could see the expression on his face from all the way up here. I wished I knew how he looked – relieved, triumphant, afflicted? He was untied and was at least able to stand.

'He made it,' I said. 'Nothing happened to him.'

Bacon held his bandanna onto to his head as he leaned over the side to look down. 'Limping a bit, looks like. But, yeah, you're right, dude: he survived.'

'So what's the problem then? He did it, I can too.'

'You saw him, right? Looked like a right gym-jockey to me, man. And then I look at you . . .'

I hated him for being so right.

'Hey, it's not called an *extreme sport* just because it sounds cool. This kind of thing's easier if you're a fit dude and your body can take it. And listen, yeah? Best not ignore the stats either, okay?'

'The what?'

'Statistics, man. It's something like one in every thousand jumpers ends up with permanent injury. You know, their neck or back, maybe their legs – knees pop or something.'

'Bollocks.'

'It's true, man. It hurts me that you think I'd lie. One in every thousand, yeah? On average.' He turned to Dunc. 'Hey, Dunc, man. How many jumpers we had this week?'

'Nine hundred and ninety-nine,' Dunc said.

And they both laughed.

Again I told myself he was just winding me up. The more scared I looked, the more dramatic the photo . . . The problem was, it was working.

I stood on the narrow gantry looking 160 metres back down to the ground. The roped-off area where I was meant to land seemed too small. What if I hit someone in the crowd?

Inside my head I was swearing at myself, but how else were we going to pay for Kenny's ticket?

'I'm ready,' I said to Bacon. 'Give me the money.'

Bacon counted it out; the edges of the £10 notes were ruffled by the breeze.

'Where're you gonna put this poster?' I asked as I shoved the money deep down in my back pocket.

'Everywhere. You, dude, are gonna be famous. That's part of the dealio, right?'

I wished it wasn't.

Dunc was winching up the cord from the previous jumper and motioned for me to join him at the open end of the gantry. 'You get weighed?' he asked.

I showed him where it was written on the back of my hand.

He adjusted the cord and gave me a harness to wear around my waist. He sat me down, wrapped a towel around my ankles then looped the bungee around a couple of times, and in between, tugging on it, before fastening it to the harness. Bacon kept asking me if I was sure it was tight enough. I ignored him, but watched Dunc's every move. The final knot, however, he left me to tug on myself – as hard as I could. Maybe it was his version of an escape clause, I thought. If it all came unravelled, and I hit the beach with a crunch, he'd remain blameless because that final knot I'd tightened myself.

That got me thinking more than any of Bacon's digs. This could all go wrong, couldn't it? I could die. I didn't believe Bacon's statistics, but there was a slim chance this might be the last thing I ever did. And a slim chance was still a chance.

I thought about Ross. Was it better to be like him and not know how quickly your last breath was approaching? I thought about him being dead from some stupid accident, and here I was risking my life in a way that people paid for and was meant to be fun. Nobody wanted to die, but we seemed to get a kick out of purposely coming close.

Dunc helped me to my feet. I hoped he didn't notice the traitorous trembling in my knees. I was shuffled to the edge. I could feel my heart, hear my breathing. I felt like I wanted to sit down and stay there a while.

I looked at Bacon, who grinned at me. 'Fingers crossed, dude. Fingers crossed.'

I took one more toe-tingling step towards the

edge, the tips of my trainers poking out at thin air.

'Look out at the tower,' Dunc told me.

I did as I was told.

'Don't look down,' Bacon said.

But, of course, the second you hear someone say that . . .

And it was a long, *loooong* way down. My heart kicked; I shuddered, closed my eyes. Bacon laughed.

I wondered if I'd ever risked my life before. Had I ever done anything genuinely life-threatening? I didn't think so. Tipping the ton in Sim's brother's car? No; didn't count, not really. Had my life been so dull, so easy? In fifteen years of living had I never once been worried that I might not wake up tomorrow? Did that mean I was boring too?

And then I thought about Ross again. Did people think he'd led a boring life? Which parts had flashed before his eyes when that car hit him? Did he get slow-motion replays of his favourite bits? I wished he was here to watch me. But if he was here, I wouldn't be doing this. If he was still alive we'd never have left Cleethorpes.

'I'll count down from three,' Dunc said.

I nodded.

'Three . . .'

I wobbled.

'Two . . .'

I went. Didn't wait for 'one'.

Head first. Arms out – my best Superman impression. I noticed the camera's flash, then . . .

The rush. The speed. And the crush of noise in my ears. The plummet as I fell.

I could feel the downwards hurtle. I could feel the air I sliced through, dived through. I could feel it against my outstretched hands, feel it against my face, even feel it against my eyes. It rattled my eyeballs in their sockets as I fell.

There was no snatch of gravity, no grab of an invisible hand. I was with it all the way. I was racing it, chasing it. Like a swoop or a dash. A brain-flashing, eye-blurring plunge.

What a rush. Wow! What a RUSH!

The beach zoomed up at me. It leaped towards me in a single blink of my eye. Far then close – so suddenly close. And I thought I was going to touch it with the tips of my fingers.

The jerk of the cord was a surprise. I hadn't felt it stretch or tighten. I was yanked back up and a rolling weightlessness filled my stomach. Think of a roller coaster; multiply it by a hundred. Or what you imagine the nightmare of a malfunctioning lift might be like.

But I felt good. Great. Incredible.

Awesome.

And at the height of my bounce I could see Dunc and Bacon up on the gantry, leaning over, watching me. In that slow second as I hung in the air I was looking right up at Bacon with his stupid facial hair and his ludicrous red and black skull-and-crossbones bandanna.

I gave him the finger.

Then fell again.

Fifteen

Still in one piece – pretty much. My legs were shaking, buzzing with the adrenalin, but that was okay because it meant they were still attached. The only thing missing was my stomach, which I seemed to have left a hundred metres or so back up there.

The *Bungee! Blackpool!! Bungee!* assistant was quick to untie the cord from my ankles and offer to help me to stand, but I wouldn't let him. I wanted to do this by myself. I was loving the applause from the gathered crowd.

I looked back up. I really had just jumped from there, hadn't I?

I wanted to walk up to strangers and let them pat me on the back. I wanted them to see my face and make sure they knew it was me, yes me, who they'd just witnessed being courageous enough to leap out into thin air at the height of 160 metres.

I also wanted to see my photograph – the one

snapped of me as I'd jumped. I wondered if there was a way of persuading Bacon into giving it to me. It would be the ultimate, undeniable proof that I'd done what I'd done. It would be something to flash in the face of people like Munro at school. (I wanted to show it to Nina.) But I doubted he'd give me the photo – I reckoned he'd want to charge me forty quid for it.

I saw an orange T-shirt coming at me through the crowd. Kenny was waving, excited, beaming, big-eye amazed. And that made me feel very cool. Sim, Joe and Gus were following him and I went over.

Kenny grabbed at me, pawed me. 'I'm telling you,' he said. 'Honest, Blake. Really . . . I'm telling you. I really am.' He nodded hard, to prove he meant it.

'Thanks.'

Sim grinned at me from behind his sunglasses. 'You've got balls this big,' he said, holding his arms wide to show me just how big.

'Why d'you think I weigh so much?'

Joe clapped me on the back. 'We didn't think you were going to do it for a minute there. But you proved us wrong. Right, Gus?' And Gus nodded, winked at me.

'What was it like?' Kenny asked. 'I want to do it now. Was it really scary?'

'Scariest thing I've ever done in my life,' I said, bloated with pride. 'But it felt amazing.'

'I wish I could do it,' he said. 'D'you reckon Bacon'll let me . . . ? You know, seeing as he let you?'

'He didn't exactly *let* me, Kenny.' Again I wanted to see the photo, to see how I was going to look on a poster.

'You want to wait for Bacon?' Joe asked.

I looked up at the lift as it descended. I wanted the photo but I was worried he might not be happy with it, might try to insist I jumped again. 'No time,' I said. 'Let's get to the station.' And we jogged across the beach heading for where we'd parked the taxi.

I think I went on a bit to Joe and Gus as we drove to the station – saying how great it had been meeting them both, and how much we really appreciated their helping us out. My mouth ran on so much I sounded like Kenny. But I was on a massive high, still on top of the world, and wanted to share the feeling. As we pulled up outside the station I promised we'd send them the petrol money we owed.

Joe switched off the taxi's engine. 'You might not

owe us anything. If Bacon gets more customers because of this poster with you, we'll have a job and that'll be payback enough. Right, Gus?'

Gus was lighting another cigarette. He shrugged; nodded.

As we climbed out onto the pavement Joe's mobile rang. A brief burble to signal a text message. He dug the phone out of his jeans pocket, then swore when he saw what had been sent.

'What's up?' I asked.

'It's Bacon. And he . . . Not really sure you want to know, to be honest.' He showed it to Gus, who tutted, shook his head. Joe was reluctant to pass the phone to me.

I read Bacon's message. *My new poster.* Below it was the photo of me as I'd jumped. The quality wasn't great – but you could tell it was me even if the look on my face was that of a petrified child frozen mid-howl. You could see the sweat stains under the arms of my T-shirt and the way it had rucked up as I'd dived, exposing my pale, flabby belly as it bunched up over the harness. It looked like a saggy balloon in a wind tunnel. Underneath Bacon had written: *If Fat Boy can do it, so can you! I dare you!!*

The phone burbled again. This time the message read: *Best £40 publicity I ever spent!!!*

I felt like shit.

'Hey, listen,' Joe said. 'You're an optimist, right?'

'Hope so.'

'Then you're gonna do fine.'

We shook hands in a weird, formal way. It certainly wasn't something I was used to doing. And I felt bad giving Joe such a half-hearted shake, but I'd come back down to earth with a bump. The thought of that photo being made huge and plastered on view for thousands of tourists, and even put in the newspapers, made me feel sick with embarrassment. The thought of it was worse than how it had felt standing on top of that bungee platform. I wanted to get out of Blackpool as soon as possible.

Joe wished us luck with our 'mission'. 'Got to admit to being kind of curious about how it's all going to turn out. Let us know what this Ross place is like. If it's cool enough, never know, maybe Gus can take my ashes there too. Seeing as there's nowhere called *Joe*.'

'There's somewhere called *England*,' Kenny told him.

Sim and I grabbed him to pull him away.

But he wanted to shake Gus's hand first. And he said, 'Can I ask you something? Don't you ever say anything? I mean, you *can* talk, can't you?'

Sim rolled his eyes. And I thought, Oh God, here we go.

Gus seemed surprised by the question. He stepped away from Kenny and squinted at him, took a long hard look at him. He blew smoke. 'Nice T-shirt,' he said.

Sixteen

Crappy, geriatric train from Blackpool to Preston. Changed onto what we all agreed was a 'proper' train, a smart Virgin Pendolino with comfy seats and a bit of oomph, to Carlisle. Sim not letting Kenny keep hold of his new ticket – just in case.

The two of them had been doing their best to leave me alone, allowing me to stew in my self-pity. Any time they tried speaking to me I'd only snapped back anyway – badmouthing Bacon, bungees and Blackpool every opportunity I got. Which then made Kenny keep repeating how sorry he was.

'Honest, Blake,' he'd go. 'I'm telling you: I know it's all my fault for losing my ticket, but I'm really *really* sorry. Honest I am. And I shouldn't have said about advertising or posters either. Sorry for that too.'

His solemn face and heartfelt apologies had begun to grate on my nerves. We were sitting on opposite sides of the aisle, me looking one way up the carriage,

Kenny and Sim facing the other. I'd leaned across and hissed, 'Say sorry one more time, just once more, and I'll punch you. Okay?'

Since then he'd let me be, played I-Spy with Sim and bemoaned his lost Travel Scrabble instead.

'. . . something beginning with M.'

Kenny though about it. 'Man.'

Sim shook his head.

'Magazine.'

'No.'

Kenny pointed at an ugly woman further up the carriage. 'Minger.'

Sim nodded. 'Yeah. Your go.'

Kenny had a good look around. 'Okay . . . Something beginning with S.'

Sim pointed a finger in Kenny's face. 'Shithorn.'

It was a little after seven – nine hours since I'd been sitting with Caroline in the Fells' claustrophobic kitchen, and yet it felt like far too much had happened. The June evening speeding by outside the train's window was still sunshiny bright, but a whole week's worth of stuff had gone on, hadn't it? I was beginning to realize how tired I felt. And we still weren't anywhere near where we were meant to be going yet.

I'd kept my rucksack on the seat next to me. I got the map out.

'Everything okay?' Sim asked. He leaned across the aisle and kept his voice down. The train was busy and I suppose we couldn't help wanting to stay secretive even this far from home. 'We're definitely going the right way?'

I nodded. 'But I still don't know if there's any way we can make it to Ross tonight – we should have been there by now. I was just trying to think where we ought to stay. We've got to change trains at Carlisle, so we could try and find somewhere there. Or go all the way to Dumfries.'

'What d'you reckon'll be best?'

'Not sure. Where would you vote for, Kenny? I suppose we should think about where's going to be cheaper.'

'Can I vote for food instead?' Kenny asked. 'I'm starved. We left the last of the Mars Bars in Joe's taxi.'

And as if on cue, my stomach rumbled.

'I'd rather have something to eat too,' Sim said. 'I reckon we should just keep going as far as we can. Get the train to Dumfries. And how far is it from there to Ross? What, ten miles or something? We can walk that if we have to. Just keep going.'

'Might actually come to that,' I admitted. But it looked a good bit further than ten miles on the map to me. Closer to thirty.

'I don't think I could walk even two miles at the minute,' Kenny said. 'Not without something to eat.'

My stomach rumbled again. 'We've got fifty p more than last time, thanks to the change from Bacon's forty quid after buying your ticket. My vote is we keep every penny of it until we get to Dumfries, because it's gonna be cheaper than buying anything on a train.'

Kenny pulled a face. 'But that's ages.'

'Couple of hours at the most,' I said with my mouth. *Gimme something to eat*, my stomach replied. I decided to listen to my stomach.

'Just get the cheapest,' Sim said.

Our money was in the side pocket of my rucksack, and as I rooted around for it my fingers accidentally closed over something else that was also in there. I made sure Sim and Kenny were too busy looking at the map to see what I was up to as I grabbed my mobile and slipped it into the front pocket of my jeans.

'Back in a minute. Watch my bag,' I told them, hoping it would stop them from following me.

I made my way through the carriages towards the train's shop with my phone feeling hot enough to burn. I kept my eyes well averted from the other passengers in their seats as I passed. I checked over my shoulder twice to make sure Kenny and Sim weren't behind me. And the first toilet I came to, I ducked inside.

It was a huge cubicle – a Tardis toilet, looking like the kind of place Doctor Who would take a dump. I waited for the automatic door to slide into place behind me and pushed the flashing button to lock it. Feeling both sneaky and nervous I took my phone out of my pocket and switched it on. I watched the screen light up and blink – it chimed a little welcome. It searched for my network. I saw the little bars grow taller as it found the signal.

It surprised me how anxious I felt. I suddenly wasn't sure I wanted to know who'd been trying to contact me. But too late. The phone beeped with every text message and missed call. And I thought it was going to keep beeping until the seas dried.

Thirty texts. Thirty missed calls. It was full. It didn't have the capacity to store any more.

I swore under my breath. Switched off the phone and shoved it back into my pocket. Not wanting to know. Really, really not wanting to know. I stabbed at the button to open the toilet door and got out of there as quick as I could. Almost ran for the shop.

But standing in the queue with two packs of sandwiches, a bottle of 7-Up and a big bag of crisps I could feel my phone heating up once more, even hotter this time, scorching my thigh through my jeans pocket. I knew all the missed calls and texts would be my mum, my dad, maybe Ross's mum and dad, even Caroline. They'd all make me feel guilty – and petrified about going home to face the furore we'd caused. But what if Nina had called . . . ?

We're too far away, I told myself. Doesn't matter what they say, we're not turning back now. We can't.

And yet I knew my mum might very well have some sly, fiendish trick up her sleeve that would make me want to. She was the Queen of Emotional Blackmail.

I realized I'd been mumbling to myself, and not heard the shop assistant in his red Virgin uniform talking to me. I apologized and fumbled to pay. £7.63. I should have been worrying about losing nearly a quarter of our cash in one chunk but could only think about my phone.

Thirty texts. Thirty missed calls.

On the way back to Kenny and Sim I ducked inside the toilet again.

I pushed the button to lock the door. Then pushed it again to be sure. I told myself I would check just one missed call and one text – that was it, no more. I put the sandwiches and crisps in the hand basin and sat down on the closed loo seat. The train rocked one way then the other; it sounded much louder in here than in the carriages. I took my hot phone out of my pocket, switched it on. And assured myself I'd flush the bloody thing if it dared to ring right now.

I only wanted to check the last missed call, and although the phone confirmed that the last person who'd tried to contact me had been my mum, it also told me I'd missed nineteen of her calls in total – which was something I would have rather been left in the dark about. Was she angry, or worried? I guessed both. I couldn't think about it, forced the guilt right to the back of my mind and checked the last text that had been sent. It was from Nina:

Everybody wild. Please. Are you okay?

It was spelled and punctuated correctly, same as all of Nina's texts. That was her way. It raised a small smile. I felt happy but flustered. Against my better judgement I started to type a reply. Then stopped. Then swore. Huffed and puffed a bit. Then did it anyway.

all ok.

Problem was, now I felt tempted to listen to my voicemail. It would be great to hear Nina's voice. I dialled before I could talk myself out of it. But then got nervous it was going to be my mum or dad . . . Or, worse, Ross's mum. I thought of how she'd looked at the top of her stairs that morning. So sad and pale and weak. Like a soft wax ghost. I worried she might have left a message asking us to take her son back to her. It worried me because it might be so hard not to.

I wanted to delete them, get rid of them. But I had to listen to them to do that. I held the phone to my ear with my left hand and made sure the first finger of my right was ready on button 3. At the sound of the speakers' first syllable I hit that delete button. Even so, I knew who everybody was.

Mum, Mum, Dad, Mum, Dad, Dad, Mr Fell, Mum, Mum . . . On and on.

Until a voice I didn't recognize surprised me. Made my deleting finger pause. A man's voice – deep as a dungeon, solid and thick as a prison wall. I almost dropped the phone when he called himself Detective Sergeant Cropper. But I stabbed button 3 and shoved the phone back in my pocket before he could say much more than '. . . *caused a lot of trouble and worry . . .*'

I sat very still, not quite daring to move at first. When we were little kids Ross and I used to poke sticks into wasps' nests we found under bushes at the park. Those wasps were in my belly now. I felt more scared than I had when I'd been standing on that bungee platform – ten million times more.

I walked back to Kenny and Sim with paranoia crawling up my spine, checking the passengers' faces as I passed in between their seats. I knew it was ridiculous, of course I did, but I was looking for someone who might be chasing us. Or someone who might look like the police. But what if they were CID – Coppers In Disguise?

'You all right?' Sim asked, spotting how pale and twitchy I was.

'Is this all they had?' Kenny asked, turning his nose

up at the goat's cheese and sun-blush tomato sandwiches.

'Fine,' I told Sim. 'Shut up and eat it,' I said to Kenny.

I didn't know whether to tell them or not.

Kenny ripped open the bag of crisps. Sim gave me a funny look. 'You not having any?' he asked me.

'Feeling a bit travel sick,' I lied.

And then my phone started ringing.

Seventeen

My phone blared. But not as loud as Kenny.

'Your phone! You switched it on! You said . . . You agreed you'd . . .'

Sim just said, 'Don't answer it.'

I realized I'd been stupid enough to shove it back in my pocket without thinking to switch it off. As I fumbled to dig it out again I prayed it wasn't going to be Detective Sergeant Cropper. But when I read the name on the caller display I was reluctant to turn it off. It was Nina – she might be able to tell us what was going on. I saw the looks of betrayal on Kenny and Sim's faces, however, and hid my reticence as I jabbed at the power button and killed the noise.

'Who was it?' Sim asked.

I thought about lying, but: 'Nina.'

'Why's she calling?'

'By the looks of my missed calls, everyone's calling.'

'You should have answered it if it was her,' Kenny

said. 'Told her to shove it up her hole, whatever it is she wants.' The way he was carrying on was drawing stares from the other passengers.

'Simmer down, Kenny,' I told him.

'Bollocks to what you say! Bollocks to you, Blake. You agreed not to use our phones and that's exactly what you've been doing. In fact, I want to use mine now. I want to know what my mum's been saying.' Then he remembered his mobile was in his bag. 'Bollocks!'

'I know we agreed,' I said. 'It's just . . .'

'You've let us down,' Kenny said. 'You've let Ross down.'

I didn't like that. 'Hold on a minute. Who the hell are you to say something like that. I didn't realize I was the one who refused to help him out on the day he died.'

Kenny looked like I'd punched him.

Which first made me think, *Good*. But then, *Shit*. 'Sorry. I didn't mean that.'

Kenny was furious. 'Yes, you did. Why'd you say it if you didn't mean it? That's what you think, isn't it? You think that if he *did* kill himself, it's because of me.'

Sim turned on him. 'Christ-on-a-bike, Kenny! What're you on about?'

'Blake's blaming me—'

'I'm not blaming you for anything.'

'And Ross didn't even kill himself,' Sim said, eyes like snooker balls. 'So shut up before I shut you up, all right?'

Kenny thumped his whole body back into his seat, like a petulant child getting over a tantrum.

I waited for all the nosy passengers to look the other way. 'I'm sorry, Kenny, okay? I didn't mean it – I opened my mouth without thinking.' He wouldn't look at me but I ploughed on anyway. 'And the phone thing ... I just thought something might have happened that we needed to know about.'

'And?' Sim asked. 'Has it?'

I was scared that if I told them about Detective Sergeant Cropper they'd want to turn back. And I didn't think I wanted to do that, not yet.

'I don't know,' I said. 'I guess so. I started looking to see how many missed calls and texts I had. And it's loads. My mum mostly, but I reckon Ross's parents too. But, you know, I can tell we're in big trouble – it's obvious, isn't it?' Again I almost told them. Again held it back. 'Put it this way: I don't think we're gonna get banners and balloons and a welcome home party when we go back. I don't think people are gonna understand.'

'We'd guessed it was gonna be like that anyway,' Sim said. He shook his head. 'But it was easier when I didn't know for definite.' He put on his sunglasses and slumped down in his seat. 'I just don't want to know about that kind of stuff.'

'Nor me,' Kenny said. He stuffed his face with crisps and turned to stare out the window. 'I *know* my mum's gonna kill me. Don't need anyone else to tell me that, do I?'

I didn't know what to do. They were saying they didn't want to know, but . . .

I felt like a traitor twice over. I turned to the window next to me, watched the hills of the Lake District rise up against the evening sun. We were a long way from home, and getting further by the second. Maybe we should go back. I thought again of Mrs Fell standing at the top of the stairs, shrunk and softened by grief.

I wasn't sure if Sim had his eyes open or not behind his sunglasses. I reached across the aisle to nudge his arm. 'Here,' I said, and dropped my mobile in his lap. 'Make sure I don't use it again.'

'I don't want it.' He tossed it back to me. 'I can't stop you, can I?'

'Take it,' I said. Then, pointing at my belly: 'Look at me. When have I ever had any willpower to conquer temptation?' I got a smile out of him at least – and that felt good. But he still wouldn't take my phone. 'I just want to say I'm sorry, okay. This is all about the three of us sticking together, right? No matter what.'

'We've got to,' Sim said. 'If we don't stand up for one another and just go around blaming each other, it's gonna be much worse when we get back home. We're already in deep trouble anyway, aren't we?'

I held my hand high, showing him exactly how deep I thought it was – about as tall as I guessed a detective sergeant with a scary voice stood. 'Up to here.'

He sighed. 'But maybe I don't care, you know? Maybe I still reckon it's the right thing to do. For Ross. Because I was just thinking, he didn't even die at a good time, did he?'

Kenny paused long enough between crisps to ask, 'What d'you mean?'

'Well, it's not like there's ever a good time to die, I suppose. But you've got to admit, he had kind of a crappy last week, didn't he?'

'So you reckon if Ross had died while he was having a really good time, like if he'd still been with Nina or hadn't been beaten up by Munro, it would've been better?'

Sim shrugged. 'I don't know. Maybe.'

'Sounds a bit weird to me,' Kenny said. 'To die when you're having a good time.'

'Yeah, but at least you know you've had a good time. Ross probably died thinking everything was always going to be crap.'

'So you should die when you're on holiday or something?'

'How should I know? But maybe you should only die when you don't mind dying.'

'Like *after* you've just passed all your exams,' Kenny said.

Sim laughed. 'Yeah. Or *after* you've just got a good look at Ross's sister's tits in the shower. Yeah, I'd die happy then.'

'I thought you hated her.'

'Doesn't mean she hasn't got massive tits.'

'Okay,' Kenny said. 'I'm only going to die on the day *after* I've just spent the last pound of the eighteen million I'm going to win on the Lotto.'

'Exactly,' Sim agreed. 'Why die when you're still losing? *Die on a high*, that's my new motto.'

'Good idea,' I said. 'But there's a problem with that, isn't there? Because if it happens once, who says it's never going to happen again?'

They both shrugged, not sure what I was getting at.

'It's like, sitting here now, I don't think I'm ever going to see Caroline's tits, do I? And okay, it upsets me, but it seems like a total impossibility – so I don't worry about it. Because if I ever *did* get to see them in all their glory, it would seem like *nothing* was impossible, wouldn't it? It'd be like, I've seen them once, so maybe, just maybe, if I was lucky, I might get to see them again. And I'd always be thinking that, wouldn't I? I'd always be waiting for my second chance. So I'd rather die knowing something was impossible and was never gonna happen. It'd be a less frustrating death.'

Sim thought about it. 'Maybe.'

'It's what I'd be missing out on that would worry me,' Kenny said. 'I'm telling you: it'd be just my luck if someone was gonna invent a hovercar on the day after I died.'

Sim and I exchanged a look. '*Hovercar?*'

'Yeah. Don't you think they'll just be so cool when they're invented? I'm definitely getting one. I've always wanted one. I really hope they get invented before I die or go blind and can't drive them or something. That's what's so bad about Ross dying, isn't it? There's so much he's going to miss out on.'

'Like hovercars?' Sim asked.

Kenny nodded. 'Yeah. Because he's probably already seen his sister's tits, hasn't he? But think about it – not just hovercars, maybe the first man on Mars too. And computers inside your head. And just loads of brilliant stuff like that. Ross won't get to see any of it now.'

'England winning the World Cup again,' I said.

'All those beautiful women and all that sex he's not going to get,' Sim said.

'And even being a writer,' Kenny said. 'He'll never be a famous writer and have his books made into films.'

The train flashed through the bulging hills of the Lake District. We were quiet, thinking about how wrong it was that our best friend was going to miss out on so much.

Eighteen

Kenny saw the three girls first. 'Good-looking birds at three o'clock,' he said, rolling his eyes, nodding his head, coughing in their direction – all very unsubtle. 'What d'you call a bunch of birds, Sim?'

'A flock, obviously.'

'Yeah, that's right,' Kenny said. 'I knew that. But what do you call a flock of *good-looking* birds?'

Sim shrugged. 'Kenny-dodgers?'

We were waiting on yet another platform in yet another station. This one was Carlisle, and it was our sixth today – I wondered if it was some kind of record. It was only twenty past eight and still nowhere near dark, still nowhere near cool. The heat of the day was settling like sediment. We'd been waiting ten minutes or so for the train to Dumfries and it made a change not to be in a rush, but the waiting was making me antsy. I was seeing Detective Sergeant Cropper peeking around every corner. I heard his heavy, serious voice in conversations behind me.

Carlisle station is an unlikely-looking place. It has proud castle walls but an ornately ramshackle greenhouse roof. And not so long ago someone must have decided that gangrene was the best colour to paint every single door and window frame. It wasn't busy; there were about a dozen or so others waiting on the platform with us. Hikers wearing backpacks and bobble hats, a family with a noisy toddler and sleeping baby, a couple of sulky-looking Emo-types dressed in black and an old man in a shabby anorak. I doubted any of them were Cropper the copper in disguise. The three girls were at the far end of the platform carrying oversized bags from trendy clothes shops. When the short train rattled and clanked itself to a halt we watched to see which carriage they got on. And then chose the same one.

Sim took off his jacket, handed it to Kenny. 'Put this on. Don't want your T-shirt to scare them off, do we? And both of you, do me a favour, okay?' He included me in his gaze now. 'I'll do the talking.'

'Why bother?' I said. 'It's not like anything can happen, is it? We've got other stuff to do.'

He gave me a funny look. 'When did you suddenly stop wanting to chat up girls?'

'Maybe around about the time we ran off with the ashes of our dead best friend.'

'It's not like we're going to tell them, is it?' Kenny said.

'And if they're from Dumfries,' Sim said, 'they might know if there's any late-night buses or some-thing, so we don't have to walk to Ross.'

'Yeah, but we're definitely not telling them why we're going,' Kenny repeated.

'Or somewhere we can stay over or something,' Sim said.

I was still reluctant. '*If* they're from Dumfries.'

Sim shrugged. 'Worth a try.'

'And they *are* gorgeous,' Kenny said.

It was another scruffy, noisy train, not even half full. It seemed to sway and jolt far more than the bigger Pendolino even though it was travelling at half the speed. We staggered through the carriage, bounc-ing off the high seatbacks on either side of the aisle. Only two of the girls we'd seen were sitting at a table near the end of the carriage – the redhead couldn't have got on. But the table across from them was empty so we took it. Kenny and Sim sat on one side, me and my rucksack sat opposite. It was obvious the girls had seen us, casting quick glances out the corners of their eyes, but they didn't seem all that interested. They had their large shopping bags underneath the table, propped up against their legs.

I couldn't help feeling awkward. I wasn't all that interested in them either, not really. But these days Kenny and Sim goggled and woofed at almost anything in a short skirt. Which was funny when you thought about it. Not so long ago we'd simply dismissed girls for their inability to achieve boyhood. How awful, we used to think, it must be not to be a boy. Nowadays, of course, women were magnetic – always making us want to point North.

Ross had been the first one of us to get a girlfriend. Sara Marsh. But she was only the first girl we'd known Ross to proclaim his love to. Nina was the sixth. Not bad going.

I don't think Sim had ever told a girl he loved her, but he liked to think of himself as the most experienced one of us. And to be fair, he did have a picture on his mobile of Julie Forde from Year Twelve wearing a black bra.

He turned and smiled at the two girls at the table across the aisle. He didn't seem to care that they were ignoring him. 'We're going to Dumfries,' he told them.

They still ignored him.

'We've never been there before.'

The girl with the short blonde hair glanced at him, but only briefly. She turned back to her mate sitting opposite. 'My brother's promised to meet us off the train,' she said. 'He'll probably have Johnny and Robbie with him too. You remember Robbie who he met in the army?' Despite the underlying threat she was aiming at us, I thought she had a lovely Scottish accent. She had a lovely face too. Her hair was white-blonde, and cut short and boyish. Very blue eyes. She looked a bit like a younger version of somebody famous. But I couldn't work out who. Maybe some-body from *Hollyoaks*? And that put me off. I hated *Hollyoaks* – always have, always will. Who got paid for that crap?

'Are there any good clubs?' Sim tried. And maybe he was trying too hard – they'd have to be stupid not to realize we were far too young to get into clubs. 'You know, somewhere for a good night out?'

The second girl laughed. 'Aye, Dumfries is the clubbing capital of Scotland, didn't you know?' But she was looking at and speaking to her friend, not

Sim. She had longer, more yellowy-blonde hair that came down to her shoulders. She was skinny – wearing a too-tight T-shirt that emphasized just how skinny. It was like you'd need four of her to make just the one of me. Her arms looked twiggy and brittle, but I liked the way they were sprinkled with freckles.

'So is that where you're from?' Sim asked.

'Maybe.' She still wouldn't look at him.

'But I'm betting the best shops are in Carlisle,' he said, pointing at their bags. 'Right?'

'Obviously.'

Sim turned to me and shrugged. He wasn't getting anywhere. I shook my head: forget it, doesn't matter.

But Kenny asked, 'Where's your friend gone?'

They were both quick to look at him. 'Who?'

And he was surprised, awkward with their sudden attention. 'I . . . I thought there was another girl with you.' He wanted me and Sim to back him up. 'Wasn't there?'

But nobody had a chance to say anything because the conductor appeared and we all had to find our tickets. Apart from Kenny, because Sim had his.

The girls beamed sunny smiles and both said a pleasant hello to the conductor when he checked their tickets. Butter wouldn't melt. And he seemed friendly enough; could have been their granddad. 'Been spending all your hard-earned wages in Carlisle?' He gestured at the shopping bags at their feet. The girls tittered and smiled.

When he checked our tickets he said, 'You've come a fair way, lads.' And again my paranoia spiked. So bad I couldn't even return his smile. Kenny and Sim mumbled some kind of reply, but both managed to look more devious than suspected train robbers hatching their plans. I was glad they didn't know everything I did. To me their guilty faces alone seemed enough to set off alarms and launch spy copters. Who knew whether or not the conductor could sense something funny going on?

He punched our tickets and the three of us craned our necks to watch him walk away. He disappeared into his private cabin at the rear of the train. Did he have a walkie-talkie or phone or something in there . . . ?

I mentally kicked myself. Told myself to calm down.

I noticed the girls had been watching him too. And when he was out of sight, the girl with the longer blonde hair nudged one of the large shopping bags under the table with her foot. Kenny, Sim and I must have looked gob-smacked as the third girl climbed out from under there. Her friends had used their huge department store bags to barricade her in, hide her from view. She was smaller and younger looking than the other two, round-cheeked and dimpled, dressed in bright flowers. Her hair was short, ruffled and red; too red to be called ginger – red enough that I reckoned it had to be dyed. She squeezed and wriggled her way out from beneath the table, all grinning and impish, so very pleased with her sneakiness.

Sim turned to Kenny. 'See that,' he said. 'See her? All that grief we went through getting you a ticket. Didn't I tell you to hide or something? But all that hassle because you're even more chicken-shit than a girl.'

Kenny looked miserable enough to want to crawl under a table himself now – and stay there. 'But I'm telling you: it's—'

'Don't tell me nothing,' Sim said. 'I'm too ashamed to even listen.'

Nineteen

The train trundled to a halt at Gretna. A couple of people got off but nobody got on. The conductor stepped out onto the platform, and I wondered if he was waiting for the special police task force.

And then I told myself to get a grip.

The girls had their shopping bags open on the table in front of them and were comparing the clothes they'd bought, holding up T-shirts with dangling price tags for inspection and admiration. They didn't seem the least bit concerned the conductor might notice one extra sitting there. But what was he going to do? He was on the platform watching nobody getting on his train. He'd just assume he'd already checked the red-head's ticket.

Kenny, Sim and I huddled around our own table with the map open in front of us. The train shuddered as it pulled away. I let out a quick breath of relief to be moving again.

'Right, now we're in Scotland,' I said. 'At last.'

Kenny was more interested in the girls. 'They're nice, aren't they? I really like them.'

'Stop drooling,' Sim told him. 'You're getting the map soggy.'

'So from here to here,' I said, pointing out both Dumfries and Ross. 'You really think we should just start walking tonight?' Scotland, I thought. We're nearly there. I knew our destination was further than it seemed just by looking at the map, but for once it felt close. And I was in a rush now. 'It's gonna be a hell of a walk,' I said.

'Sounded good when I said it an hour ago,' Sim admitted. 'But I'm knackered, and starving. Maybe crashing for the night wouldn't be a bad idea.'

'What about you, Kenny?' I asked.

He was still staring at the girls. 'Who d'you like best?'

'Genuinely, Kenny: I'm not interested right now, okay?' What I wanted to do was sneak off to the toilet to check my phone again. 'We've got other stuff to worry about.'

'Yeah, but you must fancy one of them. Come on, there's three of them. One each, yeah?'

'Nothing's gonna happen, Kenny. It's not worth getting all het up about.'

'Who's het up? Do I look like someone who's hetting up?'

'Keep your voice down,' Sim told him. 'And Blake's right, we've got other stuff to think about. But if I was on the pull . . .' He clicked his tongue. 'The one with the short blonde hair would be mine.'

Kenny wasn't happy. 'No way. She's the one I'd pick. I fancied her first. You can't pick her.'

Sim grinned. 'Tough. All mine.'

'Why? Who says? That's not fair. Tell him, Blake. Tell him he's—'

'Kenny,' I hissed, glancing at the girls, embarrassed. 'Get a grip.'

He lowered his voice. 'What if she likes me more?'

Sim just laughed.

Kenny bristled. 'I don't know why you're laughing. You think you're so cool but they've already knocked you back, haven't they?'

'Even monkeys fall out of trees sometimes,' Sim said. 'And think about it: if they knocked me back, you don't stand a chance, my friend.'

Kenny fizzed with indignation. He narrowed his

eyes at Sim, tried to shoot him dead with an invisible laser-beam glare. But then he turned in his seat, his back to the two of us. He faced the girls across the aisle and surprised us by saying: 'Er, hey, excuse me. Hi.' He pushed his floppy fringe out of his eyes and worked his most winning smile.

He'd surprised the girls too. The short-blonde acted like her seat was suddenly uncomfortable, the long-blonde looked like she'd stepped in something nasty, and the redhead just seemed plain bemused.

'I'm Kenny,' Kenny said.

The long-blonde one shrugged. 'Congratulations.' And the short-blonde one sniggered.

Sim sighed, shook his head. 'Kenny, Kenny, Kenny,' he whispered, managing to sound both sorrowful and smug.

The redhead was staring at Kenny like he was something peculiar and fascinating under a microscope. He said to her, 'So, you know, how come you were hiding from the conductor?'

The blonde girls looked at him like he was an idiot. Which, to be fair, he was.

The short-blonde said, 'Because she didn't have a ticket, obviously. What're you going to do? Tell tales on us now?' There was a needle of bitchiness in her voice.

I squirmed in my seat, embarrassment shrivelling me up.

Kenny either didn't care or didn't notice. He ploughed on. 'No, no, I lost my ticket too, you see? We're from Cleethorpes. You know, in England? And I had it in my bag but I left it on the train at Doncaster. My bag, not my ticket. Well, my ticket too, I suppose – because it was in my bag at the time, wasn't it? I had all my stuff in my bag. Lost it all. And my phone. Then we got kicked off at York when I got caught. I'm telling you: Blake and Sim were really pissed off. Sim gets really angry really quick. He's like that. But . . . But we . . .' At last he noticed the mystified looks on the girls' faces. 'So we, er . . .' He closed his mouth, bit his bottom lip. 'Um,' he said.

The train rattled along. We were jogged and bounced in our seats. Nobody said a word.

'Um,' Kenny repeated. He looked like he was drowning.

I felt maybe I should dive in to save him. But the redhead said:

'Wow. See, that's just like me. Although not totally like me because I never had a ticket anyways. Hayley, see, her brother gave us a lift to Carlisle and we all said, aye, we'd get the train back. But I spent all my money. See this top? I just couldn't resist. So I had to hide. Anyways, Hayley and Kayleigh, they got mad like your pals did with you, saying I'm always doing it. But I'm not always doing it.' She grinned, showed her dimples. 'But I am sometimes.'

Kenny blinked, twice, shocked by her sudden burst of chatter.

'I'm Kat,' the redhead said. She pointed at her friends; the short-blonde then the long-blonde. 'Hayley. Kayleigh.' And back to herself. 'Kat.'

Kenny said, 'I'm . . . Kenny.'

'See, I know that, 'cos you've said it already.'

Kenny nodded. 'Yeah. Sorry.'

'Who's Blake and which one's Sim?'

I admitted to being Blake, but Sim seemed to be trying to avoid any kind of eye-contact with her whatsoever.

'Is Sim short for "simple"?' she asked.

Kenny thought that was funny; he grinned at Sim.

And Sim punched his arm. Hard.

'Anyways, that's rude, sorry,' Kat said. 'I like the name Kenny, though. See, I had a dog called Kenny once. He was half mutt, half mongrel but we loved him. He was totally gentle and friendly. He never chased me even though he knew I was called Kat.' She laughed at her own joke. Kenny laughed too. 'He died anyways, when I was nine and three-quarters. I remember it because I wasn't ten yet. He ate one of my Barbies and the vet said he choked to death. See, and my mum bought me a new Barbie for my birthday, but I wanted another dog.'

'I've always wanted a dog,' Kenny said.

'You should get one,' Kat told him. 'But don't call it Kenny. See, it'd be confusing.'

And they both thought that was just downright hilarious.

I was astounded she'd been able to keep her mouth shut long enough to hide from the conductor. She didn't want to shut up now, that was for sure. But all the time she was talking her two friends rolled their eyes and grimaced at each other – kind of the way Sim and I did whenever Kenny opened his mouth.

Kenny turned to me, big-eyed, grinning, and silently mouthed: *She's amazing*.

Sim was also wide-eyed. He mouthed: *She's a mentalist*.

Twenty

Kenny managed to forget that Hayley was meant to have been the girl who'd caught his eye. By the time we arrived at Dumfries, he and Kat were like Velcro. The rest of us had had to shuffle seats to let them sit next to each other.

'I'm telling you: taking history at school is just stupid. All it's gonna do is get harder and harder, because more stuff keeps happening.'

'That's why I'm wanting to do geography. See, with all the global warming and everything, and all the seas rising all the time, it's got to get easier.'

It was close to ten o'clock, still light, but you could tell the end of the day was coming. The six of us walked out of the train station together. And I told myself not be stupid, but I still hesitated a second or so just to check there were no police cars waiting.

'You okay?' Sim asked.

I nodded. 'Yeah. Course.'

We stood in the car park out front. I'd expected to emerge into the centre of the town, but we seemed to be on the outskirts somewhere. There were big, posh houses opposite; tall, old and ornate. Strange as it sounds, they looked Scottish too. There was also a bus stop with a timetable printed on the outside of the glass shelter.

With Kenny and Kat getting on so well it had at least broken the ice for the rest of us. And Sim was keen to hasten the thaw with Hayley. He pointed at Kenny and Kat, who were now holding hands. 'Sweet, isn't it?' he said.

'Aye,' Hayley agreed. 'Sweet like jelly babies.'

'She hates jelly babies,' Kayleigh explained.

Sim shrugged. 'Horses for courses, I suppose.' Which at least made Hayley laugh. 'Hey, wasn't your brother and his army mates meant to be meeting you?' he asked, teasing her.

She narrowed her eyes at him. 'Aye, and he still will if I tell him you're sex maniacs.'

He winked at her. She tutted and shoved him away from her. It was a very physical flirtation.

I headed over to the bus shelter to check the times. If we were lucky there might still be a bus going our way. Problem was, I didn't recognize any of the names of the places the buses were going. Ross didn't appear anywhere. I had to dig the map out of my rucksack and hope to find somewhere as close as possible. It seemed to be my lucky night when I found a town that looked good.

'Kenny,' I called. 'Sim.'

Sim wandered over. But either Kenny hadn't heard or was trying to ignore me – too busy giggling with Kat. So I shouted again. This time he looked over at me with a scowl. I scowled back. Sim pointed at a spot by his feet, and beckoned him over with a slowly curled finger. Kenny slouched towards us across the car park like a resentful dog.

'What?'

'We can still get a bus tonight,' I said, grinning, expecting them to be as relieved as I was.

'To Ross?'

I showed them the map. 'Not quite. But close. To this place here: Kirkcudbright. It can only be about five or six miles to Ross from there.' It all seemed to be turning out easier than expected. This was great, this was brilliant. It was like a weight had been dropped off my shoulders. Everything might be going to turn out okay after all.

Kenny looked back towards Kat, who was the centre of a conspiratorial scrum with Hayley and Kayleigh. 'I thought we were gonna stay here tonight.'

'If we can get to Ross tonight, then we'll be able get back home again tomorrow. The buses run Sundays too, yeah? And the quicker we get home the less trouble there'll be.'

Kenny stared at his feet. Then looked back towards Kat. Again he said, 'But we were gonna stay here tonight.'

'I thought you were worried about your mum. You do know how much crap we're gonna have to be dodging for the rest of our lives, don't you?' I felt stressed that I had to deal with both my secret and his stiffy. 'And stay where? And with what money?'

He mumbled something at his feet.

'What?'

'Maybe we can stay with the girls,' he said.

'Have you asked them?'

'No.'

'Have they offered?'

'No, but—'

'Right, so the bus leaves at—'

Sim butted in. 'We could get the bus tomorrow. You said they're running, right?'

I turned on him. 'Yeah, but we're getting one tonight.'

'Come on, Blake. When was the last time you met a girl who laughed at any of Kenny's jokes? He's usually got to knock them out and tie them down.' Kenny let the insult fly. He wasn't so daft he didn't realize when Sim was on his side. 'Look at his face: not even his mother can love it. But he's met a girl as off her head as he is. It's Fate – gotta be. It'll be torture to make him walk away now.'

'You're only saying that because you think you're in with Hayley.'

'I don't think – I *know*. And that still leaves Kayleigh for you.'

I shook my head. 'I told you, I'm not interested in trying to get off with anyone.'

Sim scoffed. 'That'll be a first.'

'I just want to do what we came here to do, okay? You remember that, right?' I held my rucksack up in front of me, hoping the thought of what was inside would make them see sense. 'Joe said it:

we're on a mission. And there's a bus can take us—'

'Let's have a vote,' Kenny said.

I was stunned.

Kenny took quick advantage. 'Who votes we get the bus tomorrow instead?' Both he and Sim held their hands high.

I stood there, half dumb. 'Just . . . What . . .? But . . .'

Kenny was already hurrying over to be with Kat again.

Sim was grinning at me. 'I'll get Hayley to have a word with Kayleigh. You know, drop a couple of hints for you.'

'Don't,' I told him, feeling both shocked and deflated that this day had somehow managed to become even more complicated. Again. 'Just . . . Don't.'

He also wandered back to the girls. It felt like the two of them had ganged up on me. It felt like a mutiny. We often used to have these silly votes with Ross, but at least then I could rely on him to be on my side. Our friendship used to be a solid square, one of us to each corner. Things were very different as a triangle.

And I was tempted to tell them about DS Cropper, just shout it out – I knew that would halt them in their tracks. But I also knew it might make them turn right round and head back into the station, jumping on the first train south. I bit the revelation back, deciding I couldn't risk it.

I swung my rucksack over my shoulder and mooched across the car park to the group of them. 'So what've you two geniuses got planned then?' I didn't care how petulant I sounded.

'We need somewhere to stay the night,' Sim told Hayley.

'I thought you were visiting a friend.'

'Yeah, we are. But he doesn't live in Dumfries, and he's not really expecting us until tomorrow.'

'And we haven't got any money for a hotel,' Kenny said. 'Because I lost my bag? I told you? It had all my money and stuff in it. This is the only T-shirt I've got now.'

'So what are you going to do?' Kayleigh asked me.

'Don't look at me,' I said. 'Those two there, they're the brains of the outfit.'

She gave me a funny look, which I chose to ignore.

'Where's your pal live anyways?' Kat asked.

'Kirkcudbright,' I said before Kenny or Sim could say anything else.

'Where?'

'Kirkcudbright.' I showed her on the map.

Kat laughed at me. 'Ker-coo-bree. That's how you say it. Ker. Coo. Bree.'

'Kur-cub-ray,' Kenny tried, his Scottish accent not quite up to it.

'Kenny-coo-bree, Kenny-coo-bree,' Kat whispered, nuzzling up to his ear. He looked at her like she was an angel come down from heaven in a hovercar.

'Yeah, well, whatever it's called,' I said. 'That's where he lives and that's where we need to get to. The sooner the better.'

'It's ten o'clock on a beautiful summer Saturday night,' Sim said, slipping his sunglasses on. 'Chill, okay? Either we find a place to stay here, or we go there and still have to find somewhere. Let's just stay here.' He said to Hayley: 'Don't suppose you've got room enough for us three lonesome wanderers?'

'Aye, that's right,' Hayley said. 'My mum really wants some English weirdos staying with us. Who says I even care if you stay or not?'

'So forget those two. How about just somewhere I can lay my weary head?'

'You're so sure of yourself, aren't you?'

He grinned, clicked his tongue.

She elbowed him in the ribs.

'But we don't live in Dumfries either,' Kat said.

Kenny looked confused.

'We never said we did, did we? And we've got to get the bus anyway.'

'You live in Kirkcudbright?' I said, ever hopeful.

She shook her head. 'But if you come with us I know somewhere you can stay the night.' She grinned at her friends. 'We can take them to the Tramp's Hotel.'

That didn't sound good. 'Do what?'

'It's just a nickname,' Kayleigh said. 'It's an old house really. No one lives there.'

'Like, derelict?' I asked.

'Like, abandoned and haunted,' Kat said, eyes wide and rolling, grinning like a mad woman.

I looked at Kenny and Sim. I was pleased to see Kenny wasn't overjoyed at the thought of it, but Sim said: 'Hey, come on. We keep saying this is an adventure, right? I don't see what your problem is.'

'Tramp's Hotel. *Tramp's* Hotel. There's kind of a clue in the title to what my problem is. Why don't we just wear T-shirts saying: PLEASE BUGGER ME AND LEAVE ME IN A DITCH?'

Sim tutted, raised his eyebrows at Hayley. 'So melodramatic,' he said. He swung his rucksack over his shoulder and with one hand gathered up Hayley's big shopping bags. 'So, are you scared of ghosts then? D'you reckon you're gonna need protection?' He slipped his other hand around her waist as they walked towards the bus stop.

'Don't touch me,' she said, wriggling away from him – but not too far.

'Kenny?' I asked, appealing to the chicken-shit I knew lurked inside him.

'It'll be fun,' Kat giggled.

Kenny was torn for almost as long as two seconds. Then, apologetically: 'It'll be fun.' He let Kat drag him away.

The two of them followed Hayley and Sim. Which left me and Kayleigh. She brushed back her long hair with her hand, letting it fall over her shoulder. She shrugged, half smiled, then picked up her bags and followed the others.

I swore under my breath. Just when I thought things were going to get easier. I couldn't believe that we'd stood shoulder to shoulder right up until girls got in the way. But what could I do? The bus came round the corner, pulled up at the stop. I hefted my rucksack onto my shoulder and trailed along too.

Twenty-one

Hayley said, 'Parrots.'

'A company.'

Kat shouted, 'Kangaroos.'

'A mob. Come on, someone *please* give me a difficult one.'

'I'm brilliant with computers,' Kenny said to Kat, not wanting to be forgotten.

The bus took us through the centre of Dumfries. It seemed smaller than Cleethorpes and looked quieter, older. It was the kind of place my mum would call pretty. We drove across an old stone bridge over a wide, shallow river. It looked like a piece of the countryside plonked right down in the middle of the town. I spotted signs for places called Cargen, Kirconnel and New Abbey, but like every other bus I've been on, the route was too convoluted to follow. So when we got off about twenty minutes later, I didn't have a clue which of the place names we'd arrived at. If any. It looked too much like the middle of nowhere to me. Now we were walking along a narrow country road with hedges on either side of us, getting further and further into the middle of nowhere, as the sun went down. And three lots of bus fare poorer too. We were down to just over a tenner. Best not to even think about how we were supposed to get home again on that.

'Ostriches,' I said.

Sim glanced back at me over his shoulder. It was the first time I'd joined in the conversation since we'd got off the bus. And while on the bus I'd only ever tried to remind them of where we were meant to be going by pointing at my rucksack every time they looked at me.

'Yeah, a bit trickier, I suppose,' he admitted. 'Most people reckon it's a flock. But I know it should really be a pride.'

He then said to the girls: 'Did we tell you Blake did a bungee jump today? How high was it again?' he asked me. I knew exactly what he was trying to do.

And I let him. 'Hundred and sixty metres.'

'Really?' Kayleigh was impressed enough to look at me like I was crazy. The other two girls started asking questions as well, and Sim gave me a grin, a wink.

I guessed I could have stayed moody if I'd wanted to, but in the end I couldn't see the point. This trip had a life of its own. It was like trying to ride on the back of a giant snake as it wriggled and twisted beneath me. There was no way I could control it – it was far too unpredictable and dangerous. All I could do was cling on and keep my fingers crossed we'd make it there and back again in one piece.

I had to remember why I was doing this – the reason I was here in Scotland instead of back home in Cleethorpes. That reason was the one and only thing that mattered. And I hefted my rucksack higher up on my shoulders.

'Where exactly is this Tramp's Hotel place?' I asked Kayleigh, who was walking closest to me, a step or two behind the other four.

'Not that far,' she said.

'Near where I live,' Kat told me over her shoulder. 'See, it's in this field where the fair used to come. And we used to dare each other to go inside when we were wee. Everyone said it was haunted back then. So you had to be real brave and go in or the older kids'd beat you up.'

'Have you ever been inside?' Kenny asked.

'Oh, aye. Plenty of times. But those two never have.'

'You only went in so's you could get off with Malky Smith,' Hayley said.

'Aye, so?'

'Who's Malky Smith?' Kenny asked.

Kat gripped Kenny's hand. 'I never really liked him that much anyways. See, I just wanted him to show me his thing because everybody said he'd the biggest in Dumfries and Galloway.' She shrugged. 'It was okay, I suppose.'

Kenny looked anxious.

We walked by a dilapidated barn, just skeletal planks and a lopsided roof. Out front was a rusty lump of farm machinery thick with weeds – a plough or something. There was a silent, murky pond. Dark, crowding trees. Then the hedgerows grew tall again. But guarding a gap in the hedgerows was a low, wide wooden gate. The gate was chained and padlocked so we climbed over. The field beyond was up to our knees with dry grass and weeds bearing yellow or purple heads, even some thistles. It was maybe the size of a footie pitch, maybe a bit bigger, enclosed on three sides by a high, patchy wall of bushes. But there was more of a mini-wood separating it from the pond and the rundown barn. I spotted a sharp glint of light, like a prolonged camera flash, in amongst that copse of trees and realized it was the reflection of the sunset on a window. There was a house hidden somewhere back there. At a guess: Tramp's Hotel.

But it wasn't our overnight accommodation that had caught Kenny's eye. 'What's that?' he wanted to know, pointing right to the very back of field.

'It's the whirligig,' Kat told him.

We waded through the thick grass towards it. I wondered if it was more abandoned farm machinery. Slumped, rusty and fast becoming overgrown, was some kind of massive, silver and red metal octopus.

'But what is it?' Sim asked.

'See, I told you the fair used to come here,' Kat said. 'But the people in the village complained about it. And when they built the new houses, where us three live, my dad started this petition going.' She put on an impression of what she reckoned her dad must sound like. '*Hello. I'm angry from Dumfries and Galloway and I hate fun. Please ban the fair. It's far too much fun for me.* Anyways, it stopped coming. But they left the whirligig behind.'

Its four giant arms were half buried in the grass, covered with a nasty rash of rust and flaky paint. The seats were like small sofa-cages and most were still attached, but they'd become matted with grass and weeds where they rested on the ground. A few of the seats had come off altogether – busted and broken by years of vandalism and decay. I'd always thought there was an engine underneath these things but this was just the structure of the ride itself. And as it lay there, its arms sprawled, it looked dead.

'How long's it been here?' I asked.

'Ever since the fair left it,' Kat said, as if I was stupid.

'Six or seven years,' Kayleigh said. 'I don't think anybody knows why they left it.'

'Can you imagine the people who run the fair when they arrived at the next town?' Sim said. 'Helter-skelter? Check. Big wheel? Check. Octopus ride? Octopus ride? Aww, shit! Who forgot the octopus ride?' It cracked us all up. 'What d'you mean you've lost it? Go backwards in your head. When was the last time you remember seeing it?'

'It's just bizarre,' I said. I walked around it, touching the metal struts and picking at the crispy paint. I could see hundreds of empty sockets along the length of the arms where all the colourful, flashing bulbs should have been. 'The day fun died,' I said.

'Piss off being so miserable,' Sim told me, dropping his rucksack to the ground. 'You sound like Ross. Look, this is still fun, this is.' He nudged Kenny towards one of the seats. 'Get in. And you, Kat.'

The safety bar was jammed down and the two of them had to squeeze and wriggle to climb in.

Sim set off on a quick walk, circling around the contraption. 'Hold tight, ladies and gentlemen. Keep your hands and feet inside the seats at all times.' He made a complete lap and started to jog. 'Scream if you wanna go faster, Kenny!'

Kenny gripped the safety bar tight. 'Yee-*ha!*'

Sim did another lap, running faster. He grabbed Hayley and Kayleigh as he passed them, dragging them round with him. 'Scream if you wanna go faster, Kat!'

She shrieked and held her hands to her face. And Sim, Hayley and Kayleigh ran as fast as they could, sprinting as they circled the whirligig. Round and round. Kenny and Kat pretending to hold on for dear life, both screaming. The two girls waving their arms as they ran. Sim put his head down and tried to haul them even faster.

'Whoo-hooo!' Kenny yelled.

And we were all shouting and cheering. It was one of the funniest things I'd ever seen.

Until Sim stumbled in the grass, tripped and fell in a headlong roll. But that was funny in a different way. Hayley and Kayleigh collapsed in panting heaps next to him. Kenny and Kat whooped and applauded.

I went over to help Sim up. 'How much more fun d'you need?' he panted as I pulled him into a sitting position – he was too knackered to stand.

'Okay, you proved me wrong,' I admitted. I took my rucksack off and propped it upright in the grass.

'Don't suppose you've got any drink left in there, have you?' he asked, sticking out his tongue to show me how parched he was after all that exertion.

I shook my head. 'But there might be a shop that's still open where we can get something.'

'You'll be lucky,' Hayley said. 'The nearest one's miles away.'

'I can get something from my house,' Kat said. 'Let's have a midnight picnic. Eat under the stars and the moon and the black holes. I've always wanted to do that anyways.'

'Sounds good to me,' Sim said. Kenny was eager too. And who was I to argue?

The three girls headed back across the field together, taking their shopping bags with them. We watched them go.

'D'you think they'll come back?' Kenny asked, his face scrunched with anxiety.

Sim gave him a reassuring pat on the back. 'No worries. You're in there.' He rolled his eyes at me but said to Kenny, 'And good luck to you too.'

'And you really like Hayley, do you?'

'Don't tell me you wanna swap. You're my best mate, but Kenny, I'm telling you—'

Kenny shook his head. 'No, no, I really like Kat. *Really* really. She's perfect, isn't she? But Hayley seems kind of, I don't know . . . kind of *spiky*?'

Sim clicked his tongue. 'That's just the way I like them. But it's not me you should be worrying about. It's Mr Celibate here.' He hooked a thumb in my direction.

Kenny said, 'Kayleigh's really pretty too, Blake. I reckon you ought to—'

I cut him short. 'Shut up, Kenny. And you,' I warned Sim, who held up his hands as if he didn't know what on earth I was talking about.

I sighed. 'Come on,' I said. 'Let's go check out where we're supposed to be staying the night.' I knew they were raising their eyebrows at each other and giving me funny looks behind my back as I strode off towards the trees, but I ignored them. Let them think what they liked.

Twenty-two

Tramp's Hotel lived down to expectations.

We had to fight through a heavy tangle of under-growth to get at it underneath the trees. Stamping down waist-high nettles and snapping off low branches. It was a squat dirty-brick cottage with half a pointy roof. I guessed it was a hundred years old – maybe more. Graffiti had spread across its walls like a dose of chicken pox in primary school. What I'd earlier thought was a pane of glass reflecting the sun was actually a sheet of metal that filled the gap where a window should be. The metal was pocked and dinted with the scars of dozens of chucked stones, but still shiny. There was no door. Just a dark, door-shaped hole.

We listened. It was silent. We peeked in. The first room was about the size of my bedroom, with two doorways leading from it. We couldn't see much in the darkness except the grass and leaves and plastic bags and crumpled cigarette packets and crushed lager cans littering the floor. It smelled earthy and damp.

'It only seems spooky 'cos it's empty,' Kenny said.

'You first then.' Sim stepped out of the way, giving Kenny space to go in if he was brave enough.

He wasn't.

Although he was probably right. I didn't like those gloomy doorways leading further into the cottage. Someone could be standing just beyond one of them, hidden by the shadows, watching us. We'd never know.

Sim led the way around the outside of the decrepit cottage, stomping down more undergrowth as he went. All the windows had been smashed and covered over by sheets of metal. One of the sheets had been pried back at one edge and Sim stood on his tiptoes to look inside.

'What can you see?'

'It's too dark,' he said.

In what would have been the cottage's back garden was a blackened patch of ground.

'Somebody's had a fire,' Sim said. He scuffed through the burned-up branches with the toe of his trainer, made them disintegrate into chunky black ash. 'Could be tramps, could be kids.'

Where the wilderness and the trees stopped, the murky pond began, separated by a tall chain-link fence. Beyond that the skeletal barn. The cottage's back door was still in place, albeit one big sheet of metal. Someone had tried unsuccessfully to force it open – there were what looked like boot prints in the scratched and dented metal.

'Why would anybody want to break in the door when all they've got to do is climb over the wall where the roof's missing?' Kenny wanted to know.

'Probably just wanted to smash it for the hell of it,' Sim said, and kicked it himself. It made the sound of a dead bell.

Which was still much too loud for me. 'Did you have to? There could be someone inside for all we know.'

'Not someone,' Sim said. 'Some *body*. A corpse all messed up and gross and rotting.'

Kenny took a step away from the cottage. 'Kat said it was haunted.'

I started walking back the way we'd come. 'Tramps, yes,' I said. 'I can believe that. But ghosts don't smoke fags, drink cheap lager and build fires.'

Sim crept up close to Kenny's ear. 'Unless they *were* tramps, but they died and were left to rot, and now they're the ghosts. Go have a look, Kenny.'

Kenny shoved him away. Sim grabbed hold of him and gestured to me. I grabbed his other arm and between us we dragged him towards the front door, getting ready to throw him inside. But he bucked and fought and kicked up weeds as he squirmed away.

'Get Blake!' he shouted at Sim. So they grabbed me next and tried pulling me towards the door. But no way could they budge me. I dug my feet into the mud and leaves and laughed at their exertions.

So me and Kenny turned on Sim instead. And Sim said, 'Touch me and die.'

The three of us messed about, acted up, jumping on each other, trying to knock each other down or trip each other up, fighting and laughing and swearing. Real grown-up stuff . . . We bombarded each other with pine cones, whapped fallen branches across each other's backs. And we were soon knackered – it had been a long day. Still grinning we moved out from under the trees back into the open field.

'Hands up if you want to sleep there,' I said.

Kenny tried hard with the hopefulness. 'Maybe we can still stay with one of the girls.'

We wandered back across the field towards the whirligig. It was getting darker as the sun slipped away.

'Maybe we can sleep here,' Sim said, pointing at one of the whirligig's seats. 'We can have one each. As long as it doesn't rain we'll be fine.'

'Wish we had a tent,' Kenny said.

Sim sighed. 'Like Ross always said: *Wish in one hand, shit in the other, and see which hand fills up first.*' He pulled himself up onto one of the whirligig's arms and sat there dangling his legs.

Kenny climbed into one of the cage-seats, crawling under the jammed safety bar. He lay on his back, testing it out for comfiness. He stared up at the darkening sky. 'You know, I'll tell you something: I'm actually having a really good time. It's, like, I know we're in trouble and everything. But this *is* cool, isn't it?'

'Very,' Sim agreed.

I sat in the grass next to my rucksack. Half of me agreed. This was an adventure, right? The other half couldn't forget the sound of the policeman on my voicemail.

'And Ross would have loved it too, wouldn't he?' Kenny said. 'He should be here with us, shouldn't he?'

We had to be quiet to think about that.

Luckily the girls reappeared and stopped us from brooding.

Twenty-three

Kat waved and the three of them climbed over the gate from the road, waded towards us through the long grass.

'I got loads of stuff,' Kat said. 'As much as I could without my dad going mad anyways.' Her shopping bag now carried bottles of mineral water, cartons of fruit juice, oatcakes, bananas and apples. All wrapped inside three thick blankets. 'See, I didn't know if you had sleeping bags or not. Kayleigh said you wouldn't be stupid enough to not have brought sleeping bags with you. But Hayley said, aye, you would be.'

Kenny, Sim and I looked at each other. 'Kenny lost his bag,' Sim said.

'Aye, that's right. Did you have a sleeping bag in it?'

Kenny looked at his feet and mumbled something.

'What did you say?'

He blushed but wouldn't look up. 'I had Travel Scrabble.'

Hayley folded her arms, looked smug.

We spread one of the blankets out on the grass and sat around in a circle. Kenny, Sim and I were quick to tuck into the food. 'This is brilliant, Kat,' I told her. 'Thank you so much.' Sim had his mouth full but nodded hard.

Kenny was rooting around inside the bag. 'Don't suppose there's any crisps, is there?'

'Do you know how unhealthy crisps are?' Kat asked. 'See, I've always said they should be banned.'

Kenny looked at an oatcake like it was something from another planet. 'Are these nice?'

Sim punched his arm. 'Eat it and say thank you.'

The girls had also brought a couple of torches, and seeing as the sun was long gone now, we switched them on. We told them a bit about Cleethorpes. They didn't have a clue where it was, but that was okay because I reckoned we wouldn't have been able to find this place on a map either – and we were here. Then Kenny told his favourite joke: 'What did the man with a steering wheel down the front of his trousers say? "It's driving me nuts!"' And after that Kat told us why Tramp's Hotel was haunted.

'I don't know all the story, but it's something to do

with a lassie that was murdered. It happened years and years ago. She was from Gretna. See, her dad was like the lord or something, but her uncle murdered her because he loved her too much.'

'Dirty old man,' Hayley explained.

'And she loved someone else anyways,' Kat added.

'So what's it got to do with Tramp's Hotel if she's from Gretna?' Kenny asked.

'See, Tramp's Hotel is where the laddie she really loved lived – when it was still a proper cottage, before it was Tramp's Hotel. He was a farmhand. And no one knew she was dead at first. Her family, they thought she might have just run away with the farm-hand. So they came here looking for her.'

'And they found her dead body in the house,' Kenny said. 'Then everyone blamed the farmhand and—'

'No, the farmhand found her body in a field near Gretna, where he worked.'

'But she haunts the house because she still wants to be near the person she loved all those years ago,' Kenny said.

Kat scowled. 'Who's telling this story? No, see, the laddie found her body in the field, but she didn't have a head. Her uncle had cut it off. *That's* what they found in Tramp's Hotel.'

Kenny looked like he wished he'd never asked. We changed the subject.

But it wasn't long before he and Kat drifted away together with one of the torches. They didn't go towards the trees and Tramp's Hotel, however, but behind the whirligig – close enough that we could still hear the murmur of their voices if not the exact words. And only a few minutes after that Sim and Hayley also wandered off, to a private spot over in the long grass on the other side of the field. Which left Kayleigh and me alone and torchless.

Neither of us really knew what to say.

'So,' I sighed. 'This is awkward.'

She gave a soft laugh.

The night was still warm, the moon and stars brilliant, like you see in movies. Kayleigh was a skinny shadow opposite me, her long blonde hair vivid in the moonlight. I couldn't quite make out her face, but her eyes glinted now and again when she looked straight at me, catching that same light from the moon. Kenny and Sim would be expecting me to make a move. They'd be disappointed in me if I didn't. And even though Kayleigh seemed a little shy, maybe she was also expecting me to. For all I knew, I might have been the only one who wasn't expecting anything.

I realized that with the moon right behind me, it was my bulk that was keeping her in shadow. I shifted a little to one side as I munched on an apple and tried not to appear embarrassed or uncomfortable. I hated myself for it. I'd spent years being self-conscious of my size around girls but I'd thought that these days, thanks to Nina, those kinds of feelings had been consigned to the past. I could talk to girls, I could make them laugh, but it had always been rare for them to want anything other than friendship from me. And I've never been as smooth as Sim. Or as opportunistic as Kenny. Or as desperate as Ross.

Kayleigh and I sat there trying to pretend we didn't know we were the only ones *not* getting off with each other. In my head I was willing Hayley to slap Sim's wandering hands and come stalking back over. Or Kenny to say something too stupid even for Kat.

I got up, stretched. 'I want to sit in the whirligig. I didn't get to have a go earlier. You coming?'

She followed me to the nearest cage-seat. It had the safety bar jammed up and was easy enough to climb in. The seat was wooden and solid, but it felt good sitting so close to her, side by side. And now that I wasn't blocking the moonlight I could see her better too. I reckoned that if I liked skinny girls, I'd like her a lot. We were squeezed up against each other, but it was far from uncomfortable.

I asked, 'Have you known Hayley and Kat long?'

'For ever really.'

'You're all at school together?'

'Kat's in the year below Hayley and me.' I loved her gentle accent – sounded great in the dark.

'How old are you?'

'Sixteen. How old are you?'

'Yeah. Sixteen,' I lied. Then changed the subject. 'Is her name Katherine, then? Or Katrina?'

Kayleigh giggled. 'No, it's Patricia. But don't tell her I told you. She decided she hated it so forced everybody to call her Kat. She won't even answer her dad or the teachers if they don't call her Kat.'

'But you're definitely Kayleigh?'

'Aye. And you're really Blake?'

'Through and through. Like a stick of rock.'

I couldn't tell for definite, but I think she was leaning closer in to me. I stayed still and let myself be leaned against. Her hair smelled of coconut.

After a while she said, 'So tell me about your pal?'

'Who, Kenny or Sim?'

'No, the one you're going to visit tomorrow.'

'Oh, right.' I'd put another apple in my pocket and I took it out, polished it on my T-shirt, gave myself time to decide on an answer. I decided a little bit of honesty wouldn't matter. 'He's called Ross. He's an old friend.'

'There's a place near here called Ross.'

I bit a chunk of the apple. 'Is there really?'

'Well, along the coast a wee bit. And there's a lighthouse.'

'I'll have to ask him if he's heard of it.'

'Is he from Cleethorpes too?'

'Yeah. He's our best friend.'

'Why's he in Kirkcudbright?'

'Where?'

'Kirkcudbright. You said that's where he lived.'

'Oh, yeah. Yeah, that's right.' I swore at myself inside my head. 'He lives there.'

'Has he lived there very long?'

'Yeah. Well, about a year, I think.' All I could do was make it up as I went. 'Bit longer maybe.'

'Do you know which school he goes to? I've got some pals who are at—'

'Not a clue.' I forgot to chew and swallowed a far too big chunk of apple that scraped its way down my gullet.

Even though it was dark, I knew I'd be able to see the look on her face if I turned towards her. So I didn't. But I didn't need to be my usual genius self to realize she was beginning to wonder how much of our story to believe.

'We met at school,' I said, trying to win her over again. 'Well, Kenny and Ross had been friends all through primary – their mums knew each other. They weren't mates with Sim at first. He was a *bad lad*, you see. They were more like geeks – back then, not now. But Sim hung around with this moron called Sean Munro, and a bunch of other head-cases. They used to pick on Kenny all the time, beat him up on a regular basis.'

'So how come they're friends now?'

'Kenny hit him back. Sim was picking on him one day, same as any other day – Kenny was probably crying. But out of nowhere Kenny just suddenly punched Sim in the face. And it was a lucky punch. Lucky because it hardly touched Sim at all, but he jerked his head back so quick he cracked it on the wall behind him. Knocked himself out.'

Kayleigh laughed. 'No . . .'

'Straight up. Smacked his head back, *bang*, and went down. He was off school for a whole week, I think. But when he got back all his hard mates took the mickey all the time, and somehow, not really sure how, he kind of drifted in with Ross and Kenny. I guess he didn't feel welcome with his old mates any more. Weird, yeah?'

'Aye. Very.'

'But trust me, he has a habit of making Kenny's life a misery now and again. It's like the world's slowest revenge, I reckon.'

Kayleigh laughed again. She was so close. I tingled all down the side where we touched. I realized it might be very easy to turn towards her and kiss her. Easy and tempting. But I stayed very still. I said, 'Then I came along in secondary school. My parents split up and I moved to live with my mum, so started at their school.' Sitting next to Kayleigh, our bodies touching, was far enough.

We heard giggles from Kat and Kenny. A cool

breeze had come out of nowhere and it rustled the tops of the trees.

Kayleigh said, 'So is Ross a real person, then?'

I didn't know how to reply for a second. I stumbled for words. She felt me go tense.

She said, 'Hayley doesn't think he's real. But we can't work out why you'd be here if he wasn't. Kat thinks you might be running away.'

I heard myself say something stupid like, 'What d'you mean, is he a real person? That's . . . you know, isn't it?' And cringed.

'If he's real, then he's definitely not your best pal.'

I felt on firmer ground here, with something solid to defend. 'He's the best friend I've ever had. Him, Kenny and Sim all are.'

'But how can he be your best friend if you don't even know where he lives?'

'We do. I told you: Kirkcudbright.'

'No, you told us *Kerk-cud-bright*. And you said he's lived there a year? So how come after a whole year he's never told you how it's pronounced?'

I squirmed. 'Well, it's just outside where he lives. You know, not quite in the centre, exactly.'

She shook her head.

'But he's real,' I said. 'I promise. Ask Kenny and Sim. He's absolutely our best mate. All four of us, we're all best friends.'

She was quiet, thinking it over.

I could hear the wind getting stronger and feel it stealing away the summer warmth. I said, 'I could do with a jumper.' Fetching my rucksack was a good excuse to climb out of the whirligig. The side of me she'd been leaning against was quick to chill without her warmth.

She followed me over to the blanket. 'I don't know if boys even really have best friends.'

I was shocked. And offended. 'Of course we do.'

'Do you buy Kenny, Sim and Ross birthday presents?'

'No.' It came out a bit too scornful.

'Boys never do, do they? Girls buy each other presents for Christmas and birthdays because it's like showing how special their friendship is, showing how much we care about them. I was ill in February, and was only off school for two days, but Hayley and Kat still came to see me and gave me get well cards. Then, last week, I had a piano exam. They gave me a good luck card too. Boys never buy each other cards.'

I thought, Thank God for that. But what I said was, 'It doesn't mean we're not friends.'

'Girls always talk to each other. We tell each other everything.'

'We always talk.'

'When?'

'At school. At home. Whenever we see each other.'

'*We* phone each other every night, and send each other texts all the time too. It's not only when we see each other. Boys don't talk to each other about proper things. I know I can talk to my pals all the time any time I want and tell them *anything*.'

I knew there were one or two things I would never dream of telling Kenny or Sim. But maybe I would have talked to Ross about them . . . 'You're being a bit unfair, aren't you?' I said. 'Okay, maybe we don't talk all the time, but maybe we don't need to. I know Kenny and Sim would be there for me if I needed them. In fact, just today with that bungee jump? The guy who ran it was a total arsehole, but Kenny and Sim were right by my side all the time.' I was surprised by the strength of my feelings. I felt wronged, mis-understood. 'What we do for each other's just not always said out loud.'

She wasn't convinced. 'I've seen boys. Most of you would rather fight then admit you liked each other.'

'Most isn't everyone,' I said.

'We know everything about each other. I know what size clothes Hayley and Kat wear. And we share too. I bet you don't share clothes with Kenny.'

'Shit, no. Have you seen that T-shirt he's wearing?'

'So what do you do? I've got two brothers, see? All my little brother and his pals do is play computer games all day. And Calum, the older one, all he does is either ride his motorbikes, clean his motorbikes, or mend his motorbikes. He likes them better than real people. Unless he's playing football.'

'Well, yeah. We play football and computer games. But that's still being with your mates, isn't it?'

'No it's not. It's just trying to win – competing with each other.'

'I'd do anything for Kenny and Sim.' I did feel a bit weird, a bit embarrassed, saying it out loud like that. Because we were mates – nothing more. But no way did I want Kayleigh to think anything *less*. 'It's just the same as you with Hayley and Kat. And me, Kenny and Sim would do anything for Ross. I mean, look what we're doing for him now, coming all this way to

Scotland. You don't do what we're doing for someone unless he's your best friend. It's all because we miss him, isn't it? I really, really, genuinely, one hundred per cent miss him. D'you know how much I wish he was here right now, because—?'

And I suddenly had to swallow my next words, but the big lump in my throat made it difficult. I missed him. I had to gulp back some surprised tears. He should be here. Now.

'I miss him.'

'But does he know?' Kayleigh asked. 'I bet you've never told him any of this stuff to his face.'

I went cold. I had goose pimples. My voice faltered. 'I . . . No,' I admitted. 'No, I never told him.'

I was scared I was going to erupt into tears in front of this girl who I'd only just met. And I knew I'd never live it down if Kenny and Sim found out. I was thankful my face was dark to her and dropped my head.

The wind was rustling the treetops. Clouds blew across the dark sky. It felt like a sharp storm was brewing. I dug in my rucksack for my jumper. I had to unwrap it from around Ross and was tempted to tell Kayleigh everything. Just to prove her wrong. When I pulled my jumper over my head I was able to give my face a surreptitious scrub to dry any leaks. It was only when my head popped out of the hole that I saw a torch bobbing over the field towards us. Someone had climbed the gate at the road.

'Who's that?'

Kayleigh looked behind her, just as whoever it was shouted, 'Hayley!' He was Scottish, and big by the looks of his chunky silhouette.

Over in the grass off to our right I heard swearing and a hurried rumpus. Hayley's torch flicked on. I saw Sim's annoyed and confused face squinting into light, then the beam whipped across the field towards the newcomer.

Who shouted again, 'Hayley!'

Kayleigh looked worried. She snatched up the blanket, started bundling it back into the shopping bag.

'Is it her dad?' I asked.

But Kayleigh shook her head. 'No. Calum's my older brother.'

'So why's he want Hayley?'

'Because she's his girlfriend.'

Twenty-four

It could have gone really badly, but the rain came. It lashed it down. Nobody wanted to fight in that kind of downpour. But neither Calum nor Sim wanted to be the first to back down.

They squared up to each other in the dark, and I hoped Kayleigh took note of the way Kenny and I were there at Sim's side. Calum was about twenty, I reckoned, wearing a thin shirt smeared with what I guessed was motorbike grease. A big bloke, with a square jaw and rock-star stubble. Better looking than Sim, so maybe more worried about getting his face damaged. He didn't look like he was going to be the first to throw a punch anyway. Hayley grabbed his arm and tried to pull him away. The rain flattened his hair and dripped off the end of his nose.

I said to Sim, 'Leave it. It's not worth it.' I could tell Sim fancied his chances.

He ran a hand over his hair, spattering rain like

when you flicked the bristles of a toothbrush. 'He's got to walk away first.'

Hayley gave another tug on her boyfriend's arm. 'Nothing happened, Calum. God, I hate it when you get like this. Come away. Come on.'

'I came looking for you,' he said, his accent sounding thicker than any of the girls'. 'Your dad said you were with Kat so I knew you'd be here.'

'See, she *is* with me,' Kat said. 'And we *are* here. So why're you getting your knickers all in a twist?'

Calum stuck a finger close to Sim's face. 'Because he's here too.'

Sim looked like he wanted to snap that finger off at the knuckle.

'Come on, Sim. Leave it,' Kenny said. And then as if we hadn't already noticed: 'It's raining.'

'I'm getting soaked,' Hayley said. She let go of her boyfriend's hand and started walking away across the field, back towards the road. Kayleigh turned to follow, gesturing at Kat to do the same.

Calum swept a hand over his face to clear it of rain. Sim took a step towards him. I shivered in my sagging, wet and chilly jumper.

Kat gave Kenny a quick hug. 'So wait for me, aye?

I'll come back tomorrow morning.' Then she went after her two friends.

Calum watched them go. Then said to Sim, 'You're a lucky boy.'

Sim narrowed his eyes. 'You're a chicken-shit.'

And maybe Calum would have swung for him then, but Hayley shouted, 'Come away, Calum.' She climbed the gate to the road.

'Very lucky,' he growled at Sim and at last followed the three girls.

He tried to swagger as he walked away, tried to look cool. He just looked wetter. The girls were waiting for him by the gate. He stopped halfway across the field and started to light a cigarette but struggled to do it and hold his torch at the same time. Hayley shouted at him to hurry up, then strode off down the road out of sight, her friends at her heels. Kat waved to Kenny once. Calum threw his soggy cigarette away, ambled to the gate and disappeared over onto the road. We couldn't tell in the dark if he looked back at us or not.

'I could've had him,' Sim said. 'Who did he think he was?'

'You were messing with his girlfriend. He's kind of got the right to want to slap you.'

'What if he comes back?' Kenny asked. 'With some friends?'

Sim didn't answer. He snatched up his bag and the torch the girls had left, then stalked away towards the trees and the shelter of Tramp's Hotel.

We pushed through the undergrowth to the derelict cottage. I wanted to shine the torch around inside before we went in – just in case a tramp was already in there dossing down for the night. But Sim barged right on into the shadowy first room. He threw his bag on the ground and rummaged inside for a dry T-shirt. I went in after him, but made sure I had a good look around. Nothing seemed to have changed since we'd peeked in earlier – same leaves and mud on the floor, same graffiti-stained walls – but now the two doorways leading off deeper into the cottage were much, much gloomier.

I put on a clean T-shirt, gave Kenny my last one. He was kind enough not to say it was far too big for him, so I didn't comment on how pleased I was to see the back of his orange monstrosity. We hung our wet clothes over our rucksacks in the hope they'd dry a bit. Kenny didn't look happy being here. He jumped at his own shadow as Sim swung the torch around.

Then refused to turn his back on those two darkened doorways and sat facing them. Sim and I slumped down either side of him, leaning against a wall that crumbled like biscuits when you ran your fingers over it. Neither of us said as much, but I reckoned we didn't like the idea of having our backs to the shadowy rooms beyond either. Sim put the torch at our feet, aimed to one side and casting the arc of its beam just wide enough for us to keep an eye on those doors in case someone came sneaking through.

Outside the storm went from blustery to nasty. Lightning unzipped the night sky in Zorro slashes and let the rain streak down. We listened to it shake the trees and rattle the old roof, and were thankful the wind wasn't gusting the rain through the open door. It would have been pitch black without the torch.

At last Kenny said, 'I need a pee.'

'Do it outside,' Sim growled.

'But I'll get soaked again if I go out there.'

'And you'll get punched if you do it in here.'

'But what if there's someone out there? Hayley's boyfriend?'

'He won't come back in this weather.'

'What about a tramp then?'

'Ask him if he's got an umbrella.'

Kenny muttered but stayed where he was, deciding to hold it in.

'I could've had him,' Sim said. 'I could, couldn't I?'

'It wouldn't have been worth it,' I said.

'Who did he think he was? It's not like Hayley even let me do anything.'

I shrugged. 'Who'd have thought Kenny would be the one to get lucky?'

Kenny grinned. 'She's coming to see me tomorrow morning before we go. That'll be okay, right? I really do want to see her again.'

'As long as she gets here early enough. We can't hang around.'

'I should've just asked him who the hell he thought he was,' Sim said. 'He didn't scare me.'

'It happened,' I told him. 'Forget about it. Just one of those days. I get a poster of my overweight arse leaping off a bungee spread across the whole of Blackpool, you nearly get into a fight in a field in Dumfries, while Kenny falls in love with some mad Scottish bird. And all because we stole our best mate's ashes. Like I said: just one of those days.'

Sim grunted half a laugh, but I could tell he was still boiling inside.

The wind in the trees was so loud, like an industrial roar. I began to wonder if we were about to see the end of Tramp's Hotel for ever – if, after all these years, the storm was going to peel the roof and walls apart.

'I'm really going to have to go,' Kenny said.

'So *go*,' Sim and I said together.

Kenny shuffled, fidgeted. 'Can I have the torch?'

Again simultaneously: 'No.'

Kenny swore under his breath but still stayed sitting.

'I hate backing down,' Sim said. 'How many times have you ever seen me back down?'

'You didn't back down,' I told him. 'Not really. You were with his girlfriend. If it was the other way round, I wouldn't have even tried to stop you.'

He mulled this over. 'Big Scottish shitbone bastard.' But I could tell he was at last simmering down a bit. 'He's lucky I didn't punch his sporran in.'

I nodded. 'He's lucky you didn't knock his haggis off.'

Sim laughed – and meant it. 'Yeah. Maybe next time I will.'

Kenny said, 'Will one of you come with me then?'

'What's up, Kenny?' Sim asked. 'Scared of the headless ghost?'

Kenny didn't answer, looked down at his feet.

'Christ-on-a-bike, Kenny . . .'

'You come with me then.'

Sim said nothing.

'Why don't you just go through there?' I pointed to the dark doorways. 'Just do it far enough away from us so we don't have to hear the splash and see the trickle. There's no need to go outside then, is there? Doesn't smell like anybody else ever does anyway.'

'I'll still need the torch.'

Sim and I looked at each other, rolled our eyes, sighed and muttered, as if it was all for Kenny's sake that we were both going with him. But deep down neither of wanted to be left in the dark by ourselves.

I had the torch so I had to go first. I chose the door on the left. Then changed my mind and went for the one on the right. While we'd been sitting there I'd had the weird feeling we were being watched – like chilly, prickling needles at the back of my neck. I'd not said anything to the others, had done my best to ignore it. I reckoned it was either Hayley's boyfriend come back to have a go again, or some tramp annoyed that we were invading his doss house. But I could have sworn I'd felt eyes. As I walked across the room with Kenny and Sim behind me I thought I could sense someone waiting, listening, in the room through the door on the left. That's why I went through the one on the right.

But before I stepped in I swept the beam around the room slowly enough that we could all see nobody and nothing was lurking in between the shadows. It was about the same size as the first room, just as littered with detritus, both natural and unnatural. There was also a half-ruined stone fireplace set into one wall, full of black ash, with a stained and scabby mattress on the floor in front of it. A doorway leading to the room I didn't want to go in was to our left. I stepped away from it, moved closer to the fireplace and the mattress.

'Someone really does live here,' Kenny said.

'Well, sleeps here anyway,' I said. The rain rattled down hard on the old roof. 'Just hurry up and have your piss.' I wasn't able to keep the edginess out of my voice.

'I can't do it where someone sleeps.'

'You wanna go looking for the gents, you do it on your own,' Sim told him.

'What about through there?' Kenny asked, turning to the door and the room I was avoiding.

'Kenny, just—'

Sim grabbed my arm. 'Shh!'

'What?'

'Did you hear that?'

'Through there.' Kenny pointed. 'I heard—'

'Shut up!' Sim hissed.

And we all heard scuffles in the other room.

Cold fear, genuine fear. I was stuck to the spot. Frozen. Nobody breathed. I managed to lift the torch to aim at the empty doorway but all it did was throw shadows into the room beyond. Nothing could be seen through there.

Kenny had bobbed his head, dropped his shoulders, clenched his fists; he was ready to run. Sim still had hold of my arm, gripping it tight enough to hurt. Then the noise again. And he squeezed so hard I gasped out loud.

'Oh shit,' Kenny whispered. 'Oh shit oh shit oh shit.'

The storm kicked and screamed. The whole

battered cottage groaned. And we stood very, very
still. Moving didn't seem sensible. We listened almost
painfully hard, but couldn't hear anything except the
storm now.

'It's the wind,' I said. I hoped. 'It's blowing in
through a window or something.'

'It's not. I'm *telling* you: it's not. Oh God. Oh
bloody hell.'

But apart from the rain and the wind outside it was
silent. Even so we stayed where we were, didn't move,
held our breath, strained to listen.

'It could've been an animal,' I said. 'A fox, or a
badger, or . . . something.'

Neither Sim nor Kenny replied.

I took a deep breath, pulled myself together. 'Have
your piss, Kenny. Then let's go.'

'But . . .'

I jiggled the torch around, pushed it as far through
that door as I could. 'Look – there's nothing—'

But all three of us saw the girl's head on the floor.

Sim swore in a rush of breath. Kenny wailed. I
almost dropped the torch. We saw her face, her eyes,
her hair. We were all springing back, turning to
run.

Then: 'It's a football,' Sim said. 'Look, can you see? Jesus. Wow. See it? It's a football.' His laugh was giddy.

I aimed the torch's beam at the half-deflated football lying on the floor of the leaf-littered room. I could see the hexagonal stitching on the worn leather, underneath the wig, behind the painted face and eyes. I sagged as I let go of all that breath I'd been holding.

'Jesus,' Sim said. 'I almost shit a hippo.'

I don't think any of us wanted to go into that room, but we had to see the football up close. Again I swung the torch around before we stepped through. I guessed this was maybe once a kitchen, with its alcove for a big old-fashioned stove and what looked like a once massive stone sink, now just broken rubble. There was an open window, and the sealed-up and vandalized metal back door we'd seen earlier from outside. On the far side of the room was half a staircase. As soon as I saw it I thought I heard footsteps on the floor above us, but told myself it was like thinking about head-lice and then having to scratch. But I thought of Ross's mum too, standing on her stairs, looking like a living ghost.

As we stepped into the room I kept the torch

sweeping into all the dark corners. Sim picked up the football. From close up it looked about as life-like as, well, a football.

'Bet it was Kat, thinking she's funny,' he said.

'Don't blame her,' Kenny said. 'You don't know her.'

'Kat!' Sim shouted. 'Come out, we know it's you.'

But the wig was full of dirt and leaves, the paint was flaked and faded. 'If it was her, she made it a while ago,' I said. 'Kind of sick when you think about it.'

'So it couldn't have been her. I'm telling you: she's not sick.'

Sim shrugged. 'So maybe just something done to scare little kids.'

'And big ones.'

Sim peered at the football again, turning it over in his hands. He took a step towards the open window and drop-kicked it through. 'Come on, Kenny, have a slash already,' he said.

Kenny went over to the alcove where the stove would have been. And once he started Sim and I needed to go too. So the three of us stood there and went, side by side. 'Don't cross beams,' Sim said. Then we were quick to get back to our place in the first

room, sitting close to the front door with our
rucksacks.

'We still heard a noise, though, didn't we?' Kenny
said. He picked up the torch and pointed it all around
the room yet again, checking, making sure we were
one hundred per cent alone.

Sim seemed to be deep in thought. I said, 'Just a fox
probably. We scared it off.'

'Kat's story could be true. You were scared too,
Blake. Don't tell me you weren't.'

I took the torch off him, put it back at our feet. 'I
told you before, it's not ghosts you want to be worried
about in a place like this. If tramps really do use this
place to doss down in, it's them we should be worried
about. Solid, live people can be a bit more of a
problem than see-through ones. Meeting bearded
madmen with big knives in the middle of nowhere is
what scares me.'

'How do you know there's no ghost?'

'Because there's no such thing. Because they're not
real. Because they don't exist.' I shrugged. 'Want me
to go on?'

'But you don't know that, do you? You can't prove
it.'

I sighed. Looked to Sim to back me up.

But: 'I believe in ghosts,' he said.

'You what? Bloody hell, I'm surrounded by mentalists!' I made a joke of it, but my surprise was genuine.

'I don't believe in headless girl ghosts who come back looking for ex-boyfriends or whatever. But something's got to happen to us when we die, hasn't it? We've got to go somewhere, right?'

'Bollocks.'

'No, seriously.'

'Yes, seriously. *Bollocks.*'

'Don't you believe in God?' Kenny asked.

'What's that got to do with anything?' I wanted to know.

'Well, heaven and hell and stuff. Where we go when we die. Don't you believe in life after death or anything like that?'

'Nope.'

'So you reckon you're what? An atheist?'

'Yep.'

'I don't believe you.'

'I don't care.'

'So what happens when we die then?'

I sighed. 'If we're lucky, our best friends steal our ashes and—'

Kenny didn't find it funny. 'You can't even talk about it properly. And that's because you know we're right. Ross believed in God.'

'No he didn't. He just had to put up with it because his mum and dad went to church. But he hadn't gone with them in ages.'

'He wrote special prayers. I saw them.'

'That was years ago.' I'd seen them too. They were the worst, most morose poetry I'd ever read. He sort of had believed, then hadn't. Then had, then hadn't. I knew these days he thought the same as me because we'd talked about it. 'He said that nobody believed in Odin or Jupiter or Zeus any more these days, so reckoned it wouldn't be long before people stopped believing in modern gods too.'

'I think what you're saying's shit,' Sim said. In the light of the torch I could see he was angry, offended. 'What you're saying is that Ross's life was a waste. But if that's what you think, then why're you here?'

'I'm not saying anything like that.'

'Yes you are. Course you are. If you don't believe in

God or heaven or life after death then why are we even bothering to do this?'

'I'm not doing this because I think Ross can see me from beyond the grave, or from some other world or something. I don't know about you, but I'm doing this because he was my best friend.' I dragged my rucksack across towards me, opened it and took out the urn. 'This is Ross now. I wish – really, really wish – he was still here. But this is all he is now. He hasn't got a clue what we're doing. You know, because he's *dead*.'

Sim was getting aggressive with me. 'So come on, what's the point then? If that's all he is now, that ash in that jar, then what was the point in him living in the first place? If there's nothing after we die, why even bother to be alive?'

I struggled to find the right words. 'Because of this,' I said at last, spreading my arms to encompass Tramp's Hotel, the dark room, and us in it. 'Yeah, okay, he's just that ash in that jar now, but if he hadn't been alive we wouldn't be here. Think of all the stuff we wouldn't have done if he hadn't been alive. We might not have even met. He knew Kenny first, then you, then met me. He got us together, didn't he? He was like a magnet pulling us together. And if he does have some kind of afterlife it's in us, isn't it? He'll always matter because we'll always remember him. We'll always be telling stories about him. That's proper immortality, that is. That's real living for ever.'

Sim still wasn't happy, but I could see by his face he was backing down. Christ-on-a-bike, I thought. Who would've guessed he'd bashed the odd Bible or two?

Outside the storm seemed to be easing; the wind in the trees was nowhere near as loud as it had been. I checked my watch. 2:20. I couldn't believe it was over sixteen hours since I'd been sitting in the Fells' kitchen. I wondered if they were sleeping tonight. Or if we were keeping them awake, angry and anxious and wondering.

Mrs Fell at the top of the stairs yesterday. The memory of how she'd looked kept haunting me. I reckoned that was the closest I'd ever come to seeing a ghost.

Part Three
Ostriches

Twenty-five

It was a fitful night. We drifted in and out of sleep. A couple of times I jumped awake without realizing I'd fallen asleep, jolting back upright against the wall. Twice I woke to find Kenny sprawled across my legs, twitching and snoring, talking to himself as he slept. Both times he woke by leaping to his feet and shouting, 'What? What was that?' It wasn't until it started to get lighter again around half-four that we felt safe enough to lie down, sharing our rucksacks as pillows, and not worry about closing our eyes. Of course, I didn't believe you only ever got murdered in the dark, but I was shattered.

The sound of scuffling woke me. It shocked me awake. I'd been dreaming of being chased by the police and I'd woken with a shot of adrenalin, my heart thumping.

I didn't open my eyes at first. Just like a little kid: if I can't see it, it can't see me. But it was the same sound we'd heard last night, I was sure of it.

Kenny and Sim were still fast asleep. I was in the middle of the two of them; Sim was the one closest to the kitchen door. He lay foetal with his back to it. I opened one eye and could see over his shoulder. But I couldn't see what was making the noise.

'Hey,' I whispered. 'Sim. *Sim.*' I nudged him.

He muttered and rolled over, carried on sleeping.

The scuffling came again. I couldn't work out what it might be. Someone searching for something?

I looked at my watch. Ten past eight. I reckoned I could be brave in daylight and so eased myself slowly, very slowly, up onto my elbows and got my knees underneath me. Taking tiny sips of breath, straining to listen, I got myself to my feet. I stepped over Sim and crept towards the kitchen door. The scuffling didn't stop. What were they looking for? What was I going to say when they saw me?

I stayed close to the wall and poked my head through the empty doorway.

The dog spotted me and ran. It leaped onto the second to bottom step of the broken stairs then bounded through the window. All I saw was a four-legged flash of mangy fur. I hurried over to the window. It was out there in the undergrowth watching me, backing away from me.

'It's okay,' I said to it. 'Hey, boy. It's okay.'

It was a skinny, scruffy mutt – no doubt a full-on flea circus. But I grinned at it, called to it. Of course it didn't come anywhere near me. It held its head down at a slight angle and watched me from a safe distance. I was sure it was what we'd heard last night. Who knew, but maybe that girl's-head football was its toy.

I sneaked back through to the first room where Kenny and Sim still slept, not wanting to wake them. I rummaged in my rucksack and found an apple from last night in the side pocket. Heading outside into the fresh morning air I made my way round the back of the cottage. The dog was still there. Again I called to it. When I tossed the apple towards it, it turned to run – probably only used to being pelted by rocks. But the apple hit the leaves a good metre or so away from it.

It was wary but curious, and hungry. Without taking its eyes off me it bent low and kind of crawled up to the apple, sniffed. I'm sure it would have preferred Pedigree Chum, but it devoured the apple in two chomps.

'That's my breakfast, you know,' I told it.

It didn't care.

It snuffled around in the undergrowth where the apple had been, searching for seconds. It looked up at me. But all I could do was hold out empty hands and shake my head. It didn't bark a thank you, didn't come any closer to lick my hand. It trotted over to the wire fence and got down low on its belly as it squirted its skinny body through a gap at the bottom. I watched it wander off around the pond towards the dilapidated barn. It cocked its leg against the corner before disappearing out of view round the back.

I could have told Kenny and Sim about the dog, but I never did. Maybe it was a bit cruel not to tell them what the night's noises probably were. Maybe. But knowing the two of them they'd be happier making up their own minds anyway. I left them fast asleep as I took the map out of my rucksack.

I walked into the field from under the trees and the early sun was already warm. It was going to be another hot, muggy day. I headed for the whirligig and climbed into the same seat Kayleigh and I had sat in the night before. I opened the map and studied the route we'd already travelled. And the best way to go today.

Twenty-six

Getting on for an hour later Sim appeared. I'd spent the time poring over the map looking at all the places I hadn't been, promising myself all the places I'd go. Sim walked across the field towards me, stretching and massaging his shoulder, looking as stiff and wooden as Pinocchio. I guessed a night on the hard floor had pushed his bones out of place.

'What you need on a floor like that is padding,' I told him, patting myself. I was relieved to see him smile. The argument last night hadn't been settled, but it looked like we were going to get along this morning all the same. 'Kenny still asleep?'

'Dead to the world.'

'It's almost nine. If his girlfriend doesn't turn up soon he's gonna be upset when we have to leave without him saying his sweet goodbyes.'

Sim leaned on the frame of the seat I was in, pulled the map round so he could see it better. 'So what's the plan?'

'Wander back the way we came and hope we find the stop where we got off the bus last night. And hope another's going to stop there today. Then just hope we have enough money for three tickets.'

'D'you think we do?'

'Your guess is as good as mine. What we haven't got is money to get home again.'

Sim sighed. 'I've been trying not to think about that. And how far to Ross if we want to walk?'

'Depends on where we are exactly.' I pointed at the map. 'I think we're here somewhere.'

'So what's that? Twenty-five, thirty miles?'

'Give or take.'

'A long way then.'

'Long enough,' I admitted. 'But you've walked that far before, haven't you?'

'Yeah, when me and my dad used to still talk he'd take me hiking along the Pennine Way. We could walk twenty-five miles easy.'

'So it's definitely doable in a day, we just have to set off as soon as we can.' I folded the map. 'Maybe we should wake Kenny – at least get him up and ready. He must have got Kat's number last night. He can call her.'

Sim was looking towards the gate and the road. 'Is that her?'

Someone was climbing over the gate. I had to shield my eyes against the bright morning sun to see who it was and noticed the glowing long blonde hair. 'It's Kayleigh.'

She ran towards us, stumbling in the long grass in her haste. Sim and I looked at each other – something was wrong. We hurried to meet her halfway.

She was out of breath and anxious, her face damp with sweat, shiny beneath her eyes. It was obvious she'd dressed in a rush too. 'You're on the telly,' she said.

That didn't make sense. 'What?'

'Aye, aye, on the news. You've stolen your pal's ashes, they said. Ross – he's dead, isn't he? He killed himself, didn't he? It's on this morning's news.'

Sim and I just stared at her, struck dumb.

'Everybody's really worried. They said you might kill yourselves too. They said it's a suicide pact you've got.'

It was getting more bizarre by the second. I had to physically take a step back, then ask, '*What?*'

She was pale, maybe frightened. She tried to catch

her breath. 'They said your pal committed suicide, and that you've taken his ashes and might be wanting to commit suicide too.'

It was ludicrous. I couldn't believe what I was hearing. What did the people on television care about anything? I was amazed. Sim was angry.

'Ross didn't kill himself,' he said, letting that anger show. 'Whoever's saying that needs their head sorting.'

Kayleigh was almost as flustered as us. 'But it's what they're saying on the telly. They're showing pictures of all three of you, and asking for anybody who's seen you to call in. My brother says he's going to phone them.'

'Who?'

'Calum.'

'But who's he gonna phone?'

'The *police*. He's going to say you're here.'

And now I was moving. I was running. All I could think was we had to wake Kenny and get going. Nothing else mattered. They were going to try and stop us from getting to Ross. I didn't want them to stop us. I refused to let them.

Sim was on my heels, Kayleigh too. We crashed through the trees and into Tramp's Hotel. Kenny was still asleep with his head on my rucksack. I yanked it out from under him, jolting him awake.

Bleary-eyed and bewildered, he rubbed hard at his doughy face and looked around trying to get his bearings.

'Come on,' I told him. 'We've got to move. We've got to get going.'

He yawned. 'I'm knackered.'

'Come on, Kenny, okay? No messing around. Remember that deep shit we're in? It just got deeper. The police are after us.'

That woke him up.

'The police?'

Sim nodded. He was chewing on his bottom lip, clenching and unclenching his fists.

I thought Kenny was going to burst into tears. 'I've got to get home,' he said. Jumping up but not quite knowing how or where to run.

'No. We've got to get to Ross,' I said.

Kenny looked at me like I was an alien. 'No way, Blake. We've got to—'

'You can't back out now, I'm not gonna let you. Sim's not gonna let you either.' We both turned to Sim, and I realized I didn't have a clue how he felt about how things were turning out, whether he wanted to keep going to Ross or thought it was time to go home to face our parents. 'Sim? You agree with me, right? You think we should keep going, don't you?'

He looked pained. 'I don't know.'

And the three of us stood there, not saying a word, not knowing what was coming next.

Would another day and night deepen the trouble even more? Undoubtedly. But that was only if it *could* get any deeper. And so what? Did I care about the trouble, about what my parents were going to say? I'd been grounded before, I could handle that. I'd had my allowance stopped for two months once, and I'd come through that okay. My parents and all their yelling and punishments didn't scare me these days like they used to when I was eleven.

But the police getting involved . . . And DS Cropper . . . Could he arrest us? Would Ross's mum and dad press charges for theft or something?

But I also believed that what we were doing now was the most important thing any of us had ever done in our lives.

I'd forgotten Kayleigh was there. 'You're not really going to kill yourselves, are you?'

'Do we look stupid?' Sim snapped.

'You don't have to be stupid to do it,' Kayleigh said. 'This boy at our school—'

'No, we're not,' I told her. 'Of course not.'

'And Ross didn't kill himself either,' Sim said. 'Okay?'

Kayleigh backed away from him. 'It's just they said on the news that—'

Kenny looked like he might faint. 'We're on the *news*?'

'Listen, yes, I admit we've got Ross's ashes,' I said to Kayleigh. 'But because we want to give him a proper funeral. All this suicide rubbish just proves that his mum and dad and everybody else didn't know him even half as well as we did. You've got to stop your brother from phoning the police.'

'It's gone too far, Blake,' Kenny said. '*We've* gone too far. I'm telling you—'

'Tell me something I care about!' I shouted in his face. Then back to Kayleigh. 'Try to talk to your brother. Please?'

'Would he do it for you?' she asked. 'Your pal – Ross. Would he do the same for one of you?'

That was the easiest question in the world. 'Yes.'

And the thought galvanized me. 'Come on, Sim. You know it's true.'

Sim seemed to brace himself, then nodded. 'I guess so, yeah.'

'Kenny?'

Kenny squirmed.

'He'd do *exactly* the same, Kenny. You know he would. No matter what happened.'

Kenny grimaced, but nodded too. 'Okay, okay, I know. But I don't ever want to go home after this,' he said. 'I'll be the dead one then. My mum, she'll . . . She really will.'

I felt better. We were moving again. We bundled up our stuff, pushed it into our rucksacks. Our T-shirts weren't quite dry but we shoved them in all the same, burying the urn underneath. I patted Kenny's back, told him it would be okay.

'Is Kat coming?' he asked Kayleigh.

I didn't let her answer. 'We can't wait, Kenny.'

'You said I could see her before we went.'

'I've never known her to get out of bed before ten if she's not forced to,' Kayleigh told him.

Kenny sagged. But Kayleigh scribbled Kat's phone number on the back of his hand. It cheered him up a little. 'Tell her how much I like her, will you?'

Kayleigh nodded.

'You were right, you know,' I said to her as I hefted my rucksack up onto my shoulders. 'Maybe if we'd just bothered to tell Ross how we felt we probably wouldn't be having to do all this.'

'Are you still trying to get to Kirkcudbright?' she asked. 'It's a really long way to walk.'

'We'll get a bus if we can. Do you know if there's any?'

'We can't get a bus,' Sim said. 'Someone's bound to recognize us if we've been on the telly.'

'But we've got to get there as quick as we can.' It felt like a race now. Them versus us. And they'd stop us the first chance they had. 'We've got to get there before they realize that's where we're going.'

Kayleigh seemed to be thinking. 'Can any of you ride a motorbike?'

Twenty-seven

The morning was already heating up. Blue, blue sky without a hint of cloud. Kayleigh lived in a renovated farmhouse just ten minutes' walk from the field with Tramp's Hotel. We ran there in five. A tree-lined and winding gravel driveway led from the road to the squat, whitewashed house, and to the adjoining stables with heavy padlocked doors. Kayleigh told us to stay hidden behind the trees while she snatched the keys.

Sim and I crouched down but Kenny couldn't stop fidgeting. 'Kat must live somewhere round here too,' he said. 'There's a village or something, isn't there?'

'Keep your head down,' Sim hissed, tugging at the back of Kenny's collar.

We waited. There was no way we could tell what was going on inside the house. Was her brother on the phone right that second? Had she been caught trying to sneak out with the keys? Were the police on their way?

Sim asked, 'You reckon we can trust her?'

'She won't grass us up,' I said, hoping it was true.

'But what about all this stuff with the news and the police? You don't reckon it's just her and her mates making it up? It's all a bit far-fetched, isn't it? It could just be their idea of a big joke.'

I knew what he meant. How come this had all got so out of hand? When had the world gone so mad? But then DS Cropper's message was on my phone, wasn't it? I'd heard it with my own ears.

'She seemed too worried and worked up for it just to be a joke,' I said. 'And she knew nothing about Ross being dead anyway. The only way she could've known was if it really was on the telly about us.'

'My mum's gonna kill me for being on the telly,' Kenny said.

'Maybe, maybe not,' I told him. 'If everybody thinks we've got some kind of crazy suicide pact, maybe they're just gonna be so pleased to see us and find out it's not true that they'll be completely over-joyed we're still alive and instantly forgive us.'

Kenny looked hopeful. 'Really?'

I shook my head. 'No.'

Sim stood up. 'She's there, come on.'

Kayleigh emerged from her house and scurried over to the stable doors. The three of us kept our heads down and stayed behind the trees as we hurried up the driveway. She looked almost as nervous as us. Her long hair kept falling in her eyes as she fumbled with the keys in the padlock and she swore at it, irritated and anxious.

'Has he called them?' I wanted to know. 'Has your brother—?'

'I don't know. I didn't see him to ask.' She pushed the heavy wooden door open just enough for us to squeeze through. Shut it behind us the second we were inside.

Even though there was still some straw on the floor, these stables no longer housed horses, but motorbikes. I counted nine. There were a couple of modern, bullet-like racers, a low-slung Hell's Angel chopper, an old-fashioned black chunky thing as big as a horse, one that looked like a caravan on wheels with its massive panniers and saddlebags, a couple of dirt-bikes and a pair of twist-and-go scooters. The still air smelled of grease and petrol. In any other circumstance I would have wanted to sit on them all.

'My dad and brother collect them,' Kayleigh said.

Kenny, Sim and I looked at each other. Could we really steal a couple of motorbikes?

Sim shrugged. 'We'll bring them back.'

'If you've never ridden before you should take these scooters,' Kayleigh said, pointing at the twist-and-goes – the kind of things that sounded like angry hair-dryers. We often saw sixteen-year-olds buzzing up and down the sea front on them back home. 'The green one's mine anyway.'

Kenny pulled a face, but I told him if he'd rather get done for nicking something twice the size and probably five times as expensive, he was welcome to do it. 'But there's only two,' he said.

'You can go on the back with me,' Sim told him.

'And there's only two helmets,' Kayleigh said, taking a white and a red crash-hat down from hooks on the wall. 'Calum must have taken his in the house with him.'

Sim gestured that me and Kenny should take them. 'Admit it,' he said. 'You two've always been softer in the head than me.'

'What's gonna happen to you when your dad finds out?' I asked Kayleigh.

She shook her head – didn't want to think about it.

'We really don't want to get you into trouble.'

'Aye, well, it's not me that's stealing them,' she said. 'I'll break the lock or something. But don't tell on me because I'll just say I never met you.'

I said, 'Thank you.' But wasn't sure I meant it any more.

She was anxious when she asked: 'You're not lying to me, are you? I'm not helping you to kill yourselves, am I?'

'You're helping us get deeper and deeper into trouble,' I said. 'But most of all, just helping us do something proper for our best friend.' I shrugged, smiled. 'Nothing else – promise.'

She nodded but didn't return my smile.

'So why *are* you helping us?' Kenny asked.

It was her turn to shrug. 'It's horrible that everybody thinks your pal killed himself. I'd hate it if people thought that about me. And I'd want Hayley and Kat to stick up for me too, like you're doing for him.'

I rocked the green scooter down off its stand. It was lighter than I'd anticipated – so maybe easy enough to ride. Sim did the same with the blue one.

'That's mine, remember,' Kayleigh said to me.

'So you could say it's only half stolen?' I asked.

'Aye, right.' But she said it in that Scottish way, the way that's far from an agreement. 'Don't crash it is what I'm saying.'

'I'll try my best.'

'And don't start them up until you're on the road and away from the house,' she warned.

'Which way do we go?' I asked. I started fumbling for the map.

'Follow signs for Kirkbean first, then Dalbeattie. It's the longer way, but maybe there won't be so many other people driving along there. And then Kirkcudbright's easy from Dalbeattie.'

If this had been a movie I know I would have kissed her. But we just left her there as we ran off down the driveway, wheeling the scooters beside us, checking the house over our shoulders again and again. She watched us go before running back inside.

Back out on the road we pushed them for another hundred metres or so before we dared climb on. Because we'd never ridden before, we began by copying TV and looked for the kick-start. Of course, these little things didn't have anything like that. Kenny was the one who said, 'Why don't you push the button?'

On a quiet, sunny Sunday morning in the middle of nowhere the buzzing engines sounded so loud. With more wobble than felt necessary or comfortable, we managed to get moving.

'You don't have to hold me quite so tight, Kenny,' Sim said. 'Not unless you fancy me.'

We started slow, but it got easier. We rode side by side. We picked up a little bit of speed with confidence. The fences and hedgerows on either side of the country road began to move by at a decent clip. I was impressed with myself when the speedo hit thirty-five, then (almost) forty. It didn't take long before I wished the top speed was even higher.

There were two or three cars that passed us. I wasn't sure how many of them noticed Sim wasn't wearing a helmet. I hoped his shaved head might fool anybody shooting by who wasn't paying too much attention. He rode closer into the grass verge, me on the outside of him, making him more difficult to see.

We were extra careful at junctions, slowing right down to make sure we knew which way to go. Not every signpost had Dalbeattie or Kirkcudbright on it and a couple of times we had to guess which road felt like the right one. We had to double back once when the road led us straight into a farmyard. I kept stopping to check the map. Our thirty-five miles per hour began to feel slower and slower.

We'd been on the road for almost half an hour, but it still seemed like we'd only travelled a handful of miles and I was a long way from relaxed. I had at least managed to push the ever-deepening trouble we were in to the back of my mind. Strange thing was, my paranoia felt nowhere near as bad as it had yesterday. Now I knew for definite that they were after us, so it was simply a race. We just had to get to Ross before they found out that's where we were going and managed to cut us off. I leaned forward and urged the little scooter on.

'Can I have a go, Sim?' Kenny shouted. 'Sim? Come on. Let me drive.'

Sim pretended not to hear.

'Sim? Can I—?'

We didn't see the police car until it was too late.

Twenty-eight

The road ahead was a slight curve and the trees blocked our view of anything coming towards us. And what was coming was a cop car. It was going fast; flashed right by us. But I saw two uniformed policemen in the front. I saw their faces turn towards us.

'They've seen us!' Kenny yelled. 'I'm telling you: they were looking right at me.'

'Of course they saw us,' I shouted back. 'It's whether they were *looking* for us or not. That's what I'm worried about.' Or if they'd noticed Sim without a helmet.

I could see them in the scooter's mirror. I swore when the red of their brake lights came on.

Sim had seen it too. He hunkered over the little scooter's handlebars and gunned it for all it was worth. Kenny was trying to twist in his seat to look back over his shoulder. But Sim had also spotted a gap in the hedgerow. He swerved off the road towards it, making Kenny yelp and cling on tighter. They disappeared through the hedge in a puff of leaves.

I hadn't seen the gap in time and had to spin my scooter round in the road to be able to follow. As I did I saw the police car trying to do the same. It was a simple enough manoeuvre for me, even on the narrow road. The cop car found it much more difficult, having to do a laborious three-pointer. It would be quicker just to run back this way. And as I thought that, I saw the passenger door fly open and an emerging copper's leg. But too late. I was through the gap in the hedge and after Sim and Kenny into the field beyond.

It was a cow field. Luckily for us the cows were a good distance away, but I still had images of stampedes flashing through my head. They raised their heads from the grass to watch us shooting by. And the field looked flat, but it didn't feel it on those scooters. It was like riding a bucking bronco. Sim couldn't go as fast as me because of Kenny clinging on the back. I soon caught him. Kenny had his eyes squeezed tight shut. Sim looked scared but determined. We raced over the grassy, tussocky ground, splatting through cowpats.

Were the police after us because we'd stolen Ross? Were they after us because we'd stolen the scooters? Or was it because they'd noticed Sim wasn't wearing a helmet? It didn't matter. I wasn't about to stop to find out.

But when I looked back the cop car was nowhere in sight.

'They're not following us,' I shouted at Sim. I could feel my hot, damp breath on the inside of the helmet's chin-guard. 'They won't be able to get through the gap in the hedge.'

Not that Sim looked like he was going to slow down any time soon. 'They'll know a way round,' he shouted back. 'They'll try to cut us off on the roads.'

We bounced and flew across the bone-shaking, spine-jarring, ball-jangling field – our little engines howling every time both wheels left the ground. I couldn't believe I was doing this. Wasn't I the kind of person who handed his homework in on time *and* got top marks? When was it I'd become the kind of person who got chased by the police across cow fields on a half-stolen scooter? It was like I was riding alongside myself, watching myself, not believing that the person on the run from the police was me.

Ross, I thought. *What kind of person have you made me into?*

The other side of the field was enclosed by another hedge, but this time there was no way through. We sped along the side of it looking for some kind of opening, the green leaves so close they were a ragged blur. And it was me that spotted a gap.

'See it? See it?' I shouted at Sim and turned sharp. He was right behind me.

There was a dip in the ground, a dry ditch where the hedge didn't grow. Riding down and up it at thirty-odd miles an hour was as bad as any roller coaster. It reminded my stomach of yesterday's bungee. The scooter's suspension banged. My foot slipped on the rests and I scuffed the toe of my trainer on the hard ground. My heart leaped. But I didn't fall off. And neither did Sim. I could hear his hot, buzzing engine right behind me.

We emerged onto an enclosed farm track. Tall trees, thick bushes and high hedgerows on either side. Purple heather splashed here and there. The track had deep ruts of mud where a tractor had driven along in the wet, then its tracks had dried. I kept my eyes glued to the ground as the scooter skittered and skidded beneath me. I had to slow, didn't dare push it too fast. Didn't trust it to stay beneath me. Didn't trust me to hang on. It felt like the handlebars wanted to twist out of my grip. All I could do was hope Sim stayed upright too – no way was I going to risk looking back over my shoulder even for a second.

Then a space between the trees into another field. We had to duck overhanging limbs, branches whipped at us. I was lashed across my arms and almost got smacked right between the eyes. But I kept my head down and refused to let go. Out into this second field and right there, across the other side, miracle of miracles, an open gate onto a road. Again the field was bumpy but I fixed my eyes on that gate and hung on all the way across. I knew Sim was still behind me and as soon as our tyres hit the smooth tarmac we twisted our throttles for all they were worth.

I was scared, wild-eyed. My bones hadn't stopped vibrating yet. My heart felt like it might never slow back to its normal rate. I ignored every sensible thought I'd ever had and kept going.

Sim caught up to ride beside me. He looked like he couldn't believe he was still in one piece. There was a crossroads and I turned without even slowing or checking for a signpost.

'Kenny,' I shouted. 'Keep a lookout for the police, okay?' I didn't dare look myself. 'Tell us if you see them.'

But Kenny couldn't tell us anything. Because he wasn't there.

Twenty-nine

'How the hell could you lose Kenny?'

'I didn't feel him let go. I don't know. Maybe it was in that ditch between the fields. Or he got hit by a branch or something. I just didn't feel him let go.'

'We've got to go back for him.'

'What if the police have got him?'

'He could be dead.'

'We weren't going *that* fast.'

'Fast enough. He could still be messed up pretty bad.'

'And the police could be with him too.'

We'd got off the scooters and dragged them into a hedge to hide them as best we could. We'd been hoping Kenny would come running along the road after us. But there had been no sign. Several cars had gone by and we'd ducked our heads. None of them had been a police car.

'He could be dead,' I repeated.

'He was wearing a helmet.'

At least that much was true.

'Jesus, Sim,' I said. 'This is really getting out of hand.'

We waited some more. My watch said it was just after half-ten. We'd been sitting in this bush for much longer than I wanted to, not knowing what to do.

'We've got to go look,' I said. 'We can't leave him lying there if he's broken his back or something.'

'We can't lose two mates in one week,' Sim said. And I knew he meant it as a joke, but I was too scared to laugh.

We decided to go back on foot so left the scooters and my helmet hidden and walked back the way we'd come. But we walked back slowly. Listening for any sound of a car. We were ready to dive into the nearest hedge at the slightest noise. We walked back along to the crossroads.

'Which way did we come?'

Sim pointed left.

'You sure?'

He shrugged.

The noise of an engine startled us and we were quick to run for the hedgerow. Too thick to dive through. We leaped straight over into the field on the other side. I winded myself as I landed on the hard ground. Then lying flat on our bellies and peering back in between the leaves and branches we saw a knackered old Mini slow at the crossroads, then trundle off across the other side.

'Look,' Sim said. 'The police are looking for three kids riding two scooters, not two kids just walking along. We can't keep jumping into bushes.'

I nodded, wincing at the pain in my chest from where I'd landed. 'We've got to be quick, though. You sure it's left?'

So we clambered back over onto the road and hurried along. Sim's memory was spot on and we came to the field with the gate. Instead of cutting straight across like we had done on the scooters we kept to the edge all the way around. We found the gap between the trees and ducked under the low-hanging branches onto the rutted dirt track. All the time I kept expecting to see Kenny's twisted body.

Sim said, 'These branches could've knocked him off if he wasn't looking.' He called Kenny's name in a half hiss, half shout.

Nothing.

We crept along the track getting closer to the dry ditch that separated it from the cow field. I was thinking if Kenny hadn't been knocked off by those trees, then this had to be where he'd fallen. But when we got there he wasn't anywhere to be seen.

'Kenny?' I called as loud as I dared.

Still nothing. And no dead body in the grass under the bushes.

I jumped across the ditch into the cow field. 'Kenny!' I shouted.

Not a thing.

'The police've got him,' Sim said. 'Come on, we shouldn't hang around . . .'

I forced him to wait a little bit longer, just a couple of minutes – just in case. But then I had to admit it too. The police finding him was the only explanation.

'D'you think he'll grass us up?' Sim asked.

'No. Never.' Then: 'God, I hope not.'

All we could do was head back towards where we'd left the scooters. I was in a rush again now and tried not to worry about any cars that might see us. If Kenny told the police where we were going they'd never let us get all the way there.

'Maybe it's not such a bad thing it's just the two of us now,' Sim said.

I didn't understand.

'After the way Kenny let Ross down,' he said. 'How hard would it have been for him to go round and sort his dad's computer out? Ross must have known his dad would go ape-shit when he found out his novel had been deleted. I bet he was bricking himself.'

'I reckon Ross would've still wanted it to be all three of us,' I said. 'Ross was never like you. He didn't hold grudges.'

I hadn't meant it to come out sounding quite as harsh as that. But I was nervy, anxious – understandably so too, I reckoned. I tried to grin to prove it was a joke, but all Sim did was grunt.

I watched him out of the corner of my eye, thinking about his grudges and how desperate he'd been to blame everybody else for what had happened to Ross. Mr Fowler, Munro, Nina, Caroline. And now Kenny too.

The sun was getting hotter. I hadn't had a shower for far too long and reckoned it was beginning to show. We stayed quiet and thoughtful as we turned at the crossroads back towards the scooters. We heard a car. It was too close for us to run even if we wanted to. So just held our heads down looking towards each other as if we were deep in conversation. We heard it begin to slow but neither of us looked up. Only as it passed by did we realize it was a police car.

We froze on the spot despite that sun. I didn't know about Sim but I was holding my breath. The cop car followed the curve of the road and the instant it was out of sight we plunged through the nearest hedgerow.

'They must've seen us,' Sim said.

'Course they did. They just didn't recognize us.'

'But I didn't see Kenny in there.'

'No. Just two coppers.'

We scurried along the inside of the hedge towards where we'd hidden the scooters. I had a horrible feeling . . . and it proved right. The police car had parked up at the side of the road. One of the coppers was pulling Sim's scooter out from the bushes.

'I thought it was hidden,' he said. 'Kenny must have told them where they were.'

'Kenny didn't even know. You dropped him, remember?'

'Don't be a shitbird, Blake,' he warned me.

We turned and headed back the way we'd come again, far enough to be well away from the police.

'So we've got to walk,' Sim said. 'We were going to anyway. Which way?'

'The opposite way to the coppers would be a good start.' I felt like I was carrying a big neon sign with the word FUGITIVE all lit up and flashing red. I dug the map out of my rucksack and we sat down to study it. 'If we knew where we were now it might be a help. Any idea?'

Sim leaned over the map, turned it this way, then that. He shook his head. 'But maybe we're gonna be better cutting across the fields,' he said. 'At least keep off the roads for a while. If we're lucky we'll see a landmark or something.'

It was the best idea we had. But then it was the only idea we had too.

With our best guess for the right direction we set off straight across the field, wanting to dodge the place we'd last seen the police. We trudged on, skirting ditches, clambering through hedges, dodging cows and sheep. There were a couple of small lochs that seemed to match the map and we had to grin and clap each other on the back when we figured out we were heading more or less the way we wanted to. We picked up our pace a bit, but I was worried about Kenny. I was worried about Kayleigh too, about what her brother and dad would do to her. And I was worried about us. I wanted to know what was going on back home, what was being said. I thought about Ross's parents. If they'd just give me the chance to explain why we were doing this then maybe I could get them to understand. I rehearsed a speech in my head.

We didn't speak much. We trudged on. It passed midday, was soon one o'clock. After that first burst of hopefulness I was beginning to doubt the map again. I was hungry, and knew Sim still had a couple of apples and cartons of juice left from last night, but didn't want to ask for them if he wasn't offering. When I looked at him it was obvious he was wilting too. But when he saw me watching he straightened his shoulders and hid his true feelings.

'I'm beginning to think we should let everyone know we're okay,' I said. 'If they know we're not going to kill ourselves, maybe they'll just let us get on with it.'

'Doubt it,' Sim said. 'Got to admit, though, I really

want to know what's happening – what's being said about us. But I couldn't call my mum or dad, they'd just go off on one. I wouldn't get a word in edgeways. They'd be too busy bollocking me.'

'Mine too,' I admitted. 'And I can't stop thinking about what Ross's mum and dad are gonna say to us when we get back.'

'Don't care,' Sim said. 'I reckon this is all their fault anyway. If they'd given Ross a proper funeral, we wouldn't have to.'

'You keep blaming everyone else,' I said. 'Sometimes it sounds like you think he killed himself too.'

He rounded on me. 'Say that again if you want a smack!'

I held up my hands. Peace.

Sim glared at me. 'I just want the people who made the last days and weeks of his life miserable to know about it.'

'Even his mum and dad?'

'If ever two parents should've split up, it's Ross's mum and dad,' Sim said. 'Come on, you know what they're like. His dad's all arty-farty, with his writing and his *masterpiece* novel, yeah? I reckon the whole reason he was so desperate for Ross to be a writer was because he wasn't one himself. But then his mum's dead strict about school and says, "You must study hard, you must pass your exams, they are the most important things in the world." Did Ross ever let you read that story of his where the boy got ripped in half by his parents? You know, like physically torn in two as they pulled at him? All that blood and stuff? I reckon that was really about him, and his mum and dad.'

I had read it. It had been one of his best.

'And d'you know what Ross said to me once? His mum's a lecturer, right? In Modern Languages? And one day Ross says to me, "Can you believe it? She speaks something like eight different languages but she still can't understand a word I say."'

We climbed over a wood and wire fence and were on a narrow road – more like a country lane. I checked the map, and if it was the road I thought it was, then we were still going in the right direction. It was a relief. But I was so tired, and so sweaty, and my rucksack seemed to be getting heavier. Ross seemed to be getting heavier. But it all had to be in my head. I guessed dead people always put on weight in our minds. And I realized Sim had now added Mr and Mrs Fell to his grudge list. So I doubted it was going to be too long before he got round to adding me.

'Look, if we're gonna call someone, who should it be?' I asked.

'Someone who won't grass us up.'

'Nina,' I said. I waited for the usual bad-mouthing of her to pass and added, 'She won't grass us up.'

Sim scowled. 'Wanna bet?'

I shook my head. 'She won't. Look, it's either call her or Caroline. Who would you rather it be?'

Getting my mobile out was a good excuse to rest. So I swung my rucksack off my shoulders and sat down on the grass with my back to a hedge. I took the phone out of one of my side pockets and held it up.

'Nina?'

Sim certainly wasn't happy but didn't say no. We both wanted to find out what was happening back home. He hovered over me as I switched on the phone. It buzzed into life. Then as soon as it found a signal it started to chime my messages. It was once more full to capacity.

'Jesus,' Sim whispered, no doubt thinking about what was waiting for him on his own phone.

I wafted a cloud of gnats away from my face and speed-dialled Nina. I held it tight to my ear.

She picked up on the second ring.

Thirty

'It's me,' I said. Sim was standing over me, nervous and expectant. 'Blake.'

There was a beat of silence. 'I know it's you,' Nina said. I'd hoped she'd sound pleased to hear from me and so the tone of her voice came as a blow. 'Where are you?'

'We're almost there.' I looked along the country lane, at the empty field over the fence. To be honest it felt closer to the middle of nowhere than ever before, so I added: 'Ish.'

'You're not there yet? You said you'd be on the way home again by now.' I could imagine the look on her face, the crease in her nose when she was angry, her wide brown eyes looking shocked. She always tucked and re-tucked her hair behind her ears when she was upset. She was probably sitting on the edge of her bed doing just that. 'Blake, you've got to come back. You don't have any idea what's going on here – what you three have done.'

'Our pictures have been on TV. The police are after us. We know that much.'

'What were you doing in Blackpool?'

That shocked me. 'She knows we were in Blackpool,' I told Sim.

'How?'

'How do you know we were in Blackpool?' I said into the phone.

'Because one of the pictures on TV is of someone who looks remarkably like you leaping off a very high bungee jump.'

'Bacon's grassed us up,' I told Sim. 'That photo of me's been on TV.' I felt a queasy bubble of humiliation. I guessed I should be feeling frightened, but humiliation was winning hands down right that second.

'What about our parents?' I asked.

'What do you think?'

'Bad?'

'You've got to come home. Everybody's upset, but Ross's mum looks terrible. And was it you three who've been spraying graffiti about Ross everywhere? My dad's gone wild.'

'Why, what's wrong with him?'

'Because you sprayed it all over his garage doors too.'

'No,' I said. 'We . . .' I stared hard at Sim. He must have been to Nina's late on Friday after Kenny and I had gone home. 'Has anybody tried to get in touch with you?'

'Ross's sister has.'

'Caroline? What did she want?'

'To see if I knew what was going on.'

'Did you tell her anything?'

'No. I nearly did, but . . . No. But you've got to come home or I will. What you're doing, it's hurting everyone.'

I didn't know how to answer that. The only consequences I'd been worried about was the trouble we'd be in. I'd managed to bury any concerns about how much we might be hurting people. Even though I was sitting in lush grass in picturesque countryside on a sunny morning in June I thought again of Mrs Fell at the top of her stairs, and shivered.

I said, 'We wouldn't be here if Ross's funeral had been done properly. And we're not doing this for them, we're doing it for him.'

'Are you?'

I knew what she was driving at, I wasn't stupid. She thought we were doing this for us.

I turned the subject round again. 'D'you know if they've got Kenny?' I asked.

'I thought he was with you?'

'We got split up.'

'Blake – listen. You have to come back. Just . . . it's gone too far.'

I ignored her. 'Tell everyone the suicide thing's stupid. Ross didn't. And we wouldn't either, okay?'

She was silent for a second. Then: 'Something else has happened.'

But I wasn't listening. 'You'll tell them, yeah? We're okay and we'll be back soon.'

'Blake – listen!'

'Does anyone know where we're going? Has anyone guessed?'

She sighed in annoyance. 'I don't think so, no. But—'

'Good, that's all we wanted to know.'

'Blake, you've got to—'

I pressed the button to kill the call.

I sat in the grass with my head bent and blew out a long breath. The conversation had zapped me of energy but I wasn't sure why. I stood up and said, 'We're okay for now. No one's sussed—' My phone rang. The display said it was Nina. I apologized to her inside my head as I switched the phone off again, put it back in my bag.

'We keep going, yeah?' I said. 'All she said was that we're in trouble. Which is what we already knew anyway. Everybody back home is pissed off and angry and ape-shit. It's worse than we wanted it to be, but . . . but what are they gonna do? Spank us? Ground us? Send us to "Brat Camp"? If there was ever a point of no return, I reckon we crossed it back near Doncaster somewhere. We've just got to keep going.' I swung my rucksack onto my shoulder again. 'Ready?'

Sim was watching me, unspeaking but narrow-eyed and questioning.

'For Ross,' I said.

He frowned: something was bothering him. But he nodded again, put his sunglasses on.

We walked in silence, picking up the pace again – I hadn't forgotten this had turned into a race. We tramped around the edge of the field alongside the green hedgerow through patches of purple heather, swiping at buzzing gnats and midges that got in our way. I may have been tired and anxious, but I was determined too.

It got hotter still. My rucksack felt like it weighed a ton. I was sure Sim's was as bad. The walking on the rough uneven ground of the fields was draining enough, but having to clamber over fences or through hedgerows between fields seemed to suck dry what little energy we had left. My stomach rumbled every few seconds. The map was next to useless because we weren't following the roads. All the trees, sheep and cows looked the same. It wasn't like being on a road with signposts for towns and villages that we could use. So I was surprised, but in a relieved way, when we reached the outskirts of a town called Dalbeattie just after three o'clock.

'This is fantastic,' I said, showing Sim the map. 'Look. See that? We're pretty much halfway there.' I was eager to keep going.

'I need to rest,' Sim said, not even bothering to see if I agreed.

We didn't go into the town but stayed in a field beside the main road. With a simultaneous grunt we slumped down and leaned our backs against a tall tree, enjoying the shade its branches offered. At last Sim dug the juice and apples out from the bottom of his bag and we shared. We took off our trainers to let our stinky feet breathe, sitting in silence except for the munching of apples. I closed my eyes, wanting to enjoy the time out. And now that I was sitting down, all my eagerness to keep going got up and went. But I could tell Sim was brooding. I tried to get him talking to find out what was wrong.

I opened the map across my knees. 'D'you think we're gonna make it?'

He glanced down at the map. 'It's still a long way. And tramping over these fields all the time isn't making it any easier, just making it feel longer.'

'You reckon we should risk staying on the road then?'

'Maybe we could get a bus from here. You know, split up, take a different bus each, and meet at Ross later.'

It was something I hadn't thought about. 'That might actually be a good idea.'

'How much money have we got left?'

'Just over a tenner.'

'Nothing to get home again with then.'

'It's only got to get us back as far as Dumfries. We've got train tickets back from there, don't forget.'

'I was thinking that once we've done it, scattered his ashes or whatever we're going to do, I might just call my mum and dad anyway, tell them where we are. It'll be too late for them to stop us, and we might get a lift home.'

'That doesn't sound like a bad plan either,' I admitted.

Sim was brooding again. He tossed away his apple core and lay back in the grass with his hands behind his head. I knew he'd been like this ever since I'd called Nina.

I lay back next to him. 'You okay?'

He didn't answer. I wondered if he'd fallen asleep behind his sunglasses. I didn't know whether or not to ask him again, but at last he asked, 'Why did you tell her?'

I wasn't sure what he meant.

'Nina. Why did you tell her what we were doing?' He didn't let me embarrass myself with a lie. 'The way you talked to her on the phone – it was obvious she knew what we're doing, where we're going. Why'd you tell her?'

'I felt I had to. I thought she ought to know.'

'Is that why you also wanted to tell his sister?'

'That was different – Caroline was really hurting. If you'd been talking to her you'd have seen how cut up she was and I just wanted her to know we were doing something good for her brother. I thought it might make her feel better.'

'So Nina wasn't upset?'

'Course she was. That's not what I said.'

'So she was upset, but that's not the reason you told her.'

'I don't know what you're getting at.'

Sim was quiet.

I sat up. 'Come on. What're you trying to say?'

He seemed to think about it, then asked, 'Are you going out with Nina?'

'What?'

He jerked upright and put his face close to mine. 'Did Nina pack Ross in because of those poems getting read out, and her getting embarrassed in front of everybody? Or was it because you started seeing her instead?'

I could see myself reflected in the lenses of his sunglasses. I didn't like what I saw. 'It's not what you think,' I said.

'Bullshit. Did you steal your best friend's girlfriend?'

'Sim, look—'

'Yes or no. Did you steal Ross's girlfriend?'

'I . . . Look, it just happened—'

He punched me. It really hurt. I tumbled backwards and put my hand to my bloody lip.

Sim rose to his feet, fists clenched.

I got up too, not liking him standing over me when he looked like he wanted to kill me. 'She was going to finish with him anyway. And I always got on well with Nina, you know I did. I didn't mean—'

But Sim punched me again.

'Ow! Jesus! Will you stop doing that?' I backed away from him, hands out to ward off any further blows. 'You think I don't feel shitty about it? You think I'm happy he's dead, so now I don't have to worry about telling him?'

'I never said it. But you just did.'

'Yeah, well, it's not true.'

'Call yourself a friend?' He spat at my feet. 'You're as big an arsehole as Fowler. And Munro. And all the rest of them.'

'I wouldn't be doing this if I wasn't his friend,' I

said. 'Why the hell would I be getting myself into this much trouble if I wasn't his friend?'

'Guilt.'

'You what?'

'Guilt,' Sim said. 'Guilt. You're doing this because you feel guilty.'

I didn't know how to answer. I was scared it might be true. But I was spared from saying anything because Kenny, red-faced and dripping with sweat, pushed his way through the hedge into the field. He still had hold of the helmet he'd been wearing.

'What's going on? I could hear you two shouting from all the way up the road.'

It stopped Sim and me dead. It was like neither of us believed it at first. All we could do was stare at him.

'Why're you fighting?' he wanted to know.

I unglued my mouth. 'Where the hell have you been?'

He looked surprised by the question. 'Trying to find you two, obviously. You just rode off without me when I fell off.'

'Did you get hurt?'

He turned and lifted up his T-shirt to show us the massive purple and black bruise spreading up his left side from his hip. 'It kills.'

'The police didn't get you?' Sim asked.

'I've not seen any police. I thought you'd drive on and wait for me, but I couldn't find you.'

'We went back looking for you,' Sim said.

'But I went looking for *you*,' Kenny told him.

'So how'd you get here?' I asked.

'I saw a sign for Dalbeattie, and remembered it was one of the places Kayleigh had said about.'

'You walked along the road?'

He nodded. 'I'm telling you though: my feet feel like they're gonna drop off. I've got this massive blister. And I was resting a bit further along the road – just near those houses down there, because that's Dalbeattie – and that's when I saw you two. I tried shouting at you but you were too far away to hear me. I saw you climb through the hedge and came to meet you. I was worried I'd lose you again, but I could hear you shouting half a mile away. What's going on?'

Sim and I looked at each other. I jumped in before he could say anything. 'Look, it's the three of us back together again, right?' I was trying hard for appeasement. 'Just like Ross would've wanted. Let's keep going, okay? We're almost there.'

But Sim wasn't happy.

And Kenny was still concerned. 'But what's—?'

Sim jabbed a finger at me. 'Ask him. Ask him why he stole his best mate's girlfriend.'

Kenny turned to me, shocked at first. Then sad, disappointed. 'Did you . . . ?'

'It's not how Sim's making it out to be,' I told him.

'Bollocks,' Sim sneered. Then, in a flash, he was in Kenny's face too. 'And don't you go thinking you're not as bad. You could've helped him with his dad's computer, but you just couldn't be bothered.'

Kenny was startled by the sudden attack. He staggered back a step.

'Ross would've been really scared, really shitting himself, because he knew what his dad would do when he found out he'd deleted that stupid book of his.'

'That's not fair,' Kenny said.

'He was your *friend*, Kenny. Didn't that thought even get through your thick skull.'

Kenny looked at me, appealing to me to defend him. But Sim was right. Both Kenny and I had let our best friend down.

Kenny was flustered but he managed to stand his ground. 'You can't say that. I'm telling you: you're worst of all.'

Sim lunged at him. 'What did you say?'

Kenny cowered back against the hedge, holding the helmet up to his chest to ward Sim off. 'What about Munro? You didn't help Ross then, did you? Why don't you tell Blake about that, instead of having a go at me?'

Sim looked like he was the one who'd been punched. I saw his mouth try to form words that wouldn't come out. I remembered meeting Ross after Munro had beaten him up in Haverstoe Park. I'd asked him if we should get Sim, but Ross had looked away, avoided the question.

'What happened?' I asked.

Sim didn't answer. He grunted, paced a step or two back and forth, and kicked at the ground. Then sat down like his legs had been chopped out from underneath him. He put his head in his hands.

'He didn't stop Munro beating Ross up even though he was there too,' Kenny said.

I said to Sim, 'But all that trouble with the graffiti on the bike shed . . . it only started because he let you copy his homework and didn't grass you up to Fowler.'

Sim wouldn't answer. The three of us didn't move. None of us had anything to feel proud of.

I sucked on my busted lip and stared out across the field at the sheep on the far side. I was thinking about the fuse Mr Fell had lit inside my head yesterday morning. But it glowed too hot; grew too insistent. I grabbed up my rucksack and searched the pockets for my phone. I couldn't turn it on quick enough and was impatient for it to find a signal. Kenny asked what I was doing but I ignored him. I called Nina.

I didn't let her speak, asked immediately: 'Did he know?'

'Who? Listen, Blake—'

'Please, just tell me. Did Ross know about *us*?'

She didn't answer at first, but I could hear her breathing.

'Nina?'

'He saw us together.'

That fuse in my head fizzed and sparked. I went back over what I remembered of those last few days before Ross died. And Mr Fowler, Sean Munro, Nina, me, Kenny, Sim.

Nina was saying my name.

'Yeah, I'm still here,' I told her.

'I was trying to tell you before – they've found a note.'

I squeezed my eyes tight shut. Ross had said to me, 'The day I can't stand up for myself any more is the day I roll over and die.' And all of a sudden, I knew what was coming.

'He'd been on his dad's computer,' Nina said. 'He'd damaged it or something, I don't know how exactly. But his dad was trying to get it fixed yesterday when they found that Ross had been going on the Internet to visit these chatrooms and forums. He'd tried to cover up what he'd done, delete what he'd been writing, and that's how he'd damaged the computer. But it's all come out now.'

And at last the fuse lit the bomb. And the bomb went boom.

'They were chatrooms for people who want to kill themselves.' She was crying too. 'He posted a suicide note on the same morning he died.'

Thirty-one

I thought I'd seen Sim angry before, but this was something else. I was scared of him. He smacked the phone right out of my hand and stamped it to pieces. I cowered away from him, thinking he was going to smash me up too.

'How can you say that? How can you?' He came at me and I stumbled away from him, out of his reach. 'Come on! How can you say something like that?'

'You're wrong,' Kenny told me. 'We're not going to believe it. We can't. He was knocked off his bike, wasn't he? He didn't hang himself. He didn't cut his wrists.'

'Think about it,' I said. 'His best friends, *us*, we'd all let him down. His mum and dad wanted completely different things from him; he knew he couldn't please them both. His sister humiliated him in front of all those other kids at school, because of his writing.

He was bullied by both Fowler and Munro. He must have felt like the whole world was against him. And then he thought he'd destroyed the most important thing in his dad's life. His dad, who was the one and only person who seemed to be on his side.'

Sim was still seething. 'You're saying we're to blame.'

'Maybe we are. We all ignored what was happening to him, didn't we?'

He lunged at me, knocked me over, pinned me to the ground. His face was a bruised, angry red. 'If anyone's to blame, you are. You stole his girlfriend.' He had his knee in my stomach. 'Say it.' He ground his knee into me. 'Say it's your fault.'

'Sim . . .'

'*Say it.*'

'Sim, look—'

He slammed his knee into me, making me cry out.

I managed to roll and push him off. I sat up and cradled my stomach. 'He must have done it for lots of reasons, some we probably don't even know about.'

'Then he's the biggest shithead I've ever met.' He held out his hand. 'Give me my money.'

'What?'

'I want my money back. I gave you a fiver, right? I want it back.'

'Why?'

'Because I can't believe I've come all this way and got into all this trouble for some shithead who killed himself.'

'Sim, listen—'

'Give me my money, Blake. Or I mean it: I'll take it from you.'

'We've got to go to Ross.'

He swiped his sunglasses off his face, let me see his eyes, as hard as snooker balls but glistening with tears. 'Give me my money. Just give it to me.'

I'd never seen him cry before. I dug in my back pocket for our money and gave him a £5 note. 'Don't go.' But I didn't know how to make him stay. 'At least come to Ross and—'

'Why should I? I've got problems too, yeah?' He tried to wipe away his tears. 'Why d'you think I have to copy Ross's homework? Because I'm not as clever as you three, am I? I can't do it by myself. Ever thought of that? D'you seriously think I'm gonna get into university like you?' He gulped down a hard lump of breath. 'And look at my mum and dad, and the shithole I live in. My brother couldn't wait to get out of the house, and now he doesn't even come home any more. Why d'you think that is?' His wet eyes bulged. 'Why don't I go and kill myself, yeah? I'll tell you why? Because I'm not that *weak*.' He spat the final word.

Neither Kenny nor I knew what to say.

Sim glared at us both, daring either of us to challenge him. He rubbed hard at the tears on his cheeks. Kenny and I stood there, dumb. There were no words anyway. So he grabbed up his rucksack and, forcing me to step aside, he pushed through the gap in the hedge back onto the road.

We watched him go.

I was shaking. Sim had frightened me. I needed to get moving. I stood up and hoisted my rucksack as high on my shoulders as it would go. I grabbed Sim's half-drunk juice off the ground.

'Where are you going?' Kenny asked. He was pale, bewildered.

'Where d'you think?'

He hurried to catch me up. 'Are we really leaving Sim?'

'He left us, didn't he?'

He turned back the way Sim had gone, but decided to follow me.

'Just leave the helmet, Kenny,' I told him.

We didn't talk much as we walked. He stayed a few paces behind. I knew he was crying and didn't want him to feel embarrassed about it. I found it easy enough to get lost in my own thoughts. I used the map to search for a route around Dalbeattie, not wanting to go through the town's centre and risk being recognized. I decided we should be okay sticking to the smaller roads now, like Kenny had done to get to find Sim and me. They were looking for three of us after all. So maybe it was a good thing Sim had gone. But no, I didn't believe that. I found a B road that would take us through a place called Gelston and then most of the way to Kirkcudbright. From Kirkcudbright it was still a fair distance to Ross, but it looked like a simple route with quiet roads all the way.

We kept walking. I was angry at Sim for leaving us. And I was angry at myself for ignoring what had been happening to Ross. A few cars shot by in both directions but we didn't bother to hide any more, it took too much energy. We plodded on. I wondered what it felt like to be so low, so miserable, so frightened and so lonely that you wanted to kill yourself. I kept remembering things about him. Ross sad; Ross moody; Ross secretive.

I didn't notice Kenny starting to lag further and further behind. When he called out to me he was a good fifty metres or so back down the road. I waited for him to catch up. He was limping and sunburned, with the mop of his fringe hanging wet across his eyes.

'I'm not going either,' he said, as if Sim had walked away only five seconds before instead of well over an hour ago. 'I can hardly walk with this massive blister anyway. I think I should go home.'

'But, Kenny—'

'I'm telling you, Blake! I want to go *home*.' He looked scared, like he'd seen something too big and confusing to be able to understand. Like his head had been forced open and too much stuff he didn't want to know about had been tipped in. 'Can I have some money?'

I gave him everything I had left. 'You might be able to get a bus from that place we just passed.'

He nodded. Then without saying another word he turned and hobbled back the way we'd come. I stood and watched him for too long. It made me want to go home too. I hated being alone.

With a real effort I started walking towards Ross again. My head ached with the sun and I hoped it was going to get cooler now. My feet grew a whole bunch of blisters of their own. I wondered what you called a whole bunch of blisters.

I was sorry about lots of things. Most of all I was sorry that I hadn't noticed what had been happening to Ross, that I hadn't known. But that was a lie. Of course we'd known. We caused some of it. But ignored it – buried our heads in the sand. I wished so hard that he'd talked to me. Why hadn't he talked to me? I could have helped – surely I could have done something? But then he might not have wanted to talk to the person who stole his girlfriend.

I made it to Kirkcudbright just before six. The road I was on took me right through the centre. There was a lot of traffic, people milling about the few scattered shops. I kept my head down and didn't take much notice of anything except the road signs pointing my way. I think I drew a few stares but pretended not to care. It was even smaller than Dumfries, but also had a bridge over a river on the far side of the town centre.

There were yachts and fishing boats moored in a tiny marina. I hurried along, wincing a little at my blisters.

Out the other side and back on the country roads I felt safer again. I was tempted to take a break, sit on the wide grass verge and catch my breath. But I was worried that if I sat down I might not be able to get up again. I refused to give in. I was going to do what we'd planned to do all along. My rucksack was rubbing my shoulders raw and my T-shirt was drenched in sweat but I wasn't going to stop walking. My best friend was dead: how dare I complain about anything? The pain in my feet reminded me with every step that he was never coming back.

Never coming back. Never coming back. Never coming back.

And maybe I was part of the reason why.

The walking got harder as the evening lengthened. I was grateful for every puff of cool breeze. I'd run out of juice and wished I'd saved even a dribble. A little after seven I got a jolt of much-needed energy the first time I saw a sign saying ROSS. It didn't last long. I wanted to give up. My legs were so tired. Every road got longer, every rise got steeper, every step got shorter. I was in a lot of pain – my feet, my head, my shoulders. But I refused to give up. Ross might have given up. It didn't mean I had to.

I checked the map with every bend in the road. Surely it must be round the next one.

Thirty-two

There was no sign telling me this was the place it had taken me two days to get to. The road narrowed and twisted between the trees. I passed the first house I'd seen in a good couple of miles. Then there was a tight bend and as I rounded it the trees fell away to reveal a small bay that looked bleak even on a summer's evening.

The map said this was Ross. It wasn't even a village. I only counted six houses. And an untidy heap of farm buildings – corrugated and rusty. Part of me was worried that the police or my parents had got here first and were waiting for me, but there was no one to be seen. It looked like I'd won the race after all. The feeling of relief spurred me on.

The sea had taken a bite out of the land to make an indented bay. The tide was out. There wasn't a proper beach, just mud and rocks. It was different to back home, but that was good. A lonely rowing boat rode the gentle waves at the end of its rope. On the far side of the bay was a lumpy hill of headland that sheltered the bay but blocked the view of the open sea beyond. I decided I wanted to climb up to the top of that hill and look out at the sea. I thought that's what Ross would have done if he'd ever come here.

I followed the road until it stopped being a road. It became a rubble track that skirted around the water. There was a signpost saying the track led to the Bay House Hotel. I wondered who would want to come to this lonely place for a holiday. The bay funnelled the wind and the cry of seagulls. I could smell the dank mud that had been exposed by the retreating tide. It felt empty and deserted enough now, in June. I didn't like to think how it would feel in the middle of winter.

The track curved most of the way around the water like a backwards C. I didn't follow it as far as the hotel because I came to a metal gate with a stile, and a footpath that led up and over the headland. I stepped over the stile into a field full of cows. They kept a curious eye on me as I walked between them. It wasn't a steep path but it made my tired legs ache even more as I climbed.

The view from the top was rewarding. The first

thing I noticed was the lighthouse and I remembered Kayleigh telling me about it. This one was much closer than the one at Spurn Point that could be seen from Cleethorpes beach, and I liked the idea that I'd travelled from one to another. It was a tall white tower on a tiny island the map called Little Ross, maybe a couple of hundred or so metres out into the sea. And even though the map also called this the Solway Firth, not the sea proper, it was bigger, wider and greyer than the Humber back home. It was more than good enough for me.

The footpath petered out as the lumpy hill of headland dipped down towards the water. I walked as far as I could. Again there was no beach, just a rough, bouldered edge about three or four metres high where I could sit and dangle my legs. I took my rucksack off and did just that.

I took Ross's urn out and put it in the thick grass next to me. Now that I was here, now that I'd made it, I didn't know what to do. This wasn't going to bring him back, was it? Although maybe Sim had been right and it wasn't really about Ross anyway. It was about me, and my guilt. Wasn't that what Nina had been hinting at too. So what was I expecting? Forgiveness, redemption, understanding?

I wished Kenny and Sim were here.

There was a soft breeze which cooled my sweaty face. I looked out at the sea and the lighthouse for a while. Then I lay back in the grass and stared at the evening sky.

I let it get dark around me. The beam from the lighthouse swept across the water towards me, didn't quite reach me, swept away again. The sky was cloudless and clear, and the moon and stars were bright. I pulled my jumper out of my rucksack and put it on. There was a moment of panic when I couldn't see the urn, but it had toppled to one side in the grass. I hadn't spotted it in the dark, that was all. I set it up straight.

I took a deep breath, held it as long as I could. When I blew it out again I felt a lump rise in my throat. And at last I cried. But I was angry and the tears burned my cheeks. Was what had happened enough to want to kill yourself? Was it really?

I was sorry. But I was angry too. Didn't he think about how many people he'd hurt? Didn't he care? He'd made his sister cry. He'd made his father paranoid. He'd turned his mother into a living ghost.

And he'd destroyed a friendship. Is that what he'd wanted? What kind of selfish piece of shit would do that to his family and friends? There would always be a part of me that hated him for the pain he'd caused. It wasn't fair to leave so much sorrow behind. Not on purpose.

I was ready to hurl the urn as far out over the sea as I could. What stopped me was a voice behind me, calling my name.

He was a short shadow at first, but I'd recognized Kenny's voice anyway. He came over the top of the headland, calling me. I thought maybe Sim was . . . ? But no, just Kenny. I stood up, brushed at my face to clear my tears. I waved to him, beckoned him over.

'You seem to be making a habit of this reappearing malarkey,' I said.

He bobbed his head, looked a little unsure, a little furtive.

'How'd you get here?'

'Kat's stepdad.'

I didn't understand.

He showed me the back of his hand where Kayleigh had written Kat's phone number. 'I *was* looking for a bus stop.' He shrugged. 'Then I saw this phone box, and, you know . . . But I've had to tell her the truth. She knew most of it anyway – because of the telly?'

'Where is she now?'

He pointed back over the headland. 'They're waiting in their car by the road.'

'What made you change your mind? Why'd you come?' I saw the shadows across his face twitch and added, 'I'm really glad you're here – genuinely. I just wondered why. Because you could have called your mum.'

'I knew you'd come,' he said. 'I hoped Sim would too. Is he . . . ?'

I shook my head.

He shrugged. He saw I was holding the urn. 'So what do we do now?'

'Honestly? I haven't got a clue.'

'I think what you say's true,' he told me. 'I think Ross did, you know, do it on purpose. But then, I also can't believe he really would do it either. I knew him the longest – I knew him for ever – and it's just not like the Ross I knew would ever do that. D'you think it's our fault he did?'

'Some of it. But I don't think we'd have been able to stop him either.'

'Maybe if he'd told us how he felt.'

'Maybe,' I said. 'But he never would have, would he? He was one of those people who are good at hiding everything inside – everything that really mattered to him anyway.'

'But why did he do it by getting run over?'

'Because he didn't want anybody to know. I reckon that's why he tried to cover up that he'd been to those Internet chatrooms. He was still trying to hide everything inside right up until the end.'

'Yeah, but doing that meant we couldn't help him.'

'He didn't think he wanted help. He just thought he wanted to die.'

Kenny coughed, tried to mask that he was crying. 'I don't want him gone. He was my best friend. I want him here. He should *still* be here.' He probably thought it was too dark for me to see, but the moonlight showed silver tears on his cheeks. He said, 'You know, yesterday and today have been amazing. All the stuff we've been through? And it's all been because of him. I'm telling you: we've got the best story ever. But he missed out. He's never gonna be able to tell it.' His shoulders shook as he wept.

I watched the beam of the lighthouse sweep around.

At last he gave a big sniff. A real snorter that he had to swallow. He seemed to have got himself under control again – pushed the secret Kenny who cried deep inside again. 'D'you think Sim's gonna come?'

'No. Not now.'

'Why not?'

I wasn't sure how to explain it. 'Don't take this the wrong way, but I think Ross broke his heart. I think Sim looked up to Ross more than any of us. And I bet if Sim could've swapped lives with someone, he would've jumped at the chance of being Ross for a while. He can't understand why Ross would want to throw everything away.'

'Nor me.'

I sighed. 'I reckon it's probably me and you from here on in. I hate to say it, but don't be surprised if we don't see much of Sim any more. I hope I'm wrong, but . . .'

'But you're probably not.'

I shrugged.

Kenny took the urn from me. 'So what do we do with him?'

'I don't know. I've been thinking it wouldn't be fair to his mum or dad if we left him here, would it? We've been blaming them all along, but . . . but I can't think of *anybody* who's blameless any more.'

'Maybe we should just leave a little bit here, but take the rest back. We can't come all this way and then not do something.'

He unscrewed the lid and scooped a small palmful of ash into his hand. He passed the urn to me and I did the same. It was gritty and dry. In the beginning, maybe I'd had plans for a speech or a ceremony, but so much had happened and neither of us knew what to say. We knew that this palmful wasn't really our best friend.

We threw it towards the lighthouse. The beam swept round, and it might almost have looked as if it had carried the ash away.

There was nothing left to do but head back up and over the rise of the headland towards the bay. As we reached the top we saw two cars passing by the houses on the far side, tearing along the narrow road, hardly slowing when the tarmac stopped and the rubble track began. Even in the dark, from this distance, we could see the front car was the police. As they both drew closer I recognized the second car as Ross's dad's.

'Someone's grassed us up. D'you reckon it was Sim?'

'I don't know,' I said. 'I doubt it. Maybe they just figured it out because someone local spotted us. We've left a pretty obvious trail all the way from Cleethorpes.'

The police car pulled up behind where Kat's step-dad was parked. I wondered if it was Detective Sergeant Cropper himself. Ross's dad's car screeched to a halt and he was out in flash, pointing up the hill at us.

'Here we go,' I said. 'Brace yourself. Good luck with your mum.'

Kenny had halted in his tracks. 'We really are shit-tered.'

'Are you asking me or telling me?'

He almost smiled. Almost. 'There is something I will tell you,' he said. 'I'm not glad Ross is dead, okay? You know that, don't you? But I can't help being glad we came here. I wouldn't have met Kat if we hadn't.'

I nodded to prove I understood. 'And I suppose

when you think about it, that's kind of the whole point, isn't it?'

Kenny looked across at me. 'How d'you mean?'

One of the policemen and Ross's dad were clambering over the stile into the cow field. I reckoned they didn't trust us to come down to them. Maybe they were worried we'd want to carry on running.

'Well, you never really know what's going to happen, do you? At least, not until it actually does.'

Thank you . . .

Desmond, Eric, Jane and the students from Craigroyston here in Edinburgh; Angela, Claire and the BRAW boys from St Andrew's over there in Clydebank. Clare Argar; Anna Gibbons; Lucy Juckes; Jack Merriman; Sophie Nelson; Janet Smyth; Juliet Swann and Alan Thompson. Mum, Dad and John. Especially Charlie. For ever, Jasmine.

MALARKEY
KEITH GRAY

John Malarkey is the wrong person in the wrong place at the wrong time. Up to his neck in it and on the run, he's still trying to figure out why. All he knows is that Brook High is no place for a conscience, the teachers don't run this school and he's only got twenty-four hours to prove his innocence.

Shortlisted for the Guardian Fiction Prize and the Booktrust Teenage Prize

ISBN: 978 0 099 43944 8

WAREHOUSE
KEITH GRAY

I know a place you can go . . .

'Located in the dockland of a small northern town, the warehouse is a refuge for young people who have slipped through society's safety net. Keith Gray has produced a fast-paced, convincing and moving story.'
ALAN GIBBONS

'Keith Gray's exploration of an invisible sub-culture hits you so hard it almost hurts. It has the power and realism to grip the reader and lead you into a dark, underground world of emotional outcasts.'
DAMIAN KELLEHER

'Grabbing the reader by the scruff of the neck . . . Tough, tender and true.'
GUARDIAN

Shortlisted for the Guardian Fiction Award

ISBN: 978 0 099 41425 4

THE FEARFUL
KEITH GRAY

For those who want to believe, no proof is needed.
But for those who can't believe, no evidence is enough.

The legend says that in 1699 schoolteacher William
Milmullen and his five pupils visited Lake Mou, but only
William returned. He claimed that a terrifying creature
rose from the lake and devoured the boys. But did it?
And if it all happened so long ago, does it really matter
to anyone nowadays anyway?

The legacy of that tragedy lives on in the town of
Moutonby. A town divided between those who believe
that something terrible still lurks deep down in the lake,
and those who don't.

Tim Milmullen wishes he knew. Every day he watches
the dark water, looking for a sign. Because if the
stories are true, if 'the dragon' in the lake is real,
then according to the legend he's the only one who
can stop if from killing again.

ISBN: 978 0 099 45656 8

CREEPERS
KEITH GRAY

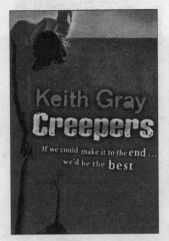

Derwent Drive was known as the Speed Creep.
A continual chain of Dashes into the Blind.
If we could make it to the end . . .
We'd be the best.

We'd all heard the story about the Creeper who
dropped Blind into a garden, only to discover he
was standing in a dog pound. It was also the longest
creep around here: twenty-five houses all in a row,
no bends, no kinks. And no Creeper had ever done
the lot. But Jaime and I reckoned we could do it.
Jaime was the best Creeper around.
He was the best buddy you could have.
And he was mine.

Shortlisted for the Guardian Fiction Award

ISBN: 978 0 099 47564 4

HAPPY
KEITH GRAY

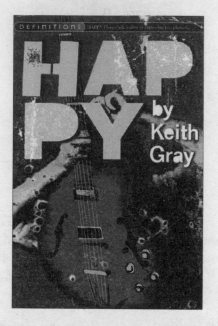

'Hundreds of people want to be in a band. They
all get guitars and they all play gigs and they all
write songs, and they still never make it.'

ock star
which
nks, car
tter not
all too